KU-165-504

£1.65

Nature's Quilt

I DO not need a patchwork quilt,
  To lay upon my bed.
For, from my casement window,
I see before me spread,
Nature's offerings, neatly set
In shades of every hue.
Changeable yet always there
Beneath grey skies or blue.

Green fields, wild moors and rolling
  hills,
Birds riding on the breeze.
Blossom in the hedgerows,
Bright butterflies and bees.
You scoff! You say it gives no warmth,
But you are wrong, my dear.
This patchwork quilt delights my soul,
Each season of the year.

Winter's sparkling frost and snow,
Springtime's mossy green,
Summer's gift of gay, fresh flowers
And autumn's glorious scene
Of russet, bronze and purest gold,
Paint such a picture fair,
It fills my heart with joys untold,
With truth I must declare.

I do not need a patchwork quilt,
To lay upon my bed.
For, from my casement window,
I have nature's quilt instead.
                    —Annie Leaver.

People's Friend Annual

CONTENTS

The Best Of Friends

by ELSIE JACKSON

O H, Shirley! Go on! Tell me who he is! I won't tell a soul.''

Shirley Black looked down at the bright, inquisitive face of the dark-haired girl sitting beside her on the Tighdearg coach, and her eyes twinkled. But she shook her head firmly.

"No. Not yet," she told Katriona Wilson for the umpteenth time. "I'm keeping him a secret until the wonderful day he asks me out or tells me he's fallen for me, too. Then I'll introduce you."

"And when do you think that'll be?" Katriona asked.

"Not until we get back to Glasgow, anyway. That's for sure." Shirley sighed, her face clouding momentarily.

"Just tell me one thing, then!" Katriona pleaded. "Is it someone I know? I'm sure it must be."

"I'm not telling you!" Shirley persisted stubbornly. "I don't want to wear my heart on my sleeve. And you'd be sure to let my secret out!"

"I wouldn't!" Katriona retorted indignantly.

"Yes you would!" Shirley gave her friend's arm an affectionate squeeze. "Why do you think we christened you 'Chatter-eena' at college? You can't help it. It's just impossible for you to keep a secret!"

"Well, honestly!" Katriona fumed, and turned to gaze out of the window in an offended silence.

Shirley smiled, as she finally got a chance to open the book which had lain on her lap all the way from Glasgow. There hadn't been any time for reading with Katriona chatting non-stop in her ear. Even now her silence wouldn't last longer than five minutes, for she was the best-natured girl Shirley had ever met. She didn't know how to be huffy or moody.

Shirley had recognised all these good qualities in her flat-mate soon after they'd started their first term at college last October. But she had also discovered that Katriona was an incorrigible chatterbox! Not that Shirley liked her any the less for that. Otherwise she wouldn't have spent the last month working with her in the City warehouse. Nor would she have invited her home to Tighdearg to spend this August fortnight with her widowed mother and her sister.

But although Shirley was very fond of Katriona, she would never dream of telling her about her feelings for Gary Davison! Otherwise the rest of Tighdearg would probably know all about it, too, before the week was out!

Katriona did know Gary, of course. He'd been working in the warehouse along with the two girls, a tall, romantic-looking art student with a beard and shoulder-length hair. Shirley had soon become aware of a very pleasant feeling whenever Gary had appeared. And the young art student began to play an important part in her daydreams.

In reality, of course, she had thought herself fortunate when he'd told her one day that he often played tennis in Kelvingrove Park. At least when she returned to Glasgow at the end of August, she would know where to find him!

"Oh, look!" Katriona suddenly exclaimed breathlessly, as the bus reached the crest of the hill, and the blue, sparkling waters of Tighdearg Bay appeared before them. "It's beautiful, Shirley! What a fantastic spot! All those little white houses! And the boats in the bay! And the island! You didn't tell me it was like this!"

"Well, it's my home." Shirley chuckled. "I suppose I take it for granted."

Shirley hadn't told Katriona much about Roddy McLeod either, and she could see that the red-haired girl was just as impressed by him as she was by the scenery. For Roddy, bronzed from working on the farm, was waiting as usual at the pier in his Jeep to drive Shirley home. She had told him in her last letter that she was bringing Katriona, so he was prepared for two passengers.

"Which isn't always the case, I assure you!" Shirley told her friend with a grin. "I'm usually squeezed in with dogs or goats."

"Another grumble from you and you can walk home next time!" Roddy winked at Katriona before starting up the engine and setting off along the narrow shore road.

H E'S super!" Katriona breathed, after Roddy had dropped them off at the gate of the Black's cottage. "And the way you talk about him, Shirley Black! Whenever you went on about writing to 'Old Roddy,' I pictured some stodgy country bumpkin!"

"Oh, he's anything but that!" Shirley laughed. "But there again, I suppose I'm just too used to him. We've been mates for six years now, ever since his family came to Tighdearg. In fact, he's about the closest friend I have here."

Their conversation was interrupted at this point by Shirley's mother flinging open the door and asking whether they had decided to go back to Glasgow, or if she could safely infuse the tea. And the laughing, informal introductions that followed were to be the pattern for the next few days. Katriona took to Tighdearg and Tighdearg took to Katriona. And Shirley couldn't help but feel delighted that she had made the decision to ask her flat-mate to come home with her.

"She's a tonic!" Shirley's quiet, elder sister, Sylvia, pronounced. "I really look forward to all her chatter and jokes after a dull day in the bank."

And Roddy, too, was of the opinion that Katriona was "a real character." To begin with, Shirley had wondered whether her old friend might not resent a third party coming on their evening walks. But Roddy didn't seem to mind. And on the fine evenings that followed, the trio would walk along the long stretch of beach, talking and joking, to end up at the Bay Hotel where they'd have supper in the spectacular glass-walled lounge and watch the sun set behind the island.

ONE evening Shirley guided Katriona carefully round a patch of lighter coloured sand, which was exposed because the tide was further out than usual.

"I had the biggest fright of my life here, Katriona," she said, with a meaningful smile at Roddy. "Roddy hadn't long come to Tighdearg and we were out fishing one evening. We beached the boat near here. I was busy with our tackle and when I looked round I couldn't see Roddy anywhere."

"And she suddenly remembered, that I didn't know about that patch of quicksand there. She thought I'd been swallowed . . . big, black wellies and all!" Roddy chimed in.

"It wasn't funny!" Shirley said. "I've never felt so awful in my life! Then the great clown popped up from behind those bushes at the top of the beach. He'd been playing hide-and-seek! Would you believe it?"

"I'd believe it." Katriona laughed, blue eyes shining as she looked up at the handsome young farmer.

If Shirley had been worried that Katriona might find a holiday at Tighdearg on the dull side, she couldn't have been more wrong. Coming from a small, industrial town in Lanarkshire, she revelled in the West Coast countryside. And she loved nothing better than to tramp across the moors or up in the hills.

Inevitably on these long walks Katriona did her best to find out who Shirley had lost her heart to back in Glasgow. And once, she was nearly caught.

"I wonder what he'll be doing just at this moment — your heart-throb I mean," Katriona murmured innocently one afternoon.

"Playing tennis, I expect," Shirley replied without thinking, then gave a squeal of rage and stuffed a fistful of heather down her delighted friend's neck. "You won't catch me like that again," she vowed. And she kept her word.

THEN during the second week of Katriona's visit, a tiny cloud appeared on Shirley's horizon. Roddy began to act strangely. He avoided her eyes, for one thing. His glance would slide away as though he had something to hide from her. And once, when she and Katriona had walked up to the McLeods' farm for eggs, she saw Roddy deliberately set off up the hillside away from them.

When he did come down to the bay, it was Katriona that he talked to, Katriona he smiled at. And still the truth never dawned on her. Not until the Wednesday evening of that second week when her sister came out with it!

Sylvia, on her way home from work, had just walked up from the bus terminus at the pier. And on her way she had passed Katriona, hurrying down to the post office for some stamps.

"And who should be waiting outside the post office but our Roddy!" Sylvia remarked with dancing eyes. "Now there's a coincidence."

Shirley, who had been laying the table, looked up at her sister with a frown. "What do you mean?"

"Just that it's the third time this week I've met that pair having a long chat outside the post office!" Sylvia laughed.

"Oh, Sylv! Don't be so daft!" Shirley retorted with unusual sharpness. "Roddy always goes down to the post to collect the mail at that time."

"And Katriona's always running out of stamps at that time."

Just then Katriona burst in on them and one look at her face told Shirley that there was every chance Sylvia and her mother were right. Katriona's eyes were really sparkling. In fact, she looked radiant.

"Just met Roddy," she announced breathlessly, "and he says the fair's coming to the Kirk Field tomorrow evening. And did you remember?"

The Peace Within

CLOSE the door for just a while
And seek the peace within.
Shut out the world and all its noise
And let the silence in.

Close your eyes for just a while
And let your spirit rise.
To find your own serenity
Beyond all earthly ties.

Close your mind for just a while
To daily hopes and fears.
Uplift your thoughts in harmony
To reach celestial spheres.

Close your ears for just a while
Until you only hear
That still, small voice that whispers,
"All is well, for I am here."

Myra Greenall.

"No, I'd forgotten, as a matter of fact," Shirley replied slowly, her mind in a whirl. "Did you want to go, Katriona?"

"Oh, yes!" Katriona fairly bubbled, dancing over to set the cups and plates out on the table. "Roddy says he'll meet us there at eight . . . So shall we stay in this evening? I'd like to wash my hair."

"Yes. That's a good idea," Shirley murmured, as she went through to help her mother dish up the meal.

B Y nine o'clock the following evening Shirley was feeling positively wretched and still bewildered by the emotional turmoil which had suddenly overwhelmed her. After all, Roddy and Katriona were her closest friends. She should have been glad that a romance had sprung up between them, that they had wandered off together now to some quiet corner of the fairground.

A small, hard lump was beginning to form in her throat when someone tapped her gently on the shoulder. She turned to find Roddy looking down at her.

"You don't look happy," he said abruptly. "Can I help?"

"I'm fine!" Shirley assured him, forcing a smile. "Where's that Katriona got to?"

Roddy coloured slightly. "Don't think I'm being rude, Shirl, but I'm afraid Katriona's non-stop chatter gets a bit much for me. I've passed her over to Alisdair Strang. He seems more than happy to be looking after such a pretty girl. And she's quite happy with the arrangement, too." He grinned.

"You've . . ." Shirley's voice died suddenly as her eyes met Roddy's. And for a moment she saw his face through a mist of tears, so that she had to put a hand on his shoulder to support herself.

"What is it?" Roddy's arms encircled her, and his voice wavered between incredulity and delight.

"I thought that you and Katriona . . ." she began. "You were acting so strangely . . . and I suddenly realised . . ."

Roddy's arms tightened around her. "But what about this romance of yours back in Glasgow? Katriona told me you'd really fallen in love. It was like the end of the world . . ." His voice broke off as Shirley hugged him fiercely.

"Oh, that Chattereena!" she exclaimed, half-laughing and half-crying. "Who would ever have thought that wagging wee tongue of hers could have done so much good? It's you I love, Roddy McLeod."

"And I love you, too, darling," Roddy whispered. "And I thought I'd left it too late to tell you!"

"Come on, you two!" Katriona's gay voice suddenly urged. "Alisdair and I are going to the shooting gallery. Let's see if we can win a teddy bear apiece!"

"A teddy bear!" Shirley exclaimed, turning to grin mischievously at her friend. "I'm too grown-up for that sort of thing. I'm after something for my bottom drawer."

"Which is by way of being an engagement announcement!" Roddy added, putting a proud and protective arm around his bride-to-be. □

Two Sides

by Margaret Johnston

SHARON looked at the wad of notes Donald had put down beside her plate and knew they were some kind of ultimatum. She looked up at her husband and down again at the money, but Donald still didn't speak. He hadn't said a word as he'd dropped the notes casually in front of her. He hadn't even bothered to count them.

Sharon tried to guess how much there was. A lot, she decided. Much too much to spend on one dress, even if it was to wear to the Country Club.

Her eyes lifted to him again, pleadingly, but Donald's expression didn't alter. He'd thrown down the challenge, and now it was up to her. With a sigh, and an awkward movement, Sharon crushed the money into her hand. She loved Donald and she didn't want to lose him, but she felt they were coming dangerously close to the end.

"Thank you," she said quietly, and for a fraction of a second Donald's face relaxed, but then the mask was back.

"I'll try not to be late," he said, picking up his briefcase and heading for the door.

Sharon sat rigid. Donald had never left her without a kiss before. She knew she should go to him but her legs felt weak, and fear made her throat dry as he opened the door. She bent her head, unable to watch him leave, so that she was startled when his hand came down on her shoulder and his lips brushed her forehead.

She put up a hand to catch his but he was gone, as swiftly and quietly as he had crossed the room towards her.

When the sound of his car faded, Sharon began to clear the table. All that had passed between them was running round and round inside her head.

Donald was wrong. Of course she wanted him to succeed at his job. He worked so hard, he deserved success. How could he believe she didn't want him to be successful? She had said as much to him when he had hurled the accusation at her.

"Oh, don't be silly. Of course I want you to get on."

"Then why won't you come out on Wednesday?" he'd demanded. "Any other woman would be glad to eat a dinner she hadn't cooked herself, to spend an evening in pleasant company. And it's not just that. You know this sort of thing is important to me. I've been trying to get this order for days now. If I play my cards right . . ."

Sharon had muttered that she hadn't anything to wear and it was then that Donald had given her the bundle of notes. The memory of those bitter moments drove her to pick up the telephone.

"Liz? It's Sharon. Can you baby sit for us on Wednesday?" she asked when her friend answered.

"Wednesday? Free as the wind, my child." Liz always talked like this and Sharon found herself smiling.

To Every Story

"Good. We're going to the Country Club," she added, a note of pride slipping into her voice.

"Hey! Have you two come into a fortune?" she teased. "You're going up in the world, aren't you?"

"Come off it, Liz. Surely it's not that grand. Anyway, this is business. Donald's got a client he wants me to sweeten. I'm even to buy myself a new dress." Sharon began to feel excited and her earlier fears left her.

"Make it something special, then," Liz commanded with her usual candour. "Not one of your buys which will come in useful for a host of other events."

Sharon felt herself blushing. Liz was too wise by far. Hadn't she already been wondering if the money would stretch to a new coat for four-year-old Roger?

"And mind you spend every penny Donald gave you," Liz went on. "As well as anything extra you can scrape from the housekeeping."

Sharon replaced the receiver thoughtfully. Liz's remarks had alarmed her. Was the Country Club really as exclusive as she implied? Sharon knew it was expensive, but from what Liz said it sounded so much more than that. She was worried. Had her father been right all along?

"He's not our sort," Mr Mather had said when Sharon had suggested they might get engaged. "Oh, I'm not saying anything against the lad, but he's been used to different things; holidays abroad, a grand house."

Sharon had cut him short, laughing gleefully. "Dad! You can't mean it! He's not our class," she mimicked. "That's what you mean, isn't it? Things like that don't matter these days."

She had said it with every confidence and her mother had backed her up.

"Frank Mather, are you implying I didn't bring up our children properly? Sharon can take her place anywhere. She knows what's what, and don't let me hear you suggesting anything else. We're as good as the next person."

Her father had subsided into silence, but now Sharon was beginning to wonder if his views might not have been right after all. Donald's public school, his years at university, his holidays abroad and his home had all left their mark; an indefinable something Sharon knew she lacked. Confidence was one name for it.

S HE hadn't missed it when they were first married. Donald had warned her that his father's position wouldn't make things any easier for them. Mr Haslam was a self-made man and Donald was expected to carve out his own life. Throughout those first years the differences between them hadn't been evident. Evenings out, like the one Donald was planning, had been few and far between, and never, Sharon suspected, on the scale of this one.

But when Donald got his first promotion, he suggested they began to entertain more often and that's when Sharon began to worry. The first dinner party had been a disaster. For days Sharon had pored over cookery books. She'd always prided herself on being a good, plain cook, but clearly this called for something more.

But though the meal was fine, and arrived on a beautifully-laid table, Sharon, herself, had suffered in the process. Her hair, newly and expensively set for the occasion, hung in lank tendrils round her face, and she looked anything but the cool, poised hostess she wanted to be. Her nerves, already frayed, tightened like violin strings knowing how she must look, and she could scarcely bring herself to speak to their guests.

Later, much later it seemed to Sharon, Donald tried to console her.

"Don't worry, love. You'll do better next time. You've simply got to relax."

14

But Sharon didn't want to relax. All she wanted was for life to go on as it had before. She enjoyed the informal nights when they entertained their friends; she loved the quiet evenings she and Donald spent together, and she had to admit that she found their increasing wealth very pleasant. It was fun to be able to dine out occasionally, to buy a dress without worrying about the cost, to seek the sun in some far-off country for their holidays. Why couldn't Donald be content with what they had? Why must he strive for more? Especially if it meant dragging her along on these nerve-racking occasions.

But despite her doubts, Sharon bought her new dress, and Donald whistled his approval when he saw her in it.

"Hey! Keep well away from Les Brown tonight. I want him to keep his mind on business, and . . ." he added quietly, hugging her close to him ". . . I don't want to lose you."

His remarks made Sharon feel much better. She twirled before the mirror, knowing she looked her best. Then her qualms returned as she caught sight of Donald's reflection. He looked so calm, so confident. Even though this meeting mattered to his work, there wasn't a trace of diffidence about him. Not for him the fumbling fingers when it came to handing over her coat. He wouldn't stumble as they followed the waiter. His cutlery wouldn't grow heavy, and unmanageable, or his wine glass unsteady.

Well, there's no turning back, Sharon thought. Somehow she had to get through the evening without disgracing herself.

"Let's get this show on the road," she said, her voice brittle. But Donald didn't seem to notice.

"That's the idea, darling." He piloted her into the sitting-room where Liz was already reading Roger's bedtime story.

"I think I can start planning how to spend my commission, don't you, Liz?" he teased. "Isn't she something?"

Liz grinned, but spoiled the effect by saying something about counting one's chickens, and Sharon knew her friend hadn't been deceived. She knew Sharon was scared.

T HE evening was all Sharon had feared and Liz looked at her sympathetically when they arrived back home, much too early. She squeezed Sharon's fingers as she followed Donald to his car.

"I'll ring tomorrow," she whispered.

Sharon was in bed when Donald came back from dropping Liz at her flat. She was curled into a ball, her face turned away from the door, pretending sleep. But she knew Donald wasn't taken in. The way he moved around told her that.

"I hope you're pleased with yourself." Donald's words burst from him. "I hope you realise I can say goodbye to the Area Managership after tonight's fiasco. All I needed was one really good order to clinch things, but you had to go and behave like a kid right out of school. And not a very good school at that," he added, cuttingly.

Sharon flinched and Donald misinterpreted the movement.

"Oh, don't give me that 'I wasn't educated at a private school' excuse. That's got nothing to do with it. You only had to act like a normal, civilised human being. But it's not just that, is it?"

All at once Donald was bending over her and pulling the covers from her face.

"It's some strange idea you've got into your head," he went on. "Just because your parents were poor and happy, you think there's no other way. Well, my parents were happy, too. Don't you see? Your parents were happy *despite* the fact that they hadn't much money, not because of it."

Sharon didn't know whether he expected an answer but she didn't give him one, and after a moment she felt the blankets descend around her again, and heard Donald stride across the room. As his hand found the door knob he spoke again, his voice softer.

"If you do really believe all that about not knowing how to behave you could learn, you know. But, you won't, will you?" He gave her time to speak, then the door slammed shut behind him.

Sharon burrowed deeper under the covers. She understood what Donald was telling her, and she knew he was right. It was only confidence she needed. But you can't buy that, she argued, silently. Anyway, why should I change? We were happy before. We've got a nice home and . . . and everything. It's him who's spoiling things, not me. He just isn't satisfied, she decided, pummelling the pillow ferociously.

In the kitchen the next morning, a half-full mug and the heel of a badly cut loaf showed that Donald had tried to get himself some breakfast. But there was no sign of his brief-case or the car. Sharon went back upstairs to fetch Roger.

The little boy lay listlessly waiting for her, his face flushed, and Sharon remembered that Liz had said he seemed a little feverish the night before.

Wrapping him in his dressing-gown and a blanket, she carried him downstairs and settled him on the settee.

FAIRY PRINCESS

THEY tell a lovely tale about Alexandra, Queen of Edward VII.

Once she received a grubby, poignant note. From a child long months in bed.

"I will send her flowers!" the Queen said.

Just give the order? Not her way. She chose the flowers; she wrote the note tucked in the gilded basket.

And then the touch of a fairy princess! A Royal carriage halts at a humble door. A footman, clad in scarlet livery, presses flowers into a sick child's hands.

For when the Queen was a child in Denmark, Hans Andersen came to the castle, to tell her his fairy tales.

She never forgot when the chance occurred in later years to play the part of a fairy princess.

Rev. T.R.S. Campbell.

Two Sides To Every Story

"You'll be better there, my love. Mummy will bring you some breakfast in a moment."

Sharon's own head ached, and she wasn't sure which of them felt the most wretched. She wasn't altogether happy when Liz arrived.

She knew her friend meant well, but right now she didn't want to be told where she had gone wrong, or how she could put things right. She led the way through to the kitchen.

"Was there something you wanted?" she said, ungraciously, avoiding the sharp way Liz looked at her.

"How's Roger? I see he's not better. Too quiet by half." She chuckled.

Sharon felt on safer ground. "No, like you said, he seems to have a cold. But you know children, he'll be all right, shortly."

"Don't I just," Liz agreed feelingly. "You can't know how I welcome half-term. I need a break from teaching every once in a while."

Sharon relaxed, smiling across at her friend. "One's enough for me, at least for the time being . . . perhaps for good," she added, her voice rising as a crash and a loud wail came from the other room.

"What is it?" she cried, bursting in on Roger. "Oh, Roger! What were you doing?"

THE boy was lying on a pile of books which were scattered across the floor. He was crying lustily, evidence that he wasn't seriously hurt.

Sharon ran to pull him to his feet. "You naughty boy! You were climbing, weren't you? And on a pile of books. How often have I told you not to climb?"

"But I couldn't get my plane. I couldn't reach."

He saw Liz behind his mother and appealed to her. "I made a plane, just like you showed me, Auntie Liz. And it flew! But it went up there, and I couldn't get it down. I didn't want to shout for you, Mummy," he said, his eyes turning tearfully to Sharon.

"You were so cross, before," he mumbled. "And I could have got it. I could! But the books fell over." He aimed a kick at those nearest to him, but Sharon couldn't chastise him. His words had hurt.

Slowly she hugged him, wiping away his tears with her fingertip. "I'm sorry, love. I didn't mean to be cross. See, I'll get your plane right away."

As she handed the paper toy back to her son, Sharon bent down to ruffle his hair. "Silly lad. Why didn't you get something to hook it down? Daddy's umbrella, perhaps? Now pop back under that blanket. Mummy's not feeling very well, either, so Auntie Liz is going to make all of us a hot drink."

Obediently, Roger tucked himself under the blanket and, as Sharon began to pile the books back on to the shelves, she heard her friend running water into the kettle.

Really, the whole thing was getting out of hand. If only she didn't feel so awful she might find a solution to the problem, but as it stood, she and Donald obviously just weren't going to agree.

B   17

L IZ was busy in the kitchen, ladling sugar into a mug of steaming coffee, when Sharon came in.

"Sweet and hot for shock." Liz smiled. "Or for anything else which might be troubling you, I always say." She pushed the mug towards Sharon and picked up a cup for Roger.

"Won't be a minute, then we can talk."

Sharon wasn't sure she wanted to talk, at least, not about what was the cause of her bad temper. But Liz didn't speak directly of the night before.

"There's one thing about being a teacher," she began, picking up her own drink, "you don't get so emotionally involved. But you do come to know something of how they tick. Take Roger now, he has to stretch himself, Sharon. Has to strive after things, try to do the things which are still beyond him. It's only natural." She gave Sharon a beaming smile. "Don't they say you can't keep a good man down? I suppose it's in the nature of the beast."

Abruptly she drained her beaker and looked swiftly at her watch. "Sorry, love. I've got to dash. Ring if you want me, and if I can give you any more words of wordly wisdom," she chuckled, "don't hesitate to ask."

She was gone before Sharon had collected her thoughts. It was clear there had been more in her friend's words than appeared on the surface, but right now she was content to allow the warm drink to seep through her, bringing its calming relief.

A S she washed the dirty mugs, she caught sight of a small, brightly coloured booklet, which had certainly not been there a few moments before. Wiping her hands hurriedly, she picked it up, and was at the door before she realised that Liz would be far away by now.

I'll phone her, she thought, walking back, her eyes going to the words on the cover.

"Adult Education," she read and idly turned the pages. Then, as she saw that one page had its corner turned down, she smiled as she read the heading. *Etiquette For The Perfect Hostess.*

"Why, Liz Guthrie, you, you . . . you dear!"

Sharon read on. *Behind every good man there's an even better woman. Do you want your husband to get ahead?*

"Well, do I?" Sharon said, out loud. What was it Liz had said? You can't keep a good man down. Could that be true? Could it be that Donald was only doing what was natural to him? Was she holding him back? And for some silly notion of her own?

Perhaps he was right. Perhaps she had got childish, impractical ideas about love in a cottage.

Sharon picked up the telephone and dialled Liz's number.

"I think you left something behind," she said, a laugh in her voice. "But I can give you it back later, that's if you'll come and stay with Roger for an hour or so, this evening, until Donald gets in. I've found there's something I'd like to do. I'm going to enrol for evening classes."

Liz's laughter mingled with Sharon's as she agreed to help out. But Sharon didn't mind, she knew Liz wasn't laughing at her.

It was good to have a friend who really cared about her, Sharon thought. Liz would have to be the guest of honour at the first big dinner party she gave!

As she turned from the phone the front door opened and, suddenly, she was in Donald's arms.

"I had to come back," he said after he had kissed her. "I was awful to you last night. It doesn't matter, Sharon, I don't care about the managership so long as we're happy. That's all that matters to me.

"I was wrong to blame you for things going wrong — to make you feel responsible for something that wasn't your fault. As long as we're together and happy, that's all I care about. We must never quarrel again like we did last night."

Sharon thrilled at his words but she knew now how wrong she had been. Donald had been trying to do all these things for her and Roger, as well as for himself. She didn't really want a man with no ambition, no get-up-and-go.

"No, darling. You were right," she told him. "Love in a cottage is all very well, if that's all you can have. But love, if it's good and strong, ought to be able to stand transplanting to a castle."

"Well, I can't promise a castle right off, but maybe one day. And what I said is right. It wouldn't mean anything at all without you."

"Hey, don't go back on me now," Sharon teased. "A castle it's got to be. And we'll live there happily ever after, like in all the best fairy tales. But ours won't be make believe."

She kissed him, and then Donald swung her off her feet. Sharon found she agreed with all Liz had said. There was something rather primitive about a man in love.

And what's wrong with wanting the best cave in the district, she thought, smiling to herself. □

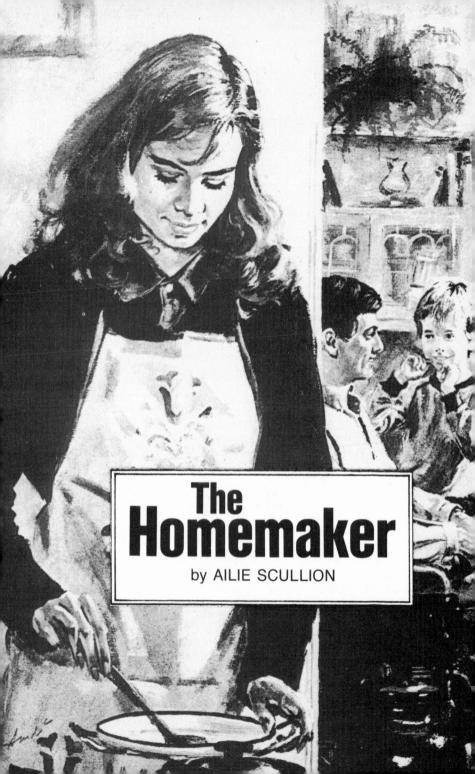

The
Homemaker

by AILIE SCULLION

The Homemaker

I KNEW I'd made a mistake the minute I saw the sign Hilltop Farm, but the advert had seemed so appealing.

Live-in housekeeper required. Sheepfarm in Clachmurrin. Good cook essential. Small boy, very independent. Applicant able to work on own initiative.

It was the last sentence that settled things. I couldn't bear to have a boss to rule over me. No, Pennygail Mirren liked to make her own rules and I told Martin Thaw so when we spoke on the phone.

Martin owned Hilltop Farm and he had been widowed now for almost eight years. I was told that there'd been a few housekeepers before, but that the isolated position of the farm seemed to put them off. He asked if I minded the quietness of the countryside.

No, I told him. After the city college I'd attended for four years and sharing a flat with three noisy students, I didn't mind the quiet countryside. And I was efficient, I assured him. I had splendid references from my tutors to prove it, and a diploma that said I could cook and do all sorts of other things besides.

The whole thing happened quickly. The journey north took up a full day so I stayed overnight at a village inn and caught the first bus that would take me to Clachmurrin. I'd burnt my boats all right, I thought, as the driver let me off at the foot of the hill.

"Hilltop Farm?" he queried. "Och, you mean Big Martin's place. Why, it will just take you a few strides, Miss, with those long legs of yours. Of course, I should warn you, the hills are turned the wrong way where you are going."

The driver was right, the hills were all turned the wrong way. They went up and up. My legs ached, and the suitcase grew heavier, then I saw it, the notice tacked on to the gate. Gate? Perhaps I should say the rusted bedframe tied to a post with rope.

Oh, Lord! I thought, what have I let myself in for?

I climbed carefully over the top of the bedframe, trying not to snag my new tights. I was wearing my best suit for I was trying to make a good impression on my new employer, but I was beginning to wonder if it was all worthwhile. I wasn't too sure that I would enjoy living in a place like this, after all.

The house, when I eventually reached it, was a simple affair, grey stone with a single chimney that sat askew the sloping roof. Smoke billowed cheerfully and I felt a little better.

The outhouses, I noticed with distaste, were somewhat dilapidated and the entire yard cluttered with rather obsolete looking farm implements. I remembered my father's spread in Northumberland with its super efficient machinery.

I marched up to the front door, and it opened immediately.

Martin Thaw had a distracted look about him. Sandy brown hair, waving naturally, seemed determined to hang over his forehead. He ran his fingers through it.

"I'm sorry, you must be Miss Pennygail Mirren. I meant to be down at the foot of the road for the bus coming in, but somehow . . ."

I looked past him into the kitchen. It was a complete shambles. There were pots and pans everywhere, one with porridge which had boiled over, and a puddle of the same had formed on the flagged floor.

"I'm sorry," he repeated. "The daily didn't turn up again and I'm afraid Nicky made breakfast."

He was looking so flustered I actually felt sorry for him.

"Never mind, Mr Thaw, I'll soon put all this to rights," I said confidently.

"Will you really?" He smiled at me then and his entire face lit up. I decided that Martin Thaw was a very inefficient man, but pleasant with it.

He attempted to show me where things were, but seemed hopelessly uninformed, so eventually I hinted that he might have work to do outside. He looked grateful.

"Well, yes, Miss Pennygail, I mean Miss Mirren, there are some fences I need to see to."

"Then off you go and leave this to me, and by the way, call me Penny."

He gave me another of his sunny smiles and disappeared like a fox into thicket.

A FTER he left I looked about and my spirits sunk lower. Then I saw the brown earthenware teapot and brightened somewhat.

After a cup of tea things wouldn't seem so bad. The place did have possibilities, I decided. I liked the huge open fireplace for a start, and the flagged floor and the large whitewood table, too. No doubt when harvest time came round this room would be filled with farm workers.

But, of course, I probably would be long gone before harvest time. My appointment was only as a temporary "live-in."

Perhaps Martin Thaw was contemplating re-marriage, I thought. After all, the house did need a woman's touch, and an eight-year-old boy required a mother, too. Yes, he probably had some woman in mind to fill the bill and I sympathised with the absent candidate. She would have her work cut out!

When I'd drunk my tea I set to with a will and had cleaned up most of the mess by the time the daily arrived. I looked at the clock. It was twenty-to-eleven.

"What exactly are your hours, Mrs Murray," I asked, as the buxom woman began to put on her pinafore.

The woman looked slightly offended.

"Nine until one, Miss, but Mr Thaw is very understanding. He doesn't really mind if I suit myself."

"Well, from now on, Mrs Murray," I said, "I want you here at exactly nine o'clock, and today you can make up the hours, by waiting on until three. I think you could start on the windows now."

She looked at me in amazement and I knew exactly what she was thinking — a young chit of a girl giving me orders. But at college I'd been taught about how to handle people. Give them some rules to obey,

The Homemaker

I was told, and they knew just exactly where they were with you.

I'll say this for Mrs Murray, once she decided to work she did so with alacrity, and the windows shone brightly in no time at all.

BY three o'clock we had the place spick and span between us and there was understanding, too. We parted on friendly terms and I was just bending over the oven to remove the steak and kidney pie I'd cooked, when I heard the voice at my back.

"That smells lovely."

Nicky Thaw, I'd been told, was just eight years old but looked older. He had his father's long legs and his serious expression, too, but that was where the resemblance ended. Where the farmer had been shy and almost inarticulate, Nicky had a great deal to say for himself.

"So you must be Pennygail Mirren. Dad and I thought the name sounded like something out of a story book, but I must say you are better looking than most of the others that have passed through. Shall I set the table?"

"How do you get up here from school, Nicky?" I asked when I could get a word in.

"By bus, of course. I walk the rest of the way from the road."

"You must get pretty wet whenever it rains."

"A bit," he admitted, "but my dad said a bit of rain never did anyone any harm. What do you think of Dad? He can't keep staff, but he's all right, you know, and he has the best black-faced sheep in the North."

He was quite the most forthright child I'd ever met and he wasn't through yet.

"Usually the 'live-ins' get annoyed when Dad forgets to come in for his meals. You see, he gets caught up on the hills and forgets that he's not eaten and I have to go up there and fetch him. Are you married or engaged or anything like that?"

I shook my head.

"Good," he said briskly. "That's something. Before, it used to give them a rare excuse to put in their notice."

I bit my lip.

"How many housekeepers has your dad had exactly?"

The boy grinned at me.

"Oh, I stopped counting after a while. Miss McFetteridge wasn't bad. She stayed for a whole month."

Nicky buttered himself a slice of bread and went to sit beside the fire. I found myself drawn towards him.

"Has your mother been dead long, Nicky?"

"Oh yes. She died when I was little. I don't really remember her. Gran was with us until I was five but then she died, too, and we've been having 'live-ins' ever since."

Poor mite, I thought compassionately. What a life he must have had.

I gave myself a shake. Why, I too, was yet another of Martin Thaw's "live-ins." No doubt I would be gone before the end of the month like all the others, and I could see what had driven my predecessors away!

Earlier young Nicky had described his father as a bit of a dreamer, but I classed him as downright inefficient. I was remembering the bed-frame gate and the obselete machinery in the yard outside.

At college we'd been taught that there was a right way and a wrong way to do things and clearly I would have to take this household to task. Start the way you mean to go on, was my motto.

What this household needed was some rules to live by. I decided to tackle my employer as soon as he chose to come home.

A T six on the dot Martin arrived in the kitchen and sniffed appreciatively as he struggled with his gumboots at the door.

He loved my steak and kidney pie and ate two helpings. Nicky didn't do badly either, I was pleased to see. I waited until he'd drunk his third cup of tea then I tackled him.

"About your daily, Mr Thaw . . ."

The farmer looked guilty. "Mrs Murray? Was she late again?"

I looked at him severely.

"You're much too lenient, Mr Thaw, and she takes advantage. Now I've taken the liberty of making a few rules."

"Rules?" He looked at me in dismay.

"Yes, Mr Thaw. If we hope to bring some order into this household we must have some rules to live by."

"What do you mean?" he queried.

"Mealtimes." I ticked off my first rule. "Breakfast at half-past five, lunch at one, and the evening meal at six on the dot. Do you agree to that?"

He ran his fingers through his hair in a now familiar gesture.

"Sometimes I forget the time Miss . . . Pennygail, I mean, Miss Mirren."

I was becoming exasperated.

"Call me Penny, please! Nicky told me how you forget the time and I happened to find this pocket watch in the top drawer of the dresser."

"That belonged to my dad," he told me accusingly.

"And a very good timekeeper it is, too."

"Are these all your rules then, Penny?"

I shook my head.

"That car in the garage. May I use it, when I need it? If it rains, I can run down to the main road and collect Nicky off the bus, and I can get into town and back with provisions and so on."

His mouth opened ever so slightly, but I wasn't finished yet.

"And my last rule is this, Mr Thaw, I must have complete say over everything that happens in this kitchen. Do you agree?"

The man nodded his head.

"The kitchen is yours completely, Penny, and the Mini, too, if you need it. But what did you mean about Nicky. It didn't rain today, surely?"

"No," I agreed, "but the boy has a cough. I'll take him into town tomorrow and let the doctor take a look at him."

"He's as strong as an ox," Martin Thaw declared, for the first time showing real resentment. "He may be skinny, but that runs in the Thaws. Nicky's not missed a day off school since he started."

"Perhaps so," I broke in, "and I intend to see that he remains healthy, so I'll just get him checked up anyway."

"Please yourself," he said huffily, and started to hunt for his pipe. I pointed towards the fireplace, where I'd laid out his slippers, his pipe and tobacco purse. Efficiency, I let him see now, paid off.

He padded across the flagged floor and sat down by the fire and buried his head in a newspaper. I had got my way so far, and I made up my mind straightaway that if Martin Thaw kept up his end, I would see that he had his creature comforts waiting for him.

That first evening flew in. Nicky showed me the entire house and where things were kept. He knew everything about Hilltop Farm and kept up a steady flow of conversation that had me blushing one minute and roaring with laughter the next.

He began to tell me about some of my predecessors. His "live-ins" as he called them. There was a Miss Furbisher who used to sweep the dust under the carpets and gave them minced steak for dinner four nights a week.

Then there'd been Miss McFetteridge whom Nicky believed fancied his dad, but she couldn't light the stove and had to get his father to do it before he started work each morning.

Anticipation

MASTER, do put on your coat and
hat;
I'm getting so bored, dozing on the
mat,
Patiently waiting just for you
To finish whatever you have to do!
It's almost time for our walk, you
know.
I wonder which way today we'll go,
P'raps if I growl, or softly whine,
You'll know that I'm ready, so make up
your mind
To whip off your specs, and put down
your book.
Why, here you are, with my lead off the
hook!
A pat on my head, as I rush to the
door,
Three hearty cheers for a walkie in
store!

Elizabeth Gozney.

Nicky didn't know why Miss McFetteridge left so hurriedly, but his father had sighed with relief and said next time they would look for someone more matronly.

I felt myself drawing in a breath as Nicky looked at me.

"Why do you wear your hair in that funny bun at the back, Miss Penny? Buns are for old ladies like my gran, and besides, my dad likes women that have long hair brushed out and . . ."

"Nicky, I don't think the way I wear my hair has anything to do with you or your father. And if you want to know, I wear my hair this way during the day for hygiene, working in the kitchen. Sometimes, in the evenings, I may brush it out."

"Oh, I'm sure Dad will like that, Miss Penny."

We had reached my own bedroom, an attic really, but with such a delightful view of the moors that I fell in love with it immediately.

Martin Thaw's room downstairs was a proper dismal affair with brown panelled walls and dark velvet curtains. If that were mine, I'd have had it papered in pale primrose and . . .

For some reason I found myself blushing as I turned towards young Nicky. "I think it's about time we got you to bed, young man."

I 'D been living for almost three months at Hilltop Farm when Nicky put the question to me.

"Why don't you and Dad get married, Miss Penny? If it's just me you are thinking about, I've no objection."

By now, I was quite used to Nicky's forthright statements, but this one made me start. I wondered just how much he knew.

It wasn't that the man had come out and said as much, but I knew Martin Thaw thought a great deal about me now-a-days, and I treasured the evenings we spent together sitting quietly in the sitting-room watching television or reading our books.

Oh, I still lived by my rules, but recently I'd mellowed a little. For one thing, I now realised how hard Martin worked on the hills and with so little help, and I saw how much his young son adored him, too. And so, when Nicky asked me his question I didn't think it unnatural.

"Why should your father want to marry me, Nicky?"

"Och, he needs a wife, Miss Penny, you have to admit it, and you're by far the best 'live-in' we've had up till now."

I laughed aloud. "Well, thank you very much, Nicky."

"Oh, and Dad likes you," he went on. "He said so the other day when we went into market to sell the yearlings."

"Oh?" My interest was roused. "What exactly did he say, Nicky?"

"That you had the nicest pair of legs he'd seen in a woman yet, but he wished you wouldn't wear jeans and cover them up so much. And look at the way he sits up at night with you. Dad used to go off to his bed and read when the other 'live-ins' were here."

I felt immeasurably cheered by this last piece of news, but guilty too, to be probing this young child for scraps of comfort. If only Martin would come out and tell me himself that he liked me.

"And you like him, too, don't you, Miss Penny? I mean, take his shirts."

"His shirts, Nicky?"

I could feel myself blushing, for I'd no idea Nicky had been monitoring my movements so closely. Martin's shirts were all badly in need of attention. I'd noticed frayed cuffs and the odd button astray. Secretly, as I thought, I'd been removing them from the wardrobe, repairing them then returning them to their hangers.

"I mean, no-one would sew shirts for someone they didn't like."

"I'm your father's housekeeper Nicky. It is my job to . . ."

The boy raised one eyebrow.

"Even his shirts?"

Really, he was far too knowledgeable for an eight-year-old boy!

Still, as we sat that night eating our evening meal, I cast secret glances at Martin Thaw. I'd grown to appreciate this rangy looking farmer, despite his absent-mindedness. He had other qualities I really admired. Such as his great courtesy and his obvious wish to please.

And he really appreciated what I did in the kitchen. Last week he bought an automatic washing machine and it sat looking so out of place in the old-fashioned room, but I loved him for it, too.

He wasn't hard to please either. Place his slippers beside the fire and his pipe at the ready and he almost purred with contentment.

"You know how to spoil a fellow, Penny," he told me after Nicky went off to bed. Martin's brown eyes glowed and I felt the familiar swell of pleasure at his compliment. I knew now that I could grow to love him and Nicky, too, but hadn't I my career to consider?

TONIGHT there was a play on television and we were both looking forward to seeing it. We made a homely scene, we two, each in our armchairs beside the fire, he with his pipe, and I knitting a sweater to replace that old one he clung to so fervently.

When the lights went out and the television went blank, I heard Martin let out a long sigh.

"Must be the fuses again, Penny. I really must think about re-wiring the house."

I could have told him that the washing-machine must have done the harm. The wiring wasn't up to such modern innovations! I heard him feeling his way out into the hall, then a yell as he struck his head on a beam.

I smiled in the dark. Inefficient, I'd once called him. Now, I was even beginning to find his shortcomings endearing. Goodness, I must be going soft.

When at last he had the fuse fixed and returned to the room, I was pouring him a nightcap. The television was switched off.

"But I thought you wanted to watch that play?" he said.

"We've missed the best part," I told him. "Anyway, I've seen it twice before. Why don't we go for our walk now?"

His eyes lit up. "We could head for the Spying Cop if you like, then back through the woods. They're lovely this time of year."

We walked companionably across the moorland, I, with my hand tucked inside his.

"You won't up and leave us now, will you Pennygail Mirren?" he asked me softly. "The others didn't matter one whit, but I couldn't bear to part with you."

We had stopped beside the wood and the grassy knoll that was known locally as the Spying Cop. These past few evenings we'd found our feet wending this way.

"I wasn't thinking about leaving Hilltop, Martin. I rather like it, working for you."

We walked on another few steps then he turned. Martin's long, craggy face seemed perplexed. My answer which should have afforded him some satisfaction only tended to make him seem disappointed.

"I wasn't exactly thinking about your employment, Penny. It was about us. You must know the way I feel for you."

It was my turn to look at him.

"No Martin, I don't know. I know you've tried hard to get Hilltop Farm into some order. You even replaced that old bedframe with a real gate! And I know you come home for meals bang on time each day, and never complain about anything I do in the kitchen. But how you feel about me, is something I don't know. Tell me, please, Martin."

He looked astonished and stared at me in silence for a very long time as though silently rehearsing what he would say. For a moment he looked very like young Nicky.

"Some mornings, Penny," he said, "I climb to the top of Torrpoint and watch a sunrise. There's something special about a sunrise up there, you know, and it makes me feel queer inside, and that's how I feel when you are near me. Even when I have to obey your daft rules I'd do so willingly just to be close to you. It's just being with you that matters."

He had my fullest attention now. And to think I imagined only young Nicky knew how to say surprising things to a girl.

"Well, that's the way I feel about you, Penny. You're the finest thing that has ever come my way. Oh, lass, when will you marry me and come down from that attic room and join me?"

"I don't like your walls," I told him quickly, "and I'd like frilled curtains and a white rug to sit in front of the bed . . ."

"More rules." He sighed. "But they are yours, every one of them."

I put up my arms and wound them about his neck.

"Oh, Martin, I'd marry you, even without a white rug, you know that, don't you? You see, I've come to love Hilltop Farm, too, and I have my own special sunrises, when I see those long legs of yours coming hurrying down from the hill just so as to arrive in time for tea. My stupid time-table! Rules! Who needs them anyway?"

And that was when he kissed me. Later, we would explain things to Nicky, although I'd a sneaking suspicion that clever lad already knew what was in the wind. But right now, we had lots of things to say to one another and the cool dark woods were beckoning. □

The village of Killin at the western end of Loch Tay lies amidst typically beautiful Highland scenery. It is closely associated with the Clan McNab whose burial place is on a small island in the river just below the Falls of Dochart. This can be seen from the road bridge. On the south side of the river, facing the village, is Kinnell House. It became the seat of the MacNabs in the 17th century and later it came into the possession of the Breadalbane family. The second Marquess of Breadalbane planted a black vine at Kinnell and it is said not to have missed a crop since 1832.

KILLIN, PERTHSHIRE

High On A Hill

by Joan Alison

IT was too late to turn back now. The plane was taxi-ing down the runway. Tears pricked my eyes as the small, inter-island plane rose into the air.

Was I really doing the right thing, beginning a new life so far away? Or being a coward and running out on the old? When I broke off my engagement to Paul, the only thing I wanted was to move right away.

Everyone had known Paul was seeing someone else — everyone except me.

I remembered my bewilderment and bruised emotions. Somehow I had found the courage to give back the ring.

We taught at the same school in Cumbria, and the atmosphere in the staff-room was uncomfortable. I couldn't concentrate on my work, so I gave in my notice at half-term.

The last few weeks were bad. I still loved Paul, but told myself that love was for the ideal, not for the person he really was. My life was suddenly empty and I grasped at whatever I could in exchange.

Impulse caused me to answer the advertisement for a teaching post on a remote Hebridean island. I was called for an interview to Stornoway, but I also chose to take the ferry to Morvay itself. I'd never been to the Outer Hebrides and wanted to see for myself what might be in store for me.

The deck of the ferry boat had been cold and forbidding then. The sea was grey and the glistening rocks were far from reassuring. But as the boat docked, a pale, watery sun shone for my first view of Morvay.

I'd booked a room at a small guest house near the pier. Mrs Johnson welcomed me warmly and insisted I had tea to drive out the cold from my bones. I began to relax.

"So you're to be the new teacher up at the school?" she asked, settling herself comfortably on a chair to watch me drink the fresh tea.

"Oh, no, nothing's settled. I had an interview in Stornoway, but I wanted to see Morvay myself."

"And have you come all the way from Cumbria just to look at Morvay?" She chuckled and shook her head. "You must be a determined young woman!"

I WALKED the short distance along the road to the school. It was a local holiday. Several boys cycled up and down at frightening speeds, turning in the middle of the deserted road, narrowly missing collision with each other. Small girls had a makeshift house on spare ground beside the telephone box.

David Craig was in the main schoolroom, hands clasped behind his back, looking out of the window. So, he'd been watching me!

He was a younger man than I expected to find as headmaster of the island school. Dark haired and broad shouldered, he was good looking except that his face was marred by a savage scar down one cheek, and a scowl which brought his black brows together in a stern line.

"Come in, Miss Hargreaves," he said, allowing no smile to soften the invitation.

He led the way to a small office in which every surface seemed to be covered by books. The window frame rattled in the breeze and I could see shirts flapping on a taut washing-line outside.

David Craig shuffled the papers in front of him.

"From what I read in your application documents, you appear over-qualified for the job here," he said abruptly.

I felt my face redden. This was a strange interview. I quickly decided Mr David Craig was ill mannered and bad tempered. There'd be no pleasure working with him.

I was just congratulating myself on the wisdom of coming to see for myself what the prospects were, when his words broke into my thoughts.

"Have you nothing to say?"

I pulled myself together.

"I'm looking for the experience of teaching in a small school," I heard myself say calmly. Only *I* knew it was not the real reason.

"You don't find big classes a challenge, is that it?" Was there a sneer in his voice? "The youngsters here are bound by the geography of their surroundings," he went on, "so it's no good trying to inspire them with lofty ideals they're in no position to realise."

I looked at the dark, curly head of the scowling man before me. Why was he talking such nonsense? He'd not looked at me. I stared at the livid scar on his cheek.

"If I'm selected to fill the vacancy, Mr Craig," I said stiffly, "I shall teach the children basic principles and encourage them to use their education to suit the circumstances."

When I returned to the guest house, Mrs Johnson had a meal ready. The smell of new-baked bread reminded me vividly of my grand-mother's kitchen above Keswick, with its black range and rows of fresh-baked loaves cooling on the fender.

"And how did you find Mr Craig, then?" Mrs Johnson asked. There was no doubt of the twinkle in her eye.

"I don't think he liked me very much." I sighed and put jam on the new bread.

"I don't think he likes women." Mrs Johnson chuckled. "He'd prefer a male assistant but nowadays there's to be no discrimination."

"His face . . ." I began, curiosity getting the better of me. "How did he get that dreadful scar?"

"I've heard he was on a climbing holiday in the Cuillins — with a friend. There was a nasty accident and the friend was killed. Mr Craig lay injured for several days before he was found, poor man." Mrs Johnson's face softened, but I thought she was wasting her sympathy.

I RETURNED home on the ferry next day. The sun shone and Morvay looked particualrly beautiful. Only one mountain, Burneval, rose from the centre of the peat hags, and a wisp of cloud lay like a halo round the uneven peak.

Some day I'd go back, but not to teach. Obviously, David Craig wouldn't commend me to his superiors.

I stood at the ship's rail and watched the gannets' black-tipped wings as they soared, suddenly twisting and diving like darts. I sighed. Ah, well. There'd be something else.

But there was nothing else. By the time I applied for other posts, they were already filled. I felt a mounting panic. What had I done? For the first time, depression reached out and tugged me down. I felt sorry for myself and life was unfair.

The letter arrived on a particularly dull morning. Brief and to the point, the Western Isles Education Authority wrote that I had been appointed assistant teacher at the school on the Isle of Morvay.

I remembered the sun-lit slopes of Burneval, the turquoise sea and the diving gannets. I smelled new bread, pictured Mrs Johnson's welcoming face. Depression began to fade even as I recalled the glowering Mr Craig.

When I read the details with more care my heart lifted. I was to stay at the guest house till I could make more permanent arrangements. It was enough to know I'd be sure of a welcome from Mrs Johnson.

Friends and family gave conflicting advice.

"You must be mad to work in such an isolated place. You'll be bored stiff," one maintained.

"What if you're ill, miles from anywhere?" another asked.

My cousin took me on one side.

"I think you're just running away, Alison," she said. "Paul's not seeing anyone. In fact, he's missing you. Can't you two get together again?"

But it was all too late. The plane was coming in to land, bumping down on to the landing strip. A small building housed the few necessary formalities and I was back on the Isle of Morvay, my future bound up with the small school and its pupils.

YOU'LL be Miss Hargreaves," a tall, fair-haired boy in fisherman's jersey said. "I'm Hamish Johnson." He picked up my suitcase and carried it to his van.

"Mother was pleased when she had the phone call asking her to take in the new teacher. She said she knew it would be you." Hamish drove out of the car park on to the road without pausing. "She didn't tell me how bonnie you were."

I hung on to a broken strap which did service as a door handle and braced my feet against the rattling floor. Twice I closed my eyes as sheep crossed in front of the van, but Hamish neither deviated nor braked and the sheep remained unscathed.

I was exhausted when the van drew to a shuddering halt outside the guest house. Mrs Johnson hurried to greet me, bidding me come away in and not waste time with the luggage. Hamish would see to that.

I was tasting the new bread and home-made jam again when Hamish came in. He sat on an upright chair by the door, his fair hair catching a ray of sunlight. I looked away but could feel his eyes on me.

"And where are you planning to stay after your first two weeks?" Mrs Johnson asked.

"I'll need to find lodgings somewhere," I said. "I can't take up accommodation you'd be filling with tourists, and quite honestly," I admitted, "I'll not be able to afford your standard of comforts on my salary."

"And who's said what we'll be charging you?" Hamish leaned forward.

"If you'd not mind taking the back bedroom with its view of the chickens and the school playground," Mrs Johnson said, "you'd be doing me a kindness. The tourists want views of the sea."

With wide-eyed innocence, she continued.

"It's not a big room but we've put in a desk, and there's an armchair."

Of course, the room was perfect. She'd not mentioned the view of

Burneval, nor the ancient standing stone outlined against the sky.

Hamish followed me up the stairs to make sure the furniture was exactly where I needed it.

"If it's not right, you say and I'll move it." His eyes were blue and unwavering.

"Thank you." I smiled, but he didn't move.

"I'd like to unpack," I said, holding the door and willing him to leave. He came out of his reverie, gave an apology and left me to my new room.

THE view of the school playground didn't dismay me at all. It reminded me of the disagreeable David Craig, but I would be teaching the children and any dealings I must have with the headmaster would be on a purely proper professional basis.

Over our evening meal, Mrs Johnson brought me up to date.

"Mr Craig moved into the school house — the one adjoining the school. He had rooms with Mrs MacSween at the other end of the village, but she's not well and is glad not to take another lodger."

She offered me a slice of rich fruit cake which I took absent-mindedly.

"When your predecessor, Mrs Fairhurst, retired and went to live with her sister in Glasgow, Mr Craig asked for the school house."

"Isn't he married?" As the words left my mouth I realised it was nothing to do with me. Who would marry such a sour individual?

"Well now, there's always talk and I don't hold with gossip. Some people's tongues won't leave the poor man alone. My sister-in-law goes in twice a week to clean. She often takes a bit of her baking for him. For the rest, he makes his own meals and does his washing."

I remembered the shirts fastened to the line outside the school-room window all those weeks before, properly pegged by their tails. It seemed a world away.

Hamish had remained silent but now he stood and fixed me with those blue eyes.

"You need any help — just anything at all, Miss Hargreaves, you ask me."

"Of course, Hamish. You're very kind."

He smiled triumphantly and left the room, whistling softly.

"You've made a hit with him and no mistake. He adored Mrs Fairhurst when he was a boy and was always round there bringing in her peats, carrying driftwood." Mrs Johnson sighed. "Now he's grown, and he's crewing aboard the Seawife. He's just a soft-hearted laddie." His mother looked lovingly at the door as though he might reappear at any moment.

School wasn't due to start till the following week. I needed the time to settle in, to become familiar with the school cupboards, the books, the conventions and taboos.

Obviously, I'd have to call on David Craig and ask for his assistance. After that I'd get on very well on my own.

I knocked on the school-house door.

"Who is it?" a wary voice demanded. "And what are you wanting?"

"Alison Hargreaves, your new assistant. I'd be glad of a few words when you can spare the time." I can be polite, I thought, even if he can't.

"Wait a moment, please." David Craig's peremptory tone made me groan inwardly. He was certainly no better than I remembered.

The door opened after several minutes and, with no apology for the delay, he asked me in. The sitting-room was sparsely furnished with old-fashioned easy-chairs and there were books everywhere.

I sniffed a familiar smell, but couldn't place it.

"What did you want to see me about?" he asked.

"I'd like to discuss my duties, arrange my timetable and see just what materials and books are at my disposal."

He looked at me, frowning, the scar puckered on his cheek.

"You can go into the school whenever you like. Here are a set of keys." David Craig pointed to them on top of a text book. "The time-table is on the wall of your class-room. No need to change it. It's worked perfectly well for the last eighteen months. You can look in the cupboards, but there's no need to move anything."

Suddenly the identity of the smell came to me. David Craig had been ironing. I'd smelled the freshly-laundered shirts and the hot iron, but they'd been whisked away when I knocked on the door.

I smiled and picked up the keys. "Thank you. I'll not take up any more of your time. You can finish your ironing in peace."

His scowl was more pronounced but at least he opened the door for me to leave.

As I explored the school I wondered what hurt the man was nursing, what pride kept him apart from everyone. The scarred face and forbidding manner made an impenetrable fence, but I believed there was a chink somewhere.

THE first day of term went well. The children were curious about me and I welcomed their questions. They had spoken with me in the village already and in such a small community information travels fast by undetected routes.

The few who prefaced every remark with "Mrs Fairhurst says . . ." soon let it slide and I felt the children's acceptance of me with relief.

On Friday afternoon I took my books to David Craig's office.

"What is it?" he barked in response to my knock.

I didn't wait his bidding but walked in.

"You'll want to look through my week's marks and records. If you have any questions about my progress, I'll be pleased to answer," I said cheerfully.

"Not necessary," he retorted, lifting his eyes briefly. "I can see you know your job. Just get on with it and I'll get on with mine."

He paused and looked up at me as I stood, stunned by his words. But it was the first time I'd seen his face without a scowl, and his face looked strained.

On Saturday I settled at the desk in my room and looked out on Burneval. My decision *had* been the right one after all. I'd not thought of Paul with any regret for days. I felt completely free. I'd not take Paul back if he came to Morvay on bended knees. The picture this conjured up made me laugh and I began to prepare lessons for the following week.

The time passed without me noticing, so when Hamish knocked and brought me a cup of tea and a plate of hot buttered scones, I was surprised.

"Mother says your meal will be ready at six, if it suits you."

I asked him to thank his mother.

"Would you like to take a walk with me down to the bay, Miss Hargreaves?" Hamish said shyly. "When you've finished your work, I mean."

Silence hung in the room. Hamish waited with a certain embarrassment.

"I'm afraid it can't be today," I said, smiling to temper the disappointment. "It was kind of you to ask."

Hamish blushed and closed the door behind him. It wasn't that I didn't like the boy, but he made me uneasy with his constant admiration. I certainly didn't want anyone getting ideas about my relationship with Hamish Johnson. And if I took a walk with him — anywhere — the local people would have our names linked closely whatever demands were made.

Family Tea

THE family are coming to tea today,
So I must put all my clutter away.
Papers and magazines, my knitting too,
All stuffed in a corner, right out of view.

There'll be daughter Jane, with her little boys,
The place will soon be littered with toys.
And my old trunk turned upside down
For Jamie's girl, dressing up to clown.

The piano thumped for the children to sing,
And the toddlers into everything.
With "Granny" this, and "Granny" that,
And forever chasing my poor old cat.

There's always so much news to tell,
Of how the twins just haven't been well.
And the others getting so clever at school,
And Johnny can swim the length of the pool.

I always bake cakes and scones for tea,
Whenever the family descend on me.
I love them all, from the depth of my heart,
But oh! What peace, when they depart!
        — Dorothy M. Loughran.

When I went downstairs just before six o'clock, Mrs Johnson switched off the Gaelic radio programme.

"My goodness, you're a hard worker and no mistake. You should get out a bit in the fresh air."

"Oh, there'll be plenty of time for that when I've planned how best to help the children." I laughed. I wondered if it had been her idea to send Hamish with the invitation he'd given earlier. It was just the kind of thing she'd do.

High On A Hill

THE following Saturday I set out along the track which led to the slopes of Burneval. After a mile, the track disappeared among rough heather, coarse grass and peat bogs. I guessed it wasn't far to the Standing Stone and from there I was sure there'd be a view of the whole western shore of the island.

As I scrambled, breathless, to the huge stone, I saw the whole perfect panorama stretching before me. I lifted my binoculars and scanned the ground between myself and the sea, then I turned and looked upwards towards the craggy tops of Burneval.

Suddenly I saw someone lying, curled up beneath a rocky outcrop. There was no movement apart from a piece of clothing lifting, fluttering in the breeze. Someone had fallen. Perhaps they were injured, unconscious . . .

I looked quickly round to judge the best way to approach. I must get up there to see if I could help then hurry down to find a telephone. I looked at the rough terrain. Without considerable care I could become a casualty myself, I thought.

I came on the person from behind and, as I approached, breathing heavily from exertion, he rolled over and sat up.

It was David Craig. I stopped, surprised.

"Are you all right?" I said. "I thought, when I saw you from farther down, that you were hurt."

"So you hurried to render first aid?" he asked, wryly.

"Well, I'd not made any plans," I admitted, smiling with relief.

David Craig was actually smiling. The transformation was staggering. Dark-brown eyes, hair ruffled by the breeze, the scar out of sight on the other cheek — he looked a different person.

"Plans can easily go wrong," he said.

We sat in companionable silence for a while. The long stretch of shore below us was deserted. Endless lines of waves rolled in, their tops falling white and random to exhaust themselves on the steep sand. I was mesmerised, relaxed.

"Did you see the buzzard?" my companion asked, picking up his binoculars from the sketch pad beside him. "He rests regularly on the Standing Stone, but never comes near enough for me to make a real portrait of him."

I'd not seen the buzzard, nor any other bird that I'd noticed.

"You know a lot about birds," I said. "Perhaps you'll help me to identify some of them."

"Perhaps," he said, non-committally. He stretched his arms above his head and yawned. "The air sends me to sleep after a week in the class-room. I'm going further up the hill," he added, glancing down at my walking boots. "You can come if you've a mind to."

I followed but he set a killing pace so before long I gave up and sat down again. Through the binoculars I could see the school and Mrs Johnson's house with peat smoke curling from the chimney. In the other direction I could pick out the tiny airstrip with its terminal building and the rocky headland beyond. It was all becoming so familiar to me and I was growing to love the place.

I WENT too fast for you," David Craig said behind me. I'd not heard him approach and turned in surprise.

He laughed at my expression.

"Tit for tat," he said. "I thought you'd fallen or twisted your ankle. Couldn't see you when I reached the top so retraced my steps to render first aid."

The original abruptness was still there but somewhat softer round the edges.

"It takes a while to get into training for this kind of countryside," I said. "No doubt I'll improve with practice. Anyway, thank you for coming to look for me."

I stood up and smiled. For a moment I couldn't look away from his brown eyes. It was almost as though I read a question in them.

By the time I arrived home, the village had seen me come down from Burneval with David Craig.

Mrs Johnson's eyes twinkled as she put down a plate of freshly-cooked fish before me.

"Mr Craig coming round a bit, is he?" she asked. "Getting used to a woman teacher, then?"

"I think he must be," I answered. "He's a very accomplished artist. His drawings of birds are excellent."

"Well, he's out in all weathers — either on the sea-shore or up the mountain when school's finished," she remarked, watching me closely.

But I made no further comment on the subject of Morvay's head-master.

A S I watched the wading birds running along the shore at the edge of the tide, I wished I knew more about them. I sat in the shelter of the dunes, binoculars to my eyes. David Craig walked by without seeing me. He stopped fifty yards further on, raised his binoculars and watched the seabirds.

I got up and joined him.

"I'd like to know the names of the different birds," I said.

He didn't seem surprised by my voice. It was almost as if he expected me.

We walked slowly along the sand till we found the track back to the village.

"I can make a drinkable cup of tea," he said.

"Then I'll come in and try one," I replied, used to the oblique form of his invitations.

"You're doing a good job here," he remarked later, spooning sugar into his cup and stirring noisily. "The children are already very fond of you."

I looked up and found his brown eyes questioning me again. They also showed me beyond doubt that he had been badly hurt by someone and that he was determined never to be so vulnerable again — never to be taken advantage of again.

"You've been very well accepted here," he went on. "It's easy to see the villagers have taken to you."

High On A Hill

"And I'm fond of them," I said. "Strange," I continued slowly, picking my way with care, "how one finds that things one undertakes with least enthusiasm often turn out for the best. I never dreamed I'd come to love Morvay so much."

He got up abruptly and put down his tea on a table behind my chair. I felt his hand on my shoulder.

"But, Alison, are you happy? Can you be sure?"

His use of my name and the pain in his voice made my heart turn over. I caught his hand and held it, warm and strong, against my face.

"Oh, I'm sure, David. I did make a mistake — once — and perhaps you did sometime in your life. My mistake taught me something."

I took a deep breath.

"I love you, David. That is my happiness."

His hand shook against my cheek. He pulled it away and came round to the front of my chair, his face bleak, vulnerable and pale. His eyes implored me not to speak anything but the truth. I got up from the chair.

He took me in his arms then, without a word, and I felt the poor scarred cheek against mine.

"I love you, David," I whispered.

He kissed me with a hunger which unnerved me, then held me at arms' length and studied me with a boyish grin. How could I have imagined this wonderful, smiling man had ever scowled at me with such resentment?

"The moment I set eyes on you, I knew it," he said.

"Knew what, for goodness' sake?"

"I knew I should fall in love with you, Miss Hargreaves, as soon as you walked in the school. I fought with every weapon I knew."

I was aghast. What presumption! He could have known nothing of the sort. Then I remembered the hint of vulnerability, the shadow across his face, barely hidden beneath the forbidding scowl whenever I was in his presence.

I'M still here on the Isle of Morvay, only I'm Alison Craig now and live in the school-house with my husband. He doesn't iron his own shirts any more and I learned to make bread almost as well as Mrs Johnson.

We're very happy together, David and I, and our family. Soon our eldest child will be going off to school in the mornings with his father.

Morvay is home to us all. The spell it cast over me when I first came here is stronger than ever, and I wouldn't dream of ever living anywhere else.

With all that I have here — David, my family and friends, I know just how lucky I am.

Hamish is skipper of Seawife and a member of the Life Boat crew. He says he's not the marrying sort, but gives me an old-fashioned look now and then when he asks if Mr Craig is in good health! □

That Lost And Lonely Feeling

by CLARE GIBBON

IT was one of those still, grey days of late autumn, when the remnants of the season's glory lie underfoot in a carpet of burnished gold. It was mid afternoon, but the light was already failing so that the stone houses flanking either side of the road, had an austere, forbidding look about them.

Neither this nor the drabness of the day were apparent to the young woman turning into the road just then. Her step was light, her heart full of hope and expectancy at thoughts of seeing Uncle Jock again. It wasn't until she'd gone away that she'd begun to realise just how much he meant to her.

That Lost And Lonely Feeling

Dawn quickened her steps towards number seven and the great stone pillars which stood at either side of the gate. It had been spring when she'd gone away and the overhanging laburnum tree had been in full bloom. Now, looking up, she saw that it had long since cast its finery and its bare branches reached skywards like outstretched arms.

Still half hidden from the old house by the high hedge, she peered through a gap in its foliage. The anticipation which had been building up ever since she'd set off on her long train journey was washed away in a sudden tide of fear.

The small garden, always her uncle's pride and joy, was a wilderness. The rose bushes were neglected and unpruned. The corner which had boasted a thriving herb plot was now choked with rambling mint. What could have happened for Uncle Jock to have allowed his beloved garden to fall into this state?

With rising unease, Dawn pushed open the wrought-iron gate and went towards the front door, peering at the unlit front-room window for signs of life. Then she remembered he wouldn't be in there anyway. Every year, once the month of October was out, he moved into the small room at the back which was easier to heat.

She placed her suitcase on the step and with trembling fingers pressed the bell. She heard its piercing ring resounding through the old house, then held her breath, waiting for some sound, some sign that would quell the fear beginning to take a hold.

Perhaps he'd gone out somewhere. But he'd never do that knowing she was arriving today. Perhaps he hadn't got her last letter. It wouldn't be the first time mail had been lost.

WHEN there was no sound from behind the heavy front door, she rang again. It would be the television, she told herself. He always had it turned high for his poor hearing. But the waiting became interminable.

Her eyes were drawn to the garden in all its disarray. There had to be a simple explanation to it all. It had been an especially wet autumn, so maybe Uncle Jock was just waiting for it to dry up before starting. But she knew in her heart such an explanation didn't hold. Since spring, she'd been so wrapped up with Rodney's illness and with getting through her course, that the thought of anything happening to her old uncle had never occurred to her.

Bending down, she peered through the letter-box but the only thing visible was the closed inner door. If only she'd not left her set of keys when she went away. At the time, going away for six months had seemed like an eternity. Besides that it had been another attempt at loosening the ties, if things should have gone differently.

All that was behind her now, all indecisions swept away for ever. She was back in Scotland, this time for good. Even as she said it silently to herself, she knew it could never again be the same as it had been before.

Resolutely, Dawn banished rising regrets and moved her suitcase out of sight under the seat of the outer porch. She'd just have to go round to the back of the house and try to get into the house that way.

A S she turned from the door to retrace her steps down the path,
Dawn thought she saw a curtain move at the house next door.

She paused, half hoping, half expecting someone to appear, but
no-one did. She had no idea who lived there now. Since almost all
the houses in the short road had been converted into flats, tenants came
and went frequently. Except for Kevin, of course. Kevin Popper had
been there for two years before moving away.

She was in the lane at the back of the houses now and found herself
looking towards the garage at number nine, even though she knew there
was no chance of Kevin's clapped-out car being there.

It had been outside that garage that they'd had their final scene. Dawn
recalled how he'd stood a little way off, his lanky frame silhouetted
against the night sky.

"But surely, Dawn," he'd burst out at hearing her news, "you're
not going to go running back to Rodney every time he calls."

"That's not fair," she'd protested. "I read you his sister's letter. You
know how it is. He's sick and he needs me."

"Huh!" Kevin had turned away. "And what are you going to tell
your uncle?"

"The truth. That I'm going on a course."

"That's only half the truth, and you know it. You'll not dare tell him
you're going to be near Rodney, I'll bet!"

Kevin was right, of course. When Rodney had broken off their
engagement, Uncle Jock had wanted to take him to court for "breach
of promise."

"Try to understand, Kevin," she'd pleaded. "I've got to go."

"Well, go if you must. Only don't expect me to be here to pick up the
pieces when you get back!"

He'd flung open the car door, climbed in, switched on the engine and
reversed recklessly into the garage.

At the time, the lump in Dawn's throat had threatened to choke her
as she'd walked back home to number seven.

The garage door had swung noisily down before Kevin had called to
her. "I only hope your going away like this doesn't kill your Uncle
Jock!"

Kevin's words, which had seemed so melodramatic at the time, came
rushing back to her now so that she almost ran across the small yard to
the back door of number seven, fear rising within her.

When there was no response to her frantic knocking, she pressed her
face against the window of the back room. In a way it was just as she
remembered it. Two armchairs faced the fireplace but there was no
sign of life, no slippers, no newspapers about the place, no fire in the
hearth, nothing to suggest anyone still lived here.

Where was Uncle Jock? Why wasn't he home? Every Saturday
afternoon for as long as she could remember, he'd settled himself to
watch the sport on television. What had happened to break this routine?

Apart from missing Kevin more than she could have ever imagined,
this had been the most unsatisfactory thing about her time away. Uncle
Jock had never been able to write very well and though she'd written

regularly, she'd only twice received any word from him. There'd not been more than five lines on either occasion. He wasn't on the telephone either, so she'd been unable to call him.

It had been through one of his scrawled notes that she'd learned Kevin had left his flat next door and moved away. But surely Dr Duncan would have let her know if Uncle Jock had been taken ill.

FEELING at a complete loss, Dawn sat on the step and buried her face in her hands. Sitting there, the smell from a garden fire strong on the autumn air, she remembered her uncle's reaction to her going away.

"Some kind of course in London, you say?" he'd probed. "Can't see what a trained nurse wants with one of them."

"Oh, it will stand me in good stead for promotion," Dawn had assured him in her well-rehearsed words.

"Promotion?" He'd raised his eyebrows. "What does a married woman want with promotion?"

"But I'm not a married woman, Uncle Jock!"

"Soon will be if that Popper lad next door's anything about him."

Dawn had avoided his eyes. "Kevin and I . . . we've . . . we'll we've broken things off."

His head came up and his shrewd gaze fixed upon her.

"Well! I suppose London's a big enough place. Mind you don't go and get tangled up again with that no-good lad you were engaged to."

Dawn had stiffened. She'd gone to great lengths in her efforts to protect him from the truth, terrified always that she'd give something away.

Now, there was no longer anything to give away. Rodney had recovered from his long illness and, equally important, she knew it was finally all over between them. It was unlikely their paths would ever cross again.

Realising she couldn't sit here much longer, she got up and peered through the kitchen window. The sink, the work-tops, everywhere was tidy, too tidy for Uncle Jock.

Dawn then looked towards the houses on either side. It was no longer the kind of neighbourhood where you could knock on a door and expect to see a well-known face. As the flats had been developed and filled with strangers, one by one the older families had moved out.

If only Kevin was still next door, Dawn thought, and a great longing filled her, a longing that had become no less acute during her months away. His words, "don't expect me to be here to pick up the pieces," came back to taunt her. She didn't know where he was even if she'd had the courage to go to him.

The solution had to lie with their doctor. If her uncle was ill, then Dr Duncan would be able to tell her. If he wasn't . . . Well, she would just have to think again. He had no family left who she could contact, and even his few friends she knew little of, except that they met during the summer at the bowling green.

She made her way to the nearest call box at the end of the road.

The People's Friend Annual

"I'm afraid Dr Duncan's away at present," the receptionist told her. "And all next week. Would you like a word with one of his partners?"

"No. No, thank you. It was Dr Duncan I wanted."

Apart from increasing anxiety, Dawn was feeling tired and dispirited. She had so looked forward to this home-coming, and it wasn't turning out at all the way she'd planned.

Ever since losing her parents in an accident, her father's elder brother had always been there and had given her a home. Perhaps she'd been wrong to go off as she had, but she couldn't have turned her back on Rodney, not then when it seemed he needed her.

Suddenly, all the loneliness of the past months in London came flooding back upon her. The relief after Rodney's recovery prior to his departure overseas and the joy of her anticipated home-coming were evaporating about her.

Increasingly, she realised that if anyone could help her find her uncle, it would be Kevin. She'd just have to try her hardest to find him.

Dawn rang the bell to Kevin's old flat a few moments later. It seemed an age before the clatter of feet on uncarpeted stairs heralded the appearance at the front door of a hefty young man wielding a paint roller.

"Hi!" He grinned. "Come to help, have you?" He indicated his paint-splattered overalls.

"No . . . no!" Dawn stammered. "I . . . I just wondered if the previous tenant left a forwarding address?"

"Oh!" He groaned and slapped his forehead. "He did, but I doubt if I can find it now. Hang on." Then he was stamping noisily back upstairs.

She waited for what seemed ages until a window opened somewhere above her head.

"Got it!" came the triumphant voice. "Park Edge. Number twenty-five."

"Twenty-five Park Edge?" Dawn repeated, her head flung back.

"That's it. Say, you sure you wouldn't like to help splosh a bit of paint around?"

TIMELESS GLORY

*I*N the springtime of her youth. She was lovely, fair and slender. She drew the artist's eyes, and on the magic mirror of his canvas, he caught her beauty at the moment of its prime.

The years rolled on; her beauty faded into age. She passed away with all her generation, many years ago.

But still, the glory of her springtime shines. For ever in the magic mirror of a painting.

Once a master artist came from God, and said to man:

"In words upon my gospel canvas, I will paint what beauty shall be yours. When man shall show to fellow man all the tender love of God.

"This no fleeting glory of the moment caught. But glory fadeless. Yours for evermore."

Rev. T.R.S. Campbell.

44

That Lost And Lonely Feeling

Dawn merely shook her head, voiced her thanks and retraced her steps down the garden path, her heart beginning to thump wildly. It was six months since she'd seen Kevin. A lot could have happened during that time. Supposing he'd met someone else.

Crossing the park, she found herself peering through the failing light at each park bench, half expecting to find her uncle sitting there, at the same time knowing he only frequented the place in the summer.

Before long, she was approaching number twenty-five Park Edge. There was a light on illuminating the diamond-shaped, leaded windows and the curtains were open. Afraid of what might be revealed there, she paused.

Then before she knew it, she was beside the white-painted door which opened straight on to the street. With a tight feeling in her throat, she raised her hand to the knocker at the same time as her eyes were drawn to the scene in the lighted room.

A television was on in one corner and two chairs were pulled up to face it, their backs to the window. There was an intimate air about the room which unnerved her.

D AWN'S hand still rested on the door knocker, and just as she was summoning the courage to lift it, she froze as a lanky figure heaved himself out of one of the armchairs and, stretching, appeared to speak to someone in the other chair. She might have known that Kevin wouldn't have been alone for long.

Even while she was thinking this, Kevin looked over his shoulder, almost as if he'd sensed he was being watched. She knew that he'd seen her.

Conquering the urge to flee, Dawn lifted the heavy door knocker, allowing it to fall noisily against its rest. Within seconds the door opened and Kevin stood there before her.

"Dawn!" was all he said, and after what seemed an eternity, he stood to one side. "You'd better come in."

"No, I'd rather not." She took a step backwards. "I only came because . . . because . . . Well, you see, I thought you might . . ." Her mouth was dry and wouldn't say the words she wanted it to. Nothing she had ever felt for Rodney could hold a candle to what she felt for this man now before her.

He stepped forward and reached an arm out towards her. "Why don't you come in?" His voice was gentle, his tone persuasive.

"No!" Panic rose in her again and she shrugged off the hand he'd placed on her arm. To know someone had replaced her in his life was enough. She didn't have to go in there and meet her.

"I just thought you might know something about Uncle Jock." For the first time she looked up into his face. "You see, he's not at home and everywhere looks . . . Well, unlived in."

"Won't you come in?" he asked again, almost as if she hadn't spoken.

Her eyes darted away from his piercing gaze then back again. What was she to do? Why couldn't he just answer her here? Just at that moment, the background volume of the television commentary rose in a roar of cheers.

"Come on, Kevin," a shaky voice called above it. "You've just missed a goal."

DAWN looked up again at Kevin and smiled at the sound of the much-loved voice.

"Perhaps now you'll come in," Kevin said, and this time she needed no persuading as she almost fell across the threshold, only to be halted by his hand on her arm.

"He may not know you right away," he whispered down at her.

Instantly, her head jerked up. "What do you mean?"

"He's not seeing too well."

"Why?" she whispered urgently. "What's wrong?"

"Just cataracts, but fast growing. That's why he's been living here with me."

"Living here with you?" Dawn leaned against the wall for support and shook her head in disbelief.

"What's going on out there?" Uncle Jock's voice rose again.

"Just coming," he replied, placing a finger against Dawn's lips to prevent her from replying. Unexpectedly he pulled her roughly to him and held her close.

Dawn could feel his heart thumping against her body. "How long . . . ?" she managed finally through her tears.

"Has he been here?" He held her head back and gazed down at her. "About a month. I came across him on a park bench and walked him home. That was when I realised how his sight had deteriorated." With one finger he traced the line of her mouth. "I told your Dr Duncan what I thought of so called nurses who went off to London deserting their dependants." Again he pulled her close. "I was all for bringing you back at first."

"Why didn't you?"

"I'm not sure. Something to do with pride, I guess. That and the fact that I felt you needed time. Time to be sure."

Dawn's heart sang with happiness. She'd tell him later that she hadn't needed time. She'd known in that first week.

"Can't anybody tell me what's going on here?" Neither of them had heard Uncle Jock come out into the hall.

At sight of him, Dawn tore herself from Kevin's embrace and, going to the old man, put her arms about him. "It's me, Uncle Jock," she managed in a choked voice. "I'm back."

"Well, lass." He pulled one arm through his and led her into the warm room. "Back to stay, are you?"

"I am that," she told him, perching on the arm of his chair.

He leaned towards the television set as if to hear better what the commentator was saying. "Suppose we'd best get along home, then," he mumbled, "as soon as the match is over."

Kevin had come to stand behind Dawn and was running his fingers through her hair. "Little does he know," he whispered, "that as soon as that match on there is over, I'm going to confront him with another, of a different kind." □

Through The Eyes Of A Child

by
Peggy Maitland

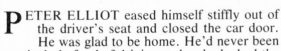

P ETER ELLIOT eased himself stiffly out of
the driver's seat and closed the car door.
He was glad to be home. He'd never been
particularly fond of driving and as he locked the
car, he was thinking that he wouldn't be sorry
if he never drove again. Somehow, he felt that he would always associ-
ate the car with old Rover's last journey.

"Mr Elliot, you've forgotten Rover!" Corrie Bennet's young voice
interrupted his thoughts. His neighbours' daughter was just four years
old but she had a way of sounding much more mature. Her tone seemed
to be reminding him that he was getting old and inclined to be forgetful.
This was true sometimes, but not in this instance.

Peter would have preferred to go straight indoors and into his study,
where he could be alone with his grief, but he couldn't hurt the child's
feelings. She was looking up at him trustingly, waiting for his response.

"Rover wasn't able to come home again, Corrie." His voice was
gruff and yet infinitely gentle.

Tears glistened on her long eyelashes.

"Couldn't the vet make him better?" she asked.

"Not this time." And as he spoke, Peter began to walk past her,
immersed again in his private sorrow.

But to his consternation, Corrie began to cry. She threw herself
against his legs, sobbing loudly.

Again, he had to put his own feelings aside in order to try to comfort
the child, but she wouldn't be soothed. When he told her that the old
dog would be happy now that he was away from all the pain he had
suffered, Corrie seemed to understand. But still she wept uncontrol-

47

lably. Peter lifted her up into his arms and stroked her golden hair.

"Shall we go and see if Mrs Elliot can give us lemonade and chocolate biscuits?" he said.

But even that suggestion had no effect on the little girl's tears. She didn't even notice that Mrs Elliot had come out to see what was happening.

As they went indoors, the elderly couple talked quietly to each other. Peter told his wife what had brought on the tears, and she told him that Corrie's mother had gone out on an errand.

"There's more to Corrie's tears than you think," Jean said. "Mrs Bennet looked pale and anxious when she asked me to keep an eye on Corrie for half an hour."

But just then their first consideration was for the child and between them, they succeeded in coaxing away her tears.

Corrie was sitting on Jean's lap, almost her usual self again, when they heard her mother's car stopping outside. Corrie's eyes flew to the window.

"Mummy was crying this morning because my daddy has left us," she said in a trembling voice.

Abruptly, she jumped down from Jean's knee and ran outside. Together, the elderly couple moved towards the back door. They saw that Corrie had taken her mother's hand and the two were hurrying into their own house. Marie Bennet looked worried and preoccupied. She didn't even glance in the Elliots' direction.

Peter Elliot put his hand on his wife's shoulder.

"The child wouldn't make up a thing like that," he said.

"Corrie was telling the truth. I'm sure of it." Jean looked up at him with troubled eyes. "It does seem incredible, though. I mean . . . they just seemed to live for each other, didn't they?"

Peter nodded.

"As for Corrie," he said, "they both dote on her."

The chore that Peter had dreaded was still tinged with sadness, but as he disposed of the dog's blanket and put the basket out in the garden shed, he found himself thinking that his dog had lived a good and happy life. Far more poignant was the plight of the little girl next door whose life had been shattered by events over which she had no control.

AFTER tea, Peter automatically went to put his jacket on. Then he remembered. There was no dog to take for a walk.

"I can't help missing the dog," he said.

"That's only to be expected. The house won't be the same without Rover," Jean said gently.

But they were both thinking the same: their loss couldn't be compared with their neighbours' suffering.

"We'll get used to it, Jean," Peter said. "I'll help you with the washing up, and then we can go through and watch the television."

They exchanged an encouraging smile. Well in advance, they had resolved that Rover would be their last dog. After he had gone they would occupy their time in different ways to keep themselves from missing their pet. At least they still had each other to share things with.

"We've been through this kind of thing before," Peter said pensively as he dried the dishes, "when the children grew up and left us one by one."

"Yes, it was a bit like this," Jean agreed, then her eye was caught by a movement in next door's garden. "There's Corrie bringing in her dolls' pram."

"It's not like her to leave her little family outside." Peter sighed. "She always takes them in for tea."

They watched her until she was out of sight, a forlorn, dejected figure trailing her pram indoors as if she wasn't interested in what she was doing.

"She's like a different child." Jean Elliot sounded close to tears. "All the life seems to have gone out of her."

"It's downright cruelty, that's what it is." Peter frowned angrily. "These two ought to be ashamed of themselves!"

"Now, Peter." Jean put a hand on his arm. "It's none of our business."

"Of course it's our business! We've loved that child since the day she was born. She's like one of our own grandchildren. And I'll tell you this much, Jean . . ."

"Stop it, Peter," she scolded. "Just you calm down."

"I'm sorry, love." He turned away from the window. "It's only that I feel so helpless having to stand by and do nothing."

"I know," she said softly, "but they wouldn't thank you for interfering."

B UT before they could discuss the matter further, their son and daughter-in-law arrived with their youngest grandson, Ian. By mutual consent they didn't mention the people next door, and in any case, the young folk had come along to comfort them because they'd been aware of the possibility that the old dog wouldn't be here any more.

Ian sat on the arm of his grandfather's chair and put his arm around his shoulders.

"I've got all the money I got for my birthday, Grandad," he said. "And Mr Kennedy along the road from us has pups for sale. At least they will be for sale when they are old enough."

"Ian!" his mother exclaimed. "You know very well that your grandfather isn't able to train another dog!"

Tears filled the boy's eyes as he looked at his grandad.

"I'd buy one for you . . ."

Peter Elliot was deeply moved by the appeal in the boy's face.

"It's good of you, Ian. But I'm getting old, you know. It would be too much for me."

The others were all talking again and Ian said no more until it was time to go home and he was walking out to the gate.

Peter felt a tug at his sleeve, and when he understood that the little boy wanted to say something he stopped and bent down.

"I won't cancel that puppy, Grandad," Ian said, whispering like a conspirator. "You'll love him when you see him. I'm sure you will."

"Ian . . ." Peter looked down at him reproachfully, but there was no time to say any more. Ian was darting through the gate and waving goodbye.

Peter Elliot couldn't help smiling. Ian would obviously need to be, convinced, but it would have to be done with great tact.

Now that they were alone the two old folk lingered in the garden, reluctant to go back into the house. But just then the Bennets' front door opened and Marie Bennet came towards the dividing hedge.

"I'm sorry I forgot to thank you for minding Corrie this afternoon, Mrs Elliot," she said. "I'm afraid I was in a bit of a state. But I shouldn't have forgotten to thank you."

"That's all right, my dear," Jean said hesitantly.

The young woman bit her lip.

"I was wondering . . . " she faltered. "Would you come in for a few minutes? I mean, if you're not busy . . ."

"No, I'm not busy." Jean glanced at her husband before she moved towards the gap in the hedge.

"Will you come too, Mr Elliot?" Marie asked. "I won't keep you long. Maybe we could have a cup of tea."

I ALWAYS think tea helps people to talk," Marie Bennet said nervously, as she poured three cups. "That was why I asked you in. I wanted to talk to you."

"Is there anything we can do to help, Mrs Bennet?" Jean asked.

The girl took a deep breath.

"I expect Corrie told you that Andy has left me." She paused briefly, watching their sorrowful nods. "That was what I wanted to talk to you about. It didn't seem right to just move out and so on without telling you. Not when you've been such good neighbours."

"We hope we're friends as well as neighbours," Jean said. "And we're as fond of Corrie as we are of our own."

"Leaving you will break Corrie's heart." Marie's eyes filled with tears. "But what can I do?"

"Are you sure your quarrel can't be settled?" Jean said.

"I only wish it was as simple as that."

"It's not for me to pry or give advice." Jean Elliot leant forward. "But you could get professional advice . . ."

"Oh no, I couldn't talk to a stranger!" Marie exclaimed. "Neither could Andy. I suppose that's the root cause of our troubles in a way. We don't talk to each other enough. When I'm angry or hurt, I just bottle it up. And Andy does the same. I think he's got to the stage of believing that I don't care about him any more."

"Now what would make him believe that?" Jean spoke soothingly.

Marie shook her head wearily. But then, as if the words wouldn't stay back any longer, she began to talk, to pour out all the troubles which had combined towards the break-up of her marriage.

The Elliots were good listeners. They didn't make any attempt to stem the flow of confidences. Instead, their caring attitude encouraged her to unburden herself. And as it became clear that there was little more for Marie to say, Jean tried to think of a way of telling the girl that they would respect her confidence. But before she could speak, her husband intervened in a surprisingly uncharacteristic way.

"Now that you've managed to say all this to us," he said, "wouldn't you consider saying it to Andy? After all, he is entitled to hear it."

"But that's what I've been telling you!" Marie insisted. "I can't talk to Andy. He doesn't listen to me."

"I'm sorry," Peter murmured, "I just thought . . ." He stopped, mentally stepping back from dangerous ground.

"It seems a pity to lose each other because of a fear of speaking out," Jean said carefully. "Couldn't you ask a friend, someone you and Andy both know and trust, to speak for you?"

"No, there's nobody," she answered in a low voice.

There was a long silence, then Marie looked up, a light of hope in her eyes.

"Unless you . . ." But as she saw the startled, uncomfortable look on the elderly woman's face, she faltered. "No, of course not. I'm sorry, I shouldn't have asked."

Jean gave her husband an appealing look.

"Peter, you could do it."

The Question

WHEN the harvest moon's a-riding
    High and golden in the sky,
And a million stars a-twinkling,
    Seemingly for you and I,
I shall ask you for an answer,
    To the words I whispered, when
In my arms I held you closely —
    Ah, my sweet, I loved you then.

At the time you seemed uncertain,
    "Wait," you said, "till harvest moon,
Tis one thing to love another,
    Something else to wed too soon."
So I courted you, impatient —
    Loving you the more each day.
With the harvest-time approaching
    Will you answer yea — or nay?
                  Violet Hall.

He shook his head vehemently, but both women were looking at him hopefully and he felt caught up in a situation he couldn't escape from.

Suddenly there was a cry from upstairs and the young mother jumped to her feet. "That's Corrie."

The old couple were left alone while she hurried to comfort the child. They didn't say anything — they didn't have to. When Marie returned to say that Corrie was all right, she must have had a bad dream, Peter Elliot had decided that for the child's sake, he would try to help.

When they arrived home, Peter strode immediately into his study and sat down at his desk.

"Peter, you can't work this out on paper. It isn't a mathematical problem," Jean said anxiously, as he pulled papers out of a drawer.

"I'm still a mathematician, Jean, even although I'm retired."

"Peter Elliot, I'm shocked at you! These two young folk are in love!"

He swung round angrily, giving her the full blast of his temper.

"Woman, will you leave me in peace!"

"No, I won't!" Jean snapped back. "There's a marriage at stake here, you know!"

Unexpectedly, Peter smiled.

"And a darling innocent child, too. Remember that, love. Surely you wouldn't want me to say or do anything to make things worse for her? That's why I must start this from a basis of logic. Do you understand?"

"Well . . ." she had to back down. "Don't work too late, you need your rest."

Jean smiled faintly, thinking to herself that if only the two next door had shouted the odds occasionally they'd have fewer problems. In her own opinion, all marriages were fraught with difficulties. It had always been so. Her generation had just had to make the best of it. But young folk nowadays wouldn't settle for less than what they imagined was perfection.

D URING the next few days, Peter Elliot was completely occupied with his neighbours' problems. His task was made easier by the goodwill of both partners and the ending of their problems, the reconciliation when it came, seemed like a personal triumph for him.

As he relaxed on his garden seat watching little Corrie playing, and listening to her chattering to her family of dolls, he thought tranquilly that the joy of seeing the child's happiness was the greatest victory of all. He felt at peace with the world as he sat in the sunshine idling away his days, smiling at Corrie when she came to talk to him, sometimes bringing him flowers she had picked from her garden.

"Are you going to cut your grass today, Mr Elliot?" she would ask him sometimes. Or she would point to the borders and tell him, "Weeds are growing in amongst your flowers, aren't you going to pull them out?"

"Maybe later." He would nod and smile at her, not in the least disturbed by her questions.

Then one day she came to him with an urgent plea.

"The handle is falling off my pram, Mr Elliot. Can you fix it?"

Without haste, he fetched a screwdriver and tightened the offending screw. "There now, that was no bother."

She thanked him and began to arrange her dolls in the pram but noticed that he sat down and put the screwdriver on the seat beside him.

"You usually always put your tools away when you're finished with them," she said bluntly.

"I will," he assured. "I will. But there's no hurry."

Suddenly Corrie straightened up and glared at him. Her elbows were bent and she pushed her fists against her sides.

"You just sit there all day doing nothing," she accused him severely.

"Maybe I'm getting lazy," he agreed. "But it doesn't matter. I've had a busy life. I'm an old man now."

She studied his face thoughtfully for a long moment.

"Do you mean that you are ready to go to heaven?"

Almost in the same instant, her mother called to her and she began to push her pram towards her own garden, without waiting for an answer.

Peter stared after her. Uppermost in his mind was a feeling of outrage. After all that he had done for her! How ungrateful could a child be? He felt bruised, wounded to the heart.

But gradually, as his angry thoughts simmered down, the stirrings of resentment within him were being turned into restless energy. His eyes were no longer tranquil as they looked around the neglected garden. There was work to be done, and only himself to do it.

J EAN noticed that he no longer sat dreaming on the garden seat and she was thankful for whatever had roused him from his apathy. In the late afternoon she came into the garden.

"You'll need to stop soon, Peter. We promised to go to tea with Joyce and Bill."

He leaned on the lawnmower, looking at her, a thoughtful look on his face. The mention of his son and daughter-in-law had reminded him of his small grandson's eager face and his generous offer.

"Have you decided what you're going to say to Ian?" Jean said. "About that pup?"

"What do you think I should say?" He frowned.

"How should I know? It's between you and him." Then, as she turned to go indoors, she spoke over her shoulder. "It's up to you whether you hurt him or not."

"Jean, we agreed that another dog was out of the question at our age."

"I must put on my other shoes." Jean neatly changed the subject.

"Jean, do you truly think it would be wise to take that pup," he asked later.

She shook her head, smiling at him.

"Never mind about wisdom. I've got eyes in my head, haven't I? You were so busy all week with the Bennets, you didn't have time to mope. Then you gave in to it this past three or four days . . . Do you think I haven't guessed it was the thought of our Ian getting you that pup that cheered you up today?"

He stared at her in bewilderment. "But it wasn't that, Jean."

"Rubbish!" she retorted. "I know you." Then in a softer voice she went on, "Ian knows you, too. He put his arms round my neck and said he loved you too much to let you be sad — which you will be without a dog about the house."

Peter's eyes were moist and there was a painful lump in his throat. Now he realised that little Corrie had posed her seemingly callous question because she cared about him. His grandson was showing his love in a more practical way.

And as for Jean . . . He thought humbly that she had been loving him in different ways for more than 50 years.

As he put his jacket on, she came over to straighten his tie, and he put his arms round her and kissed her.

"What was that for?" Jean demanded, smiling at him.

"Because I love you, of course," he said happily. □

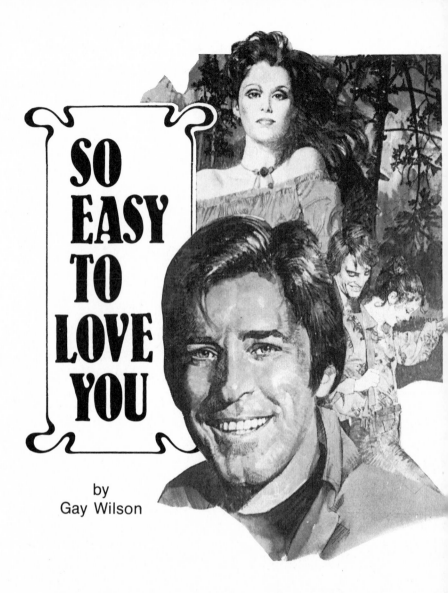

SO EASY TO LOVE YOU

by
Gay Wilson

M OST of the comforts in the flat were provided from Isobel's private
income — the new duvets, the Scandinavian rugs in the living-
room, the pictures and the stereo. She was able to indulge
herself, and did! But she was generous, and well liked by the other
students, although they envied her and told each other she was spoilt.

I was never absolutely sure why she invited me to share the flat.
Possibly, as Johnathan remarked, it was because she knew very well I
was a reasonable cook and had a tidy nature.

It was obvious to everyone why she asked Joe to muck in. He was the college "Mr Fix-It." He could sort dripping taps, stopped-up sinks, electrical failures, and windows that wouldn't open. Joe was always in demand, and not just for his handiness either. For although he could turn his hand to anything, he was the brilliant one of the four of us sharing the flat and would undoubtedly make the best doctor.

Johnathan, on the other hand, was charming, clever and thoroughly lazy. But the two boys had always been friends, and Isobel offered them the spare bedroom if they wouldn't mind sharing.

R IGHT from the beginning, I was miserably certain that Joe was in love with Isobel. Most of the male students were, or had been, at some time, but Joe seemed to be more faithful than any of the others and although things never seemed to progress between them, he always stayed around.

I'd always felt a bit of an outsider before Johnathan arrived on the scene, and I encouraged his somewhat apathetic attentions to square my pride. This seemed to fire his ardour and the situation became slightly fraught.

"Everyone thinks you're my girl," he observed mildly one day. "Why don't we have game as well as name?"

"I've got too much else on my mind to get mixed up in emotional affairs," I told him. "I haven't got such a retentive brain as you and the other two," I added as a sop to his pride. "I have to study longer hours, and it sort of uses up my . . . vitality . . . if you see what I mean?"

"Point taken." Johnathan, who was about as sensitive as a tank, agreed. "It just seems a pity to waste all that sweetness on the desert air."

I looked at him sharply. Was it possible he had guessed my feelings for Joe? Oh no, I prayed, for I'd kept them strictly under control at all times. What girl is going to lay bare her soul for a guy who is besotted with her flat-mate?

I used to lie in bed at night and yearn over Joe. Isobel took him so entirely for granted, like she did her other admirers, but she didn't understand him as I did. She found him useful, but I knew that Joe was a crusader — always fighting for the under-privileged, the less fortunate. He was special, deep, quiet and dependable. Not just ordinarily quiet, but quiet in a way which reached out to others.

I think Isobel had an inkling of the way he was. "Joe should have gone in for the ministry," she said one day. "He's a born archbishop."

I didn't contradict her, but I knew she was wrong. Joe was a born doctor. Maybe he'd never get to Harley Street, but he would scatter comfort and reassurance wherever he was. I hoped he wouldn't marry Isobel, not because I was jealous, but because I thought she would destroy him, not intentionally of course, but because of the way she was.

I used to glower behind my physiology books as the pair of them sparred affectionately, and I made it a rule never to look directly into Joe's beautiful, serious eyes, because I knew my own would have revealed too much. I couldn't see how he could possibly avoid wanting to marry her. To me she was irresistible with her glowing good looks, her charming, outgoing personality and sparkling wit. She was clever, too, as well as beautiful, and she sailed through life with complete confidence in herself, never expecting failure and never meeting it.

You couldn't help liking Isobel and I was fond of her like the rest of us, but somehow you couldn't talk to her. Not deeply, I mean. And certainly not about affairs of the heart. So I hugged my impossible secret love and concentrated all my energies on getting good grades in my examinations.

We were an odd bunch really. Isobel didn't have a care in the world. Johnathan was vague, but with an excellent academic brain and well-to-do parents who doted on him. Joe had fought his way up from the back streets of Glasgow. And me? I was struggling to be a credit to my working-class parents who were making enormous sacrifices to enable me to study.

YES, we were all so different, but we got on fine together, separating at the end of each term to take up various vacational jobs, and meeting up again when the holidays were over.

But then came the vacation when there weren't any summer jobs to be had. I knew Joe was worried, and so was I, because going home meant turning out the lodger who occupied my room. I needed both work and accommodation as desperately as he did. Johnathan never had problems of this nature!

And then, out of the blue, Isobel suddenly invited us all to spend the holidays at her home in the West Coast.

"Why don't we all go to Kilblair?" she said carelessly. "There's oodles of room at the family hovel. There's absolutely nothing to do, of course, except swim in the loch and exercise the dogs, but it wouldn't be so bad if we were all together."

My heart started to beat wildly. It sounded perfect — hills covered in heather, cold, sparkling loch water, country sounds, food and a roof over our heads.

"Do you mean all of us?" I stammered. "Won't your folk mind?"

"They'll never notice," Isobel replied. "The house is invariably full of stray relations during the summer. Dad's nearly always away, and Mum is too absorbed in her kennels to notice mere people."

Isobel's mother bred Alsatians. They were valuable and sold mostly abroad.

"Thanks a lot," Johnathan said, after a pause, "but dogs and bogs and freezing lochs aren't much in my line. In any case, my old man's just bought a villa in Spain which I think will suit me very well. I feel the need of a long, long rest in the sun."

"Poor old thing!" we chorused.

"What about you two?" Isobel said.

"I think it would be wonderful," I said, and Joe's eyes suddenly met mine with a flash of warmth and I knew that his relief matched my own.

I thought I'd never seen anything so impressive as Isobel's home. It was a sort of old, stone built mansion, which lay in a forest of fir, silver birches, rowans and oaks. It had sweeping lawns dotted with bright beds of shrubs where dogs stretched out in unexpected places.

And through the trees, we caught a glimpse of green-grey sea as we drove up the winding drive bordered with hydrangeas and scarlet geraniums.

I could see that Joe was as impressed as I was by the sheer magnificence of Isobel's home, and my heart ached for him. No wonder he tried to keep his feelings for her hidden. I knew him well enough to know how he would feel about the difference in their backgrounds. Would he always nurse a lost cause, I wondered.

I wished I knew how Isobel felt towards him. She treated him in the same way that she treated the other young men who were in love with her, affectionately but casually. She was a butterfly, but oh, what a gorgeous one. It was hard not to be envious.

The menage at Kilblair seemed to run itself. Daily women popped in and out to do the cleaning, cooking, and washing, disappearing as suddenly as they'd appeared when the day's chores were completed.

Mrs Galbraith was a handsome woman with eyes the same dark purply grey as Isobel's, and hair the colour of pewter that had been newly polished. She was completely absorbed in her kennels and paid scant attention to the house, and it was easy to see where Isobel got her vague, fey charm, and her good looks.

HIDDEN BEAUTY

THERE'S beauty in the countryside
   To gladden every eye . . .
The gentle slope of rolling hills,
   The bright blue sweeping sky.

But there's beauty in the city, too,
   In streets and cul-de-sacs . . .
In close-knit terraced houses,
   And concrete high-rise flats.

Yet the beauty here is seldom seen
   By casual passers-by . . .
For caring hearts and helping hands
   Are reticent and shy.

Such flowers of fellowship blossom
   wild,
   'Midst brick and stone and
      mortar . . .
They scatter seeds of shining deeds
   Upon the soul's high altar.
                    — Nancy Medcalf.

Living in Kilblair was wonderful after the struggle and stress of the university, and I think we all unwound during those first few weeks. Joe, I thought, seemed quieter and more thoughtful than ever. Sometimes I noticed him looking at me a bit quizzically, and I couldn't fathom this out. It was as though he was trying to convey something to me. But he didn't have to. I was well aware of the fact that I had to play gooseberry, and I did try to keep out of the way as much as possible.

The People's Friend Annual

Sometimes when the two of them had gone off for a day in the hills, I would feel terribly lonely. It was awful being the unwanted third, and I cursed Johnathan for his desertion. He would at least have made us into an even numbered party.

And then Tom Tregarthen came into our lives out of the blue. Tom was a Canadian summer student at Aberinnis Forestry School across the loch. He'd arranged with Mrs Galbraith to purchase a pup from the newest litter with a view to taking him home for breeding purposes.

I T was on one of the days when I was sitting alone, a bit forlornly, on the terrace, that he turned up. He was tall, auburn haired and strikingly attractive.

"I seem to have come in at the wrong entrance." He grinned apologetically. "I'm looking for the kennels."

"There's nobody down there until four o'clock," I explained. "Do you have an appointment?"

"Sort of." His slow Canadian drawl was fascinating. "I'm buying one of the pups, and I'm told the litter has arrived."

"Perhaps you'd like to wait for a while," I said. "Somebody is bound to be around soon."

"Sure," he agreed with obvious pleasure, and flopped into a chair beside me.

We sat in the golden light of the afternoon for at least an hour. One of the maids popped out with a tray of tea and home-made scones which Tom tucked into with undisguised appreciation, all the while telling me about the wonderful life he had in Canada.

"Say!" he exclaimed at last. "I've been talking about myself for over an hour. Tell me about yourself. What do you do for a living?"

So I told him about the medical course that the four of us were taking, and about the flat we shared in Edinburgh. He listened attentively, never interrupting until I paused for breath. Then he stretched out lazily.

"It all sounds way above me," he said. "I've been in forestry all my life. I couldn't live in a city. I'd rather die."

When the others returned, the object of Tom's visit seemed unimportant, so lively was the conversation. Isobel was on top form. It seemed as if Tom had been one of us for ever, and time simply flew by.

Eventually Isobel volunteered to take him down to the kennels, while Joe and I stayed on the terrace and watched the sun sink behind the dusky firs. Then contentedly we strolled indoors to investigate what had been prepared for our evening meal.

Isobel was strangely quiet over supper. Her glorious eyes held a dreamy expression, and she missed several remarks which her mother addressed to her.

"Did the Canadian manage to choose his pup?" Joe asked conversationally.

"He chose Rascal," Mrs Galbraith said.

"He's the rogue dog," Isobel said, suddenly becoming alert. "The wicked one. We warned him, but Tom said naughty dogs invariably have the most character, and he just wouldn't change his mind."

"He'll manage Rascal," Mrs Galbraith said with conviction. "He's a born handler. I can always tell." She smiled benignly at the three of us. "But Rascal will have to learn to obey pretty quickly."

After that first meeting, Tom Tregarthen became a frequent visitor at the house. Although the puppy wasn't ready yet to leave his mother, he spent quite a lot of time training him with the three of us watching.

Tom's vigorous presence made life much simpler for me. Now we could go places in a foursome like we did in Edinburgh. He was excellent company, full of life and vitality, and I liked him a lot — we all did. But although he enjoyed seeing Scotland, he always made it clear he was counting the days to his return home. To Tom, there was no place on earth like Prince Edward Island, and we found ourselves promising to visit some day and look him up.

THE end of the holiday came all too soon. I found myself wondering if things would be the same when we returned to Edinburgh. We seemed to be different people somehow. I couldn't put my finger on it, but it was there. Isobel, particularly, was different, quieter, more thoughtful, less flippant. She took herself off for long walks in the hills, leaving Joe and I to entertain each other.

And then she dropped her bombshell.

"I'm not coming back to university," she announced as the three of us piled dirty dishes into the sink one evening after supper.

Joe stopped dead, a pile of plates in his arms. "What's that supposed to mean?" he said.

Isobel's eyes were over bright. "It means that I'm not going to become a doctor after all," she said. "I hope neither of you is going to start persuading me to change my mind, because I'm warning you . . . I won't."

There was a moment of stunned silence.

"Has this got anything to do with Tom Tregarthen?" Joe said, at last.

Isobel flushed fiery red. "And what if it has?" she cried. "He's asked me to marry him, and I've said yes."

"You can't mean it!" Was that my voice breaking the stillness? I looked across at Joe in dismay. How could he take something like this?

"Are you quite sure, Isobel?" he said gently.

"I'm quite sure."

"Then nobody has any right to try and dissuade you."

Isobel threw her arms round his neck and burst into tears. "I knew you would understand." She sobbed. "Will you . . . will you help me break the news to my folk?"

"No." Joe's voice was deep and kind, although firm. "That is something you must do yourself. But we'll talk to them afterwards, and try to make them understand."

"Bless you," Isobel muttered, and she turned and fled from the room.

"You despatched her straight into his arms," I flung at Joe

accusingly, when the two of us were alone. "Why did you do that?"

His dark eyes widened. "She's not a child, Sue. If she's met a man she can truly love, why shouldn't she go to him? Why should I, or anybody else, try to prevent her?"

"But you and she . . ." I began wildly, and then I stopped. "I mean . . . I thought . . ."

He came near to me then, and there was something about his expression that made my heart leap.

"What exactly did you think, Susan?"

"I thought you were in love with her," I whispered.

His face suddenly cleared. "Is that why you've been at such pains to throw us together lately?"

I nodded mutely.

"You precious little idiot," he roared. "It's not Isobel I'm in love with! It's you! Surely you knew that. Surely you know how I've cursed Johnathan Steed, how I've envied him!"

"J-Johnathan?" I stammered.

"Yes," Joe said. "You gave the impression you belonged together. Isobel was sure of it."

"There was nothing between Johnathan and me," I cried. "Nothing at all. Oh, Joe, I think you've been the same sort of precious idiot, too. We've both got it all back-to-front somehow."

I was trying not to cry. I look absolutely awful when I cry, and this was the most wonderful moment of my whole life. But I couldn't help it. I couldn't hold back the tears, and it didn't matter because my face was completely hidden anyway, squashed against Joe's shirt.

He held me like this for several seconds, and then he spoke in a whimsical voice. "I hope this means you are radiantly happy."

"Radiantly!" I gulped.

"And that it's me you're going to marry?"

I raised my ravaged face at this. After all, if we were to be married, he had to see me at my worst sometime.

"Oh, Joe." I sniffed. "You did say marry . . . Or am I dreaming?"

"I think we've both been dreaming far too long." He stroked my cheek with a gentle finger, and then he kissed me with such melting tenderness, my knees went suddenly weak. "It's time now," he whispered, "to make dreams come true." □

Torridon is a pleasant little village at the heart of some of Scotland's most magnificent wild scenery. Clustered round this pretty little place at the north of Upper Loch Torridon are Beinn Eighe, Liathach, Bein Alligen and Beinn Dearg. These guardian mountains, formed of red sandstone, line both sides of the valley and are a delight for hikers and nature lovers alike. The horizontal layering of rock gives these mountains a distinctive, yet attractive, banded effect. A visit to this area will undoubtedly leave a lasting impression of splendour and beauty.

TORRIDON, WESTER ROSS

H AVE a nice day.'' The words lingered in Sally Maitland's mind
as she switched off the television set. A few hours ago it might
have applied to her. She'd been looking forward to tomorrow,
but a phone call from her sister, Jill, looked like finishing all hopes of
her enjoying her very first date with Keith Watson.

It isn't fair, she thought. Just because she worked in Lochart's and
had her half-day on a Thursday, she was always being called upon
to help Jill with the children when a crisis arose. Why couldn't Nancy
Cooper take a turn? After all, she was Jill's sister-in-law and had been
the other bridesmaid at the wedding. Surely Nancy could fit it in
somehow with her hours at the bank.

Sally sighed and some of her frustration evaporated, leaving her

As Good As Gold

by JEAN MELVILLE

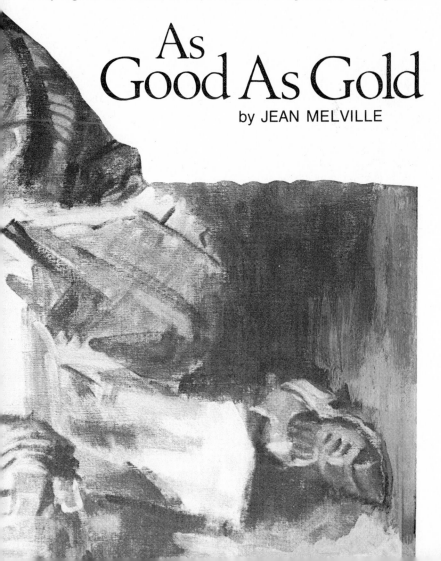

ashamed of herself. Of course Jill should always call on her only sister for help. Besides, she loved her two small nephews, even if Christopher, the older boy, was full of energy and difficult to manage at times.

If only her parents had been back home from their holiday in the Isle of Man, she might not have had this problem. Mum would have been able to help out. But Sally still had three more days on her own.

"I thought I'd told you all about it, Sally," Jill had said rather anxiously. "When I accepted the wedding invitation for Ted and me, I thought Christopher and Robbie would be at school most of the day and Mum wouldn't mind having them for an hour or two later. I didn't know the school would be closed for local elections. I mean, the 'groom is one of Ted's oldest friends and . . .''

"Say no more," Sally interrupted. "I've got a date, Jill, but I guess I can take the boys with me. We're going on a picnic to Croy Shore and Keith is borrowing a car . . ."

"Oh, Sally, am I spoiling your day?" Jill asked. "I mean, I know you've helped me out a few times, and I did ask Nancy, but she's working. I had a word with Mum before she went on holiday, and *she* thought . . ."

"I wouldn't mind in the least," Sally finished.

And her mother would have been perfectly right, normally. Sally enjoyed the company of boisterous Christopher and quiet little Robbie when she took them out on their own, but what about Keith? Would he welcome two children along on their very first date?

Sally sighed. Jill was very hard working as she strove to run a large, inconvenient house, look after the children and help Ted to run his garage. She deserved time off as often as it could be arranged.

"Have a good time," she said brightly. "I'll collect the boys on the way home from work at one o'clock and you can pick them up again in the evening. Just tell Christopher that he's got to be on his best behaviour, that's all."

"I'll make him behave," Jill promised. "See if I don't."

THE half-days at Lockhart's were staggered, some of the staff being free on Wednesday afternoons and some on Thursday. Sally had enjoyed working in the hairdressing department for the past two years, and had mixed in with the social life of the firm.

A few months ago, Keith Watson had been put in charge of the record and video department, and Sally had first met him in the staff canteen.

When he'd carried his tray to where she was sitting at a table by the window, Sally found herself looking into a pair of very dark eyes. Keith's well-cut black hair curled neatly, and his dentist was no doubt proud of his teeth. Sally had never been so strongly attracted to a man before, and to her annoyance she couldn't control her blushes when he spoke to her.

"You're Sally, aren't you?" he asked. "Sally Maitland from Hairdressing."

"Yes, I am. How did you know? You've never actually met me before."

"Asked," he replied. "I like to know who everyone is."

Sally couldn't help thinking that this might apply more to the girls than to the men, but she thrust it away. Already Keith Watson was telling her how much he liked working for Lockhart's. It was an interesting job, and so much more colourful than his brother's.

"What does he do?" Sally asked.

"Who . . . Alan? Oh, he adds up figures all day. He's an accountant. I always tell him I like to look at a different sort of fig . . . I mean, I like to look at people and not pieces of paper. That's what makes life worthwhile. Don't you agree, Sally?"

His eyes were dancing and she couldn't help responding to him.

"Perhaps. I like working with people, too, but my father is a cashier and he likes looking at pieces of paper and is none the worse for it. Each to his own taste, Mr . . ."

"Keith! Surely you can call me Keith? And I must call you Sally. I'm sure we're going to be friends."

On Monday morning he was back in the canteen when she went for morning coffee, and once again he came to join her.

"When's your half day?" he asked after chatting for a while.

"Thursday," she said shyly.

"Me, too. What about a picnic while the sun is shining? I could borrow my brother's car and we could go to Croy Shore. We can try out the Electric Brae . . . take some water in a bottle and watch it run uphill."

"Done." Sally laughed. "I'll provide the food."

She'd been so excited by the prospect, then Jill had telephoned to check that she would be able to look after the children on Thursday.

O N Thursday morning Sally made an excuse to visit the record department, but Keith was busy. She hung about for as long as she dared then gave up the attempt. He was coming to pick her up at two o'clock, and she would just have to explain about the children then.

Right after work she made her way to her sister's house to collect the children.

Normally Jill looked harassed in jeans and a sweater, with her short curly hair standing up in peaks, but this time Sally found a lovely, elegant young woman waiting for her. Excitement shone from her eyes and her cheeks were warm with colour.

"Oh, Jill!" she said. "You look lovely."

"Doesn't she, though?" Her brother-in-law appeared in the living-room doorway with a towel round his neck.

"Where are the boys?" Sally asked.

"In their bedroom, keeping clean." Jill raised her voice. "You can come down now."

Sally braced herself for the inevitable rush, but it was two rather sedate, small boys who walked downstairs to greet her. They both regarded their aunt solemnly, even after she hugged them warmly.

"Can I bring my new truck?" Christopher asked. "It's only a little model."

"And my car?" Robbie pleaded. "Mummy said that . . ."

"Bribery and corruption," Jill interrupted hurriedly. "They've got a toy each in anticipation of good behaviour."

"That's not a good idea, Jill." Sally frowned.

"I know, but I'll worry about it tomorrow." Jill bent to kiss her children. "Be good."

"I'll have to go now." Sally took each of them by the hand and picked up a bag which Jill had packed with extra clothing in case of emergencies. "I've got the sandwiches and coffee to make."

"Thanks a million for having them," Jill said gratefully. "We won't be late home. We shan't stay at the party after the bride and 'groom have left."

"Have a good day." Sally grinned.

It was unnatural, she thought, as she walked home with the children. Instead of being dragged this way and that to admire goods in the shop windows, the pair were obedient and unusually silent except for a question now and again from Robbie who was taking such an interest in everything.

That's Life!

So things went wrong!
The love is lost, that cherished plan misfired.
But was it really worth the tears
This dream your heart desired?

So things went wrong!
Don't sit and mope — the future you can face.
To love is good and you will find
In losing, no disgrace.

So make things right!
Try to forget — the past that caused you pain.
Learn by mistakes — and laugh, and live!
Love can be yours again.
Margaret Graham.

At home she left them playing with their new toys whilst she buttered bread to make the sandwiches. She included fruit, cakes and biscuits and a few small bars of chocolate for the children.

Sally barely had time to get changed. Her curls, well-cut by one of the other hairdressers, were brushed quickly and she was applying a touch of discreet make-up when Christopher's unusually solemn face surveyed her from the door.

"There's a car at the gate, Auntie Sally."

Keith had already rung the bell when she hurried to the front door and invited him in.

"I'm all ready," she said breathlessly. "I tried to talk to you this morning, but you were busy. I . . . . I'm afraid I've got to take along my two nephews. My sister and brother-in-law have gone to a wedding and my mother is still away so . . . ." She shrugged.

She saw the smile leave Keith's lips and realised he minded very much indeed, especially when his eyes lit upon her two charges.

"They've promised to be very well behaved, and they've been positive angels so far. This is Christopher, and this is Robbie."

"Hello, Uncle Keith," Christopher said gravely and Sally looked at him, startled. She hadn't asked him to say "Uncle Keith."

"Hello, Uncle Keith," Robbie parroted.

"Oh, no!" Keith groaned.

"Shall we sit in the back seat?" Christopher asked. "I can open the door."

S ALLY picked up one or two of the plastic bags she'd filled with necessities and almost reluctantly Keith lifted up the picnic basket as she pulled the front door shut. In silence he stowed the luggage into the boot of the car.

"I can't believe it!" he said, as he turned to look at her. "How can you be related to Nancy Cooper? They call her Aunt Nancy, and you Aunt Sally . . ."

"So you know Nancy!" Sally said with surprise, as she slid into the passenger seat of the car.

"Put your seat-belt on, Auntie." Christopher's voice came from the back.

"I know Nancy," Keith said heavily, "and she's already introduced me to my two extra passengers. How come you both know them?"

"It's quite simple. Jill Cooper is my sister, and her husband, Ted Cooper, is Nancy's brother. Your two extra passengers belong to both of us."

Keith started to drive with the boys breathing down his neck.

"Last time I saw this pair," he said, "was one Sunday when we took them for a walk along the banks of the River Ayr. Christopher picked up a small branch which had fallen from a tree, whizzed round and round while he held on to it, then threw it in the river. Only he forgot to let go and he followed it in. I ruined a good pair of trousers getting him out and we took him home soaking wet."

"His mother has packed clean clothes for both of them in case they get wet," she assured him. "And, anyway, Chris is being good today."

"That's a change," Keith said and Sally forgot to be dismayed that he had already coped with Christopher. She began to feel irritated.

Meanwhile Robbie was trying to smoothe down his hair which was sticking up after being blown by the breeze.

"Why does the wind blow outside the car and not inside, Uncle Keith?" he asked.

"Oh, because . . . because . . . Oh, I don't know."

"You're sheltered in the car," Sally said helpfully.

"Why is that little light flashing?" Robbie asked.

"Because we're turning right."

"Why are we turning right?"

"Because that's the way we're going! Now will you be quiet and let me drive?"

"Oh, look, Robbie," Sally said. "Look at the lovely dogs. That man has two of them and one is a very big dog."

Robbie looked with great interest.

"Why is one dog bigger than another?" he asked. "Do they know they are dogs, Auntie?"

Has he always asked things like this, Sally wondered as Robbie's questions were asked every minute or two with unfailing regularity.

WHEN they selected a picnic spot, Robbie took a keen interest in everything they did. His big solemn eyes surveyed Keith with utmost trust and confidence that he would be able to tell him everything he wanted to know. Why did sand drop through his fingers when it was dry and stick to his hand when it was wet? Why were some shells shaped differently from others?

"I don't know!" Keith shouted at last. "Now stop asking questions. I want some peace and you're driving me round the bend. And I want to ask a question." He turned to Sally. "Why on earth did you saddle us with these two?"

Sally's cheeks reddened and her temper grew. Memory was pulling at the back of her mind. She had met Nancy one day at Jill's house and asked her about her new boyfriend.

"Oh, that didn't last long," Nancy had told her. "He said he'd grown fond of me and I think he had, but he liked himself so much better. He was a bit on the conceited side."

Could Nancy have been talking about Keith Watson? Sally had a shrewd idea that she had been. But in any case, he wasn't going to criticise *her* nephews any longer. Christopher's behaviour was exemplary, though she had to admit that Robbie's continued questioning was wearing. She had asked Jill specifically to put Chris on his best behaviour, but she had taken it for granted that Robbie would be his usual quiet self.

"I told you I had to bring them," she said, "but they're with me because I want them and because I love them. They're behaving beautifully, but I couldn't care if they behaved like hooligans, I would still bring them and want them. I'm sorry you feel your day has been spoilt, Keith, but I think you ought to take us home now."

She leapt to her feet and began to pack the picnic basket. Keith also rose, staring at her huffily. He had hoped to get to know Sally Maitland much better, but how could he with two young boys looking on?

"Well . . . if that's how you feel . . ." he began.

"Why are we going so soon?" Robbie asked, but this time no-one answered and they drove home in comparative silence.

REACTION set in when Sally was once again in her own home, surrounded by towels, tissues and paper cups. Tears of anger began to well in her eyes and Christopher regarded her gravely, obviously worried.

"We were good, weren't we, Auntie?" he asked.

"You were as good as gold, both of you."

"Auntie, I've left my new toy car in Uncle Keith's car," Robbie said, the tears beginning to well in his eyes. "I've got to get it back."

Sally sank into a chair by the fireside.

"That's all I need," she said. "Oh, Robbie, I've no intention of trailing round to Keith Watson's house. It's a good half-hour's walk and I can't imagine he'll want to see any of us."

He would be ringing up his girlfriends to ask one of them to go dancing with him, she thought, but this time there was no irritation or anger. She couldn't even understand why she had ever found him attractive!

"Why will he not want to see us?" Robbie asked, his lip trembling again. "Auntie Sally, I have to get my car."

"Yes, he has to get his car," Christopher assured her.

"I'll get it for him tomorrow," Sally promised.

"No, tonight. I have to get it tonight."

"But why?"

"Because if we take these two cars back to Mummy tonight and we've been good boys and haven't made a mess, she'll wrap them both up in a pound note for us," Christopher said eagerly. "But we must show her nice clean cars . . . see?"

Sally saw. Very definitely there was something wrong with that and she would say so to Jill! But she would have to try and get the car back for Robbie.

"OK, after I've had a rest, we'll go round to the Watson house and retrieve your car."

THE weather had dulled and a rain cloud had blown in from the sea. Sally was fastening her two charges into their anoraks when there was a ring at the bell. Glancing out of the window, she saw that Keith's car was back at the door.

"Thank goodness," she said. "It's . . . er . . . Uncle Keith back again. He'll have brought your car, Robbie."

But it was a different young man who stood on the doorstep. At first glance he was very much like Keith Watson with the same dark hair and pleasant smile. But this man was older.

"Oh . . ." Sally said uncertainly. "I thought it was Keith."

"I'm Alan Watson. I'm Keith's older brother."

"The accountant?"

"The same. I found this small car on the back seat when I went to clean up the car. Keith told me where to find the owner. I thought it might be important to him."

The children had come to stand beside Sally and now Robbie ran forward.

"It's mine!" he cried eagerly. "You've found it! It's mine!"

"Well, say 'Thank you,' " Sally urged.

"Thank you." His solemn little face was alight with gratitude.

"Please come in," Sally invited. "Would you like a cup of tea and a picnic sandwich? I . . . I'm rather afraid our picnic was a disaster. Keith was . . . a bit upset . . ."

"He'll get over it," Alan said easily. "Do you know my brother well, Miss Maitland?"

"No, not well. In fact, this was our first date, but . . . well . . . I had to take the children with me, you see.

"I really don't think he enjoyed himself much though." She smiled. "Entertaining two young boys wasn't exactly what he'd had in mind . . ."

THEIR eyes met and Sally saw the hidden depths of laughter in his. She suspected that Alan Watson understood very well indeed.

"Young children have to run off their energies," he said.

"Why?" Robbie asked.

"In order to tire you out so that you sleep well at night."

"Why do we have to sleep?" Robbie probed.

"Ah, now that's a very interesting question. I don't think many people know why, except that we all feel better in the morning. Maybe when you're grown up, you can find out and tell me."

"Why am I a little boy before I'm a big man?"

"Because big men have to know a lot of things and if you start learning now, then you can keep what you learn inside you and can add to it as you grow so that you know a lot when you're a man."

"Like Mummy's bulbs which grow into flowers. Why did one of her bulbs grow into a hyacinth and the other one into a daffodil?"

"Because . . ." Alan began, but Sally stepped in.

"I think you've asked enough questions for one day," she said. "Let's set out your lemonade and biscuits, then you can take a nap till Mummy comes. Sorry about that," she said to Alan.

"No, I don't mind in the least," he assured her. "I like to hear a child asking questions, especially why things happen. I mean we can all find out what things are, or where, or even who they are, but why is the one which demands to be answered. Robbie shouldn't be discouraged now that his mind has started to grow."

Sally gave him the brightest smile he'd had in a long time and Alan blinked. She was a very attractive girl. She explained the circumstances under which she was looking after the children and Alan nodded his approval. He was glad, too, that she wasn't yet another of Keith's steady stream of girlfriends.

"We could go for a picnic on Sunday if you like," he suggested, "and take the children. I could swat up on my general knowledge before then or that young man will keep tripping me up."

Sally's heart warmed to this friendly young man who was so unlike his brother. He obviously had a great sense of humour, lots of patience — and was very fond of children. In fact, she really wondered what she'd ever seen in someone as self-centred as Keith in the first place. How lucky it was that they'd left Robbie's toy in the car!

"I think I would like that very much," she said shyly.

Perhaps they could all have a nice day! □

In His
Own Sweet Way
by KATHLEEN KINMOND

L IBBY absently pushed the twin pram up the garden path. She couldn't quite pin down the conversation at the weekly coffee morning, but she'd got the feeling that the others had been hinting that Neil didn't pull his weight like the other young husbands.

As she took off the little girls' padded track suits, she seemed automatically to be making excuses for him.

Neil was a representative for the town's big textile firm. He went quite regularly to England and the Continent on business and, as Libby's mother had pointed out, it was quite natural he should want to relax when he came home, rather than have to work at the kitchen sink or do the household chores.

"Yes, I suppose so, Mum," Libby had agreed without much enthusiasm, when last her friends had been trying to out-boast each other about how much their husbands did to help them in the house.

Libby had just finished tucking the twins in for their afternoon nap when her mother's little car arrived at the front door.

Since she had been widowed three years before, Mrs Laing would

71

pop over quite often to visit, particularly when Neil was away on one of his trips.

Libby was always glad to see her mother. They were good friends and both enjoyed the long, satisfying talks they had together.

"You've been at one of your coffee mornings again," Mrs Laing said when the two of them had settled down for a cup of tea and a chat. "And I can tell by your face the other girls were on their favourite hobby horse again."

"I'm afraid so, Mum," Libby admitted. "I really get angry with myself for letting it get under my skin. I was perfectly happy with the way Neil and I ran our life together, before I heard the other girls talking about their husbands."

She sighed as she put down her cup.

"I must admit I enjoy meeting them as a rule," she went on. "And of course, I may just be imagining they're going on about Neil."

Her husband was due home, this time from Belgium, at the end of the week and Libby was determined to put the niggling thought out of her head.

On the Friday she prepared his favourite meal, which they would have together that evening after the children were in bed.

Anne and Audrey were delighted to see their father home again and covered his face with moist, welcoming kisses.

"Daddy's back!" Anne shrieked.

"Come and see us in the bath," Audrey shouted as Libby shooed them upstairs to the bathroom.

They were halfway through the bathtime routine when Neil appeared in the bathroom, changed from his business clothes into old jeans and a sweater.

He knelt down beside Libby at the side of the bath and tickled the girls' wet tummies while Anne and Audrey shrieked with delight. Libby sat back on her heels, exulting in the happiness of her little family.

Well, at least he does help a bit with the children, Libby found herself thinking as she went through to the kitchen when the children were in bed. Then she gave herself a mental reprimanding for even thinking such a thought.

"Oh, it's just wonderful he's home," she said aloud.

NEIL sighed with pleasure as Libby brought through the meal which they always had off a small table in front of the fire.

"When I'm away," he said, "I always picture you sitting here, probably knitting something for the girls and watching television."

Afterwards, when Libby was washing-up, it seemed the most natural thing in the world for Neil to stretch his legs in front of the fire and go promptly to sleep.

By the time she had stacked away the crockery and cutlery, Libby was feeling really tired. She looked ruefully at the cream-coloured, linoleum-covered floor, and sighed. It was the bane of her life.

No matter how often she mopped or washed it, it always seemed to look grubby. Oh well, she couldn't possibly get around to doing it tonight, she felt so tired. She sat down limply on a chair.

Come to think of it, she hadn't been feeling particularly well of late. It was nothing she could put her finger on; she just didn't feel well.

She went back to the sitting-room, opening the door quietly, but even so, Neil wakened immediately and held out his hand for her to sit down on the settee beside him.

The remarks of the girls at the coffee morning flashed through her mind, and she almost told him she would have appreciated some help with the dishes. But before she could begin, he'd drawn her towards him and kissed her.

"Isn't this just perfect?" he said. "The two of us here together?" And protesting words were strangled at birth.

THEY spent a happy weekend together, and Libby felt a bit better. The niggling pain which came and went on her right side seemed to have settled down somewhat and she decided maybe it was going to be all right after all.

Neil left again on the Tuesday morning, this time for Germany, having been briefed by his boss on the Monday. Libby's mother turned up on the afternoon after he'd gone, looking more excited than she'd done for a long time.

"Hello, darling," she said. "Neil away again? Everything all right?"

Libby hesitated for a moment. She had been meaning to ask her mother's opinion about the pain, but looking at her animated face, she changed her mind.

"I'm fine, thanks," she said. "I needn't ask how you are, for I'd say there was something exciting brewing in Gran's life."

Mrs Laing laughed and sat down on the edge of a chair, as if she'd simply no time to lose.

"Yes, actually, there is. Mrs Farquharson next door has asked if I'd like to go down with her to her daughter's in Bournemouth for a fortnight. Isn't it wonderful?"

Mrs Laing stopped, quite breathless after giving Libby her news.

"How absolutely super, Mum," Libby said warmly, thinking she hadn't seen her mother looking so animated since her father died.

They had invited her to go to the seaside with them last year, but she had resolutely declined, feeling they'd have more freedom on their own. Now she was going off under her own steam with someone much about her own age, and Libby was delighted for her.

"I won't be back again before I go, dear," she said as she was leaving, "the train is booked for the day after tomorrow. I'll ring you before I go."

LIBBY realised how much her mother's quick daily visits had meant to her, particularly when that niggling pain came back just after Mrs Laing had telephoned before her departure. But she was glad she hadn't mentioned it, because her mother would probably have worried — or even cancelled her holiday.

The People's Friend Annual

This was the day of the weekly coffee morning and Libby debated whether to go or not, but the girls liked meeting the other children, and so they set off.

"Are you all right, Libby?" Catherine asked, when they arrived at her home.

"Well, I — I've a pain that niggles a bit just here." And she put her hand on her side.

"Appendicitis!" Molly Shepherd pounced on a diagnosis immediately. "How long has it been going on?"

"A little while now," Libby said cautiously.

"Well, you should see a doctor," Molly ordered. "Seriously, I mean it. It could escalate into something serious."

Libby said nothing but quietly decided to herself that she'd wait until Neil got home the following afternoon, then she could go to the late-afternoon surgery.

But it wasn't to be. She spent most of the night wandering about the house, sometimes doubling up with pain. In the early morning she decided she was just being ridiculous not doing something about it.

About seven in the morning, she rang the surgery number. It was the youngest doctor, keen and full of enthusiasm, who came at once.

"Oh, Mrs Stewart, you should have contacted me before this," he said, after examining her very tender stomach. "As it is you'll have to go into hospital immediately. Have you anyone to leave the children with?"

Libby hesitated.

"Well, not really," she said. "My husband won't be home from Germany until tonight and my mother has just gone off on holiday. I've been putting off calling you until Neil was back home."

"Any neighbour who might look after them?" the doctor asked.

Libby shook her head unhappily.

"I shouldn't like to ask them. They're all elderly and the twins are quite a handful now."

"So is my little boy!" The doctor grinned. "How old are they?"

"Twenty months."

"Fine. My lad's eighteen months. I'll take them home with me until your husband comes back. Can you contact him somewhere?"

"Not really. He'll be on his way home now."

The young doctor thought for a moment.

"I'll leave a note here for him and he can collect them from my house when it suits him."

"It's awfully kind of you to do this for us," Libby began, grimacing as a stab of pain hit her, but he waved her thanks aside.

FROM then on everything seemed to happen as if in a whirlwind. Afterwards, Libby could only remember vaguely about going into hospital and being prepared for the operation. The next thing she knew she was surfacing from a great depth and there was Neil, sitting watching her as if the end of the world had come.

"I'm all right, darling, really I am," she assured him immediately.

"I've been so worried," he said, bending to kiss her. "No wife, no children to welcome me home. I knew something was far wrong even before I saw the doctor's letter."

"Wasn't it super of him taking them until you got home?" Libby smiled.

"Absolutely wonderful. I rang his wife and she said they'd keep them until I'd been in to see you."

He glanced at his watch.

"I've been here some time waiting for you to come round. Unfortunately, I'll need to go now."

"How'll you manage, Neil?" she asked him anxiously.

He gave her a quick kiss.

"You're not to worry. I've decided to take a week's holiday now and we'll manage fine."

She watched his tall, straight figure leave the ward, and her heart sank. Oh dear, how would they all get on? If only her mother had been around, as she usually was. But she didn't want to write to her, for she deserved her break.

Libby was in hospital for a week and somehow or other, Neil managed to visit her every day.

"Are you really managing all right?" she asked him anxiously when he looked a bit worn and tired one night.

"Of course we are," he assured her. "I made lentil soup at the beginning of the

My Island Man

WE wandered far in quiet ways
On warm and sunlit summer
days.
Or rambled by the riverside
And caught a glimpse of paradise.
We saw the moonlight's silver beam
Reflected in the water's gleam;
'Twas there he told me I was fair
And twined the rowans in my hair.

The lilting of his island speech,
Beguiling, soft and ever sweet,
Held my wayward spirit fast
And lit love's candles in my heart.
I did not hear his restless sighs
Nor miss the moondust from his eyes
For gentle were his ways, and kind;
And love we know was ever blind.

For he had known horizons far
And set his course by some lone star.
Undimmed the longing in his eyes
For other lands and distant skies.
I'm glad we walked a little way
Nor would I change one whit today.
As it was, so was it planned;
My dear, my gentle island man.

Winifred Slessor.

week and it's great." He hesitated for a moment. "It's a bit thicker than you usually make it, but it's good."

"How much of the lentils did you put in?" she asked tentatively.

"A pound," he said bravely, then looked askance at her. Despite a valiant attempt to keep her face straight, she burst out laughing.

Neil laughed, too.

"Yes, it'll last us until you get home. The original condensed soup. I just take out a chunk every day and add water. The kids love it."

At last it was time for Libby's discharge from hospital. When she arrived home, the girls and Neil all earnestly helped her into the house.

Neil had laid tea in the kitchen and the twins couldn't tell their mother quickly enough how Daddy had washed the kitchen floor for her coming home!

He had indeed! Large areas of the skirting board were marked where his haphazard mop had splashed it. He hadn't gone to the trouble of moving the kitchen table or chairs, but instead had briskly whisked the mop out and in between the legs of the furniture, leaving a pattern of clean and dirty parts.

Libby tried hard to restrain the laughter which threatened to bubble up and choke her.

"Well, darling," Neil said eagerly. "Everything OK?"

"Oh yes, you've done awfully well."

"Well, in spots," he admitted modestly. "Sometimes I was completely at a loss to know what to do next. How you get through all the work the way you do is a mystery to me. I really think something will have to be done about it."

She looked at him, wondering what he meant, but he didn't seem to notice.

MRS LAING arrived home at the end of the fortnight, simply bubbling over about her holiday, but she stopped in her tracks when she saw her thin, white-faced daughter.

"Libby! Whatever is the matter with you?"

"Oh, it's all over and done with," Libby said airily. "I've been in hospital, had my appendix out and I'm back home again!"

Her mother stared at her in disbelief.

"But why didn't you let me know, Libby?" she said. "I'd have come back right away and looked after the house and the girls."

"That's just why I didn't let you know." Libby smiled at her fondly. "I didn't want to spoil your holiday."

"But however did you manage with Neil being away so much and also being, well . . ."

"A bit handless?" Libby put in, chuckling. "Well, Neil took a week of his holidays and we managed not too badly. He had one or two mishaps, I must admit, like boiling the twins' best white cardigans to get them really white and reducing them to doll size!" And the two women laughed until tears came into their eyes.

Mrs Laing was still there when Neil arrived home that night.

"Would you mind coming tomorrow morning, Gran?" he whispered as she was leaving. "I want to do a bit of shopping with Libby. I've got quite a sizeable bonus and I know how I want to spend it."

She raised her eyebrows enquiringly, but it was obviously a secret.

Saturday morning was sunny and bright as Libby and Neil left the house.

"Have your lunch out if you want to," Mrs Laing said as they left. "The children and I will manage fine."

Consequently, it was after four o'clock before they returned, Libby looking tired but very happy. Neil saw her safely into the house, then went back to the boot of the car to come staggering in, hauling a huge, ungainly package.

Mrs Laing looked on with interest.

"It's a dishwasher," Libby told her. "Isn't it wonderful? Neil says he doesn't know how I got through all the work before.

"When I was in hospital and Neil had to cope alone, he realised just how much work I have to get through every day — especially with two young tearaways like the twins to handle. They're always getting into mischief."

"And this means we'll be able to spend more time together in the evenings, too," Neil said, before disappearing into the lounge.

"Jolly good!" Mrs Laing exclaimed, watching her daughter tear away the cardboard packaging.

"But that's not all," Libby said breathlessly, plunging into her shopping bag. "We're having the kitchen floor laid with carpet tiles so that all I'll have to do is vacuum it."

"How wonderful." Mrs Laing smiled, thinking privately that it's an ill wind that blows nobody good.

"By the way," she said, "Molly phoned when you were out. She's coming round tonight. Now you'll be able to do a bit of boasting at the coffee mornings. Maybe Neil doesn't help the way their men do, but at least he tries to provide you with labour-saving devices."

Libby drew little Audrey on to her knee.

"I don't think I'll say much," she said thoughtfully. "I know it doesn't really matter what the girls think and that Neil will probably never do very much in the house like their husbands, but he loves me and tries to help in his own way."

"Where is he now, anyway?" her mother asked.

"Sleeping in the sitting-room, I've no doubt," Libby replied, and they both laughed. □

Towards A Brighter Day

by Mary Scott

THE wind caught the door, slamming it behind her as she hurried through the school corridors on her way to the staff room. Katie wasn't on lunch duty today and there'd just been time to slip out to the shops to purchase some of the things she needed for her class that afternoon.

Smiling to herself in spite of her haste, Katie Stewart had no idea how pretty she looked with her bouncing hair and wide-awake grey eyes. But Adam Fraser noticed as he held open the staff-room door for her. She thanked him shyly before dumping her shopping on the table.

"You're in a hurry, Katie." Adam grinned. "Better not let Old Grierson find out you've been shopping in your lunch hour. He doesn't approve of staff leaving the premises during school hours. Says 'it's bad for discipline,' " he mocked, mimicking the headmaster and making Katie giggle. "Still, you won't be here next term, so perhaps you're not worried."

"Oh, but I am!" Colour flew to Katie's cheeks and she wished desperately she didn't end up feeling inadequate whenever she was with Adam. Something about the way his dark hair fell untidily on to his forehead made her heart turn over. She wanted him to be interested in her but she just couldn't be herself when he was around.

She almost choked over a sandwich as she hurried to explain she'd need a reference at the end of term. Her job as supply teacher for the Christmas

term at Woodhead School was the first real teaching post she'd had since she'd finished her training. Goodness knows where her next job would be.

Katie found herself glancing across nervously to a seat by the radiator where Miss Kerr was busy marking books. The older woman had shown her the ropes when she'd arrived a few weeks earlier.

MISS KERR looked up as she heard the warning bell ring in the corridor.

"You're doing your best, Katie," she said gently, pushing her heavy glasses up on to her forehead. "But Adam shouldn't make fun of Mr Grierson. He's a good headmaster and a school is nothing if there isn't discipline and respect. Rules are made to be kept." She glanced reprovingly at Katie's shopping bag on the table.

"Oh dear . . ." Katie watched Miss Kerr go out of the room, books tucked tidily under her arm.

"Don't look so worried, Katie," Adam reassured her. "You're doing all right. How about coming to the concert at the Royal Hall tonight? Some of the other teachers are going. There's more to being a teacher than marking books."

Katie shook her head dismally, wanting to explain that she didn't have books to mark for the infant class, but she'd a whole pile of angels' wings to sew instead. Not that she could have told him the truth. It was a special secret she and her class were sharing. They'd spent hours rehearsing a Nativity play planned for the end-of-term concert.

Katie shuddered when she recollected the day she'd gone into Mr Grierson's study to ask permission to arrange the play.

"The main thing is we don't want anyone else to know," she'd burst out breathlessly as if she'd been rushing instead of hanging about nervously outside his room till he had time to see her. "I want it to be natural and spontaneous so it seems real. That's why it's important to keep it a secret just for the children and me — and you, of course."

IF only he didn't look so severe and remote, she thought. But if she'd found the courage to glance up, she'd have seen he was peering at her through his glasses with the glimmer of a smile. If only his other teachers had shown half as much enthusiasm and enterprise, he'd have been delighted. Katie would have been a welcome addition to his staff instead of just helping out while Miss Jackson was away ill.

"It will mean a lot of extra work for you," he pointed out doubtfully. "Five-year-olds can't sew very well."

"No, but they can paint scenery," Katie enthused. "Oh, it won't be perfect, but they'll have done it themselves. And I don't have anything to do in my spare time. I haven't really had time to develop a social life in the few weeks I've been in town."

Mr Grierson had suddenly relented. "All right. But the school can't provide the extra materials you'll need. It would be irresponsible to dip into school funds for anything so frivolous."

Katie had to bite down on an angry retort that a Nativity play was hardly frivolous, but Mr Grierson wasn't looking at her any more, his mind already on the new time-table for next term. Oh well, all that mattered was getting his permission. Everything else would fall into place now.

A ND so it had, though with a 101 things still left to do and only a few days to the play, she found herself close to tears. Of course, it was important to keep the play a secret and she knew the children had managed it, though they must have been bursting at times to confide in their parents. But looking at Adam, she wasn't so sure any more.

Miserably, she wished there could have been some exceptions. She just hadn't anticipated any difficulties. If she could have explained to Adam, he wouldn't have been looking so cross. There'd been occasions when she'd had coffee with him after staff meetings, and once or twice they'd bumped into each other out of school hours. But it had never been planned. This was different.

"I'm sorry, Adam," she apologised. "It's just that there's so much to be done now Christmas is near. You know, presents and things . . ." she added defensively, wishing he'd stop staring at her so blankly. She ached to add that if he'd ask her out once the school concert was over, she'd have time on her hands, but she was terrified of assuming too much. Even now he hadn't exactly suggested meeting her on her own.

"Oh, I understand all right," Adam muttered.

The school bell pealed its final warning, silencing him for a moment as they started off in the direction of their classrooms. He hesitated by his own classroom and she waited a moment, wishing he'd sound a bit more friendly.

"You're no different from all the rest," he said. "Supply teachers seldom bother to get involved with the school. No doubt you'll go back to Tarbert once term is over and forget all about us."

"Adam, that's not true and you know it," she snapped back. "I wish I could stay . . ." But her explanation fell on deaf ears. Adam had turned his back on her, shutting the door in her face.

Flushing, Katie hurried into her now subdued class. They were sitting round their small tables, modelling with Plasticine, but the moment she shut the door, they erupted noisily. Anything less like angels she'd never seen. She smiled to herself, her optimism temporarily restored.

"If you're not quiet this instant, there won't be any play and it most certainly won't be a secret," she rapped out sharply, managing to produce a stern frown that didn't fool anyone. "Look, I've got the wire and cling film to make wings and I can sew them on later," she announced, holding up the results of her lunchtime shopping expedition.

T HE afternoon flew past with the class happily engrossed. Katie drew a sigh of relief when they all reluctantly trailed off home. At least, the class had been quiet and even Miss Kerr could hardly complain! Not that she expected to see the teacher again that evening. There was nothing for it but to wait till the rest of the school staff had gone if she was going to keep the play a secret.

F   81

Keeping the secret was more difficult than she'd anticipated. What she'd have done if her landlady, Mrs Munro, hadn't produced a pile of old curtains when she'd asked if she'd any spare bits of material, she shuddered to think. She needed the material to make robes for Joseph and Mary and the Three Wise Men.

"I don't want them back." Mrs Munro had smiled, waving Katie's thanks away understandingly. Her lodgers were invariably teachers and she'd learned not to ask questions, especially at Christmas.

MRS MUNRO would have a special invitation to the school concert, Katie decided. She'd an idea her landlady would treasure that. Her own children had grown up and married, leaving home to live in England.

"If only they didn't live so far away," Mrs Munro once said to her wistfully. "When your own children are growing up and your life's busy and full, you think nothing will change. Then suddenly your bairns are parents themselves with children of their own. I hardly see them now."

Her words had left Katie feeling vaguely guilty, conscious that she hadn't seen her own gran in months.

Still, I'll see her at Christmas. She comforted herself with the thought. Her grandmother always travelled from Greenock to Tarbert to spend Christmas and New Year with the family.

By the end of the afternoon, Katie was exhausted. She was struggling to put the scenery away in the big cupboard at the back of the classroom when Mr Grierson put his head round the door.

"Working late again, Katie? Don't wear yourself out. Still, I'm glad you're here." He smiled, looking faintly embarrassed. "I found this old crib in the garage at home. If you haven't anything better, I thought it might help."

"Oh, that's wonderful!" Katie's eyes shone. "I thought we'd have to do with an old box. Everything is going to be perfect."

Incredulously, she found the headmaster insisting on giving her a lift home.

"It's not out of my way." He grinned, gathering the angels' wings into a pile. "Someone could easily see you and the secret would be out. And just tell me when you want to bring the costumes to school. I'll pick them up."

Everyone was so kind, Katie thought blissfully. Suddenly even the misunderstanding with Adam wasn't so important. She only needed to be patient and wait till the school concert. It looked like being a wonderful Christmas.

Time enough then to tell him she planned staying on in her digs with Mrs Munro. After spending Christmas at home she'd be coming back here. There'd be a better chance of finding work.

Anything, she reminded herself, that would keep her near Adam.

THE days flew by and though it hurt when Adam seemed pre-occupied and less inclined for a chat, she pushed it to the back of her mind. Most of the teachers were busy marking exam papers.

Why, even Miss Kerr looked harassed and less sure of herself! But the senior teacher still had time to keep an eye on Katie now and again.

"You're not getting enough rest, Katie," she admonished sternly, though her eyes were kindly enough. "You've got dark shadows under your eyes. When you're young, it's right to have fun, but don't overdo it."

THERE was so much she could have said, but Katie had to swallow the words, unhappily conscious that Adam was listening even though he pretended to have his nose buried in books. Her fingers stilll ached from fiddling with the wire wings and the painstaking job of sewing them on to the costumes. Thank goodness, she thought, it's the concert tomorrow and in a few days school breaks up.

That night she slept lightly, her mind alive, going over everything for the play. Mrs Munro had accepted the invitation and Mr Grierson had collected the costumes the night before. Giggling, Katie wondered what Miss Kerr would think if she could have seen the pair of them creeping through the darkened school like conspirators.

Without Mr Grierson's help, it would have been nearly impossible to keep the secret. He'd hidden the scenery away at the back of the stage in the school hall and had promised to help.

Katie smiled to herself, listening to Mrs Munro's old clock striking three down in the hall. Only twelve hours and it would nearly be over.

"We'll miss you next term, Katie," Mr Grierson had murmured regretfully when he dropped her off last night after they'd been to the school. "I hope you haven't forgotten we're expecting you to join us for supper with the rest of the staff tomorrow evening."

As if she'd forget! It would be the end to a perfect day. Hanging in her wardrobe was a dress she'd kept specially for the occasion. Adam had never seen her in anything but practical clothes.

For once she managed to get to school before Miss Kerr and she wondered how she'd get through the hours stretching ahead to the concert. But thirty excited five-year-olds kept her mind thoroughly occupied and it was while they were having lunch that she was called into Mr Grierson's study.

BREATHLESS and excited, she hurried along, imagining it was some final plan for the play. But Mr Grierson just glanced at her gravely, gesturing to the phone.

"It's your mother," he said gently. "No, she's all right," he added swiftly, seeing the colour drain out of Katie's cheeks. "I'll be in the secretary's room if you want me."

He'd gone before she could ask any questions, leaving her to pick up the phone, her heart hammering uncomfortably.

"Mum?" she whispered uneasily into the crackling phone. "Is anything wrong?"

Katie struggled to remember whether her mother had sounded anxious the last time they had talked on the phone, but it had been a family chat, full of gossip and plans for Christmas and the New Year.

Thoughts of her father and younger brothers and sisters filled her head. Surely nothing had happened to any of them? It wasn't like her mother to call her at work — especially when she'd be seeing her soon anyway.

By the time she'd put down the phone her heart was aching unbearably and the excitement about the afternoon dimmed, overshadowed by the news that her grandmother had suffered a mild stroke.

"Don't worry, love," her mother was saying, sensing her panic. "Gran will be all right. She's been lucky. But she won't be able to come to Tarbert for Christmas. We wondered if you could go and stay with her for a few weeks."

KATIE'S eyes filled with tears. "Of course I'll go, Mum," she responded steadily, hiding the quiver in her voice. "I think Mr Grierson will let me catch the train later today. It won't feel like Christmas not being with you all, but there are other years."

Torn between tears and the need to be practical, she phoned Mrs Munro, relieved when her landlady took the crisis in her stride, promising to pack Katie's things and bring them to the school.

"I shall miss you, Katie," she said honestly. "But it's your gran who needs you right now."

Replacing the phone, she felt suddenly bereft, aware that now there wouldn't be time to get to know Adam better. But then, she'd probably been letting her dreams run away with her. He'd never shown anything more than friendship and lately even that had cooled off.

Katie's tears and heartache were forgotten for the moment as she stood in the wings of the school stage, shepherding the children into their places. Rosy with excitement and nerves, the children held their breath till the curtain went up. Lopsided stars and a moon hung from the ceiling outside the stable and one huge star shimmered over the crib.

A hush from the audience made Katie panic for a second, wondering if she'd been over-ambitious. The children were so little. Then a long sigh of pleasure rippled towards her as the audience watched the familiar pattern of the play gradually unfold. Mary and Joseph, almost swamped by their robes, faltered at first till they gathered confidence.

The Three Wise Men came gravely to the infant, holding out their gifts. If one of the angels jumped up and down in an attempt to see better and a donkey's mask fell sideways, nobody minded.

Mr Grierson was next to her and glancing round, Katie saw his eyes were moist and she couldn't help sniffing herself. Only one term with the infants and she knew she'd never forget them. Oh, she'd miss them!

THEN it was over and everyone was clapping and joining in with the infants as they sang "Away In A Manger" again.

"Say goodbye to everyone for me, Mr Grierson," she implored, thrusting several Christmas gifts into his arms. "These are for the children and one or two others. I won't catch the train if I don't hurry." There was so much more she wanted to say. One glance in Adam's direction showed him chatting to Miss Kerr, unconscious of her interest.

Towards A Brighter Day

It would have been wonderful to have time to get to know him, but some things didn't happen.

THE streets were quiet as Katie made her way towards the station entrance. She sighed wearily. So much had happened today.

"Katie!" Her name was called behind her and she swung round to stare at Adam in astonishment.

Adam looked sheepish, as if he wasn't too sure of his welcome from Katie. He looked flustered and breathless, too, as if he'd been hurrying. His arms were overflowing with Christmas cards and parcels in brightly-coloured wrapping paper.

He smiled at Katie's obvious surprise at seeing him.

"I was looking for you," he said. "Then Mr Grierson said what had happened and asked if I could come after you with the presents from the children and staff. He forgot to give them to you. I was so afraid I'd be too late."

He sounded anxious and breathless and she forgot to be shy, her warm smile lighting her face and reaching her eyes.

"Adam, that was thoughtful," she burst out, accepting the gifts with trembling fingers. Then the first gladness that had swept over her faded. It didn't mean anything was different. He was just being kind. "You'll be missing the concert," she put in doubtfully.

"It's you I'll be missing." A smile lit up his face. "Look, I got it all wrong. I didn't understand why you were suddenly so busy. I thought there just had to be somebody else and it was your way of telling me. I mean you're so pretty . . . anyone would love you."

A silence grew between them and she watched him, her eyes spilling over with stars. She wasn't too sure how you coped with a dream that seemed to be coming true.

"Katie, the train's going in a minute and I have to get back to school. But can I come and see you? It's not all that far and there are holidays and weekends." His lips brushed her cheeks gently as he bent over.

AND then Adam was just a face at the window as Katie nodded and smiled, not even bothering to try to hide the tears that were running down her cheeks. How she wished the train could have waited for just one moment longer.

How wonderful life was, she thought. You could be feeling miserable one minute and up in the clouds the next. There'd be plenty of opportunities in the future for really getting to know Adam — and there'd be no misunderstandings this time.

Katie sat quietly for a long time after the train drew out of the station before she undid the parcels. But it was a card from her class signed by them all that brought the smile back to her lips.

"We'll miss you, Miss Stewart. Happy Christmas! Come and see us all soon."

Oh, she'd do that all right, she told herself happily, and before that she'd be introducing Adam to her gran. Not the Christmas she'd planned. In a way, it was better! □

HER GRANDMOTHER'S GIRL

By
CLAIRE DEMAINE

WHATEVER the big stores might say, Maggie Webster reckoned there were seven shopping days left until Christmas once the calendar was turned to November. Real shopping days, that is — days when she took her wheeled trolley and caught the bus into town.

Maggie enjoyed these trips. Deciding what extras she should buy this week brought an exciting feeling of anticipation. And the large shops were so bright and gaily decorated, with carols sounding over the address system as Christmas drew nearer. It was almost as much fun as when all the family were expected home.

Spreading the load — and the cost — over the weeks, Maggie bought biscuits, tinned soups, and Christmas puddings, all in sizes which could be eaten up later. The tree and decorations were hidden away each year, so there was no problem there, but sometimes she bought some extra baubles, or a new fairy for the top. Even if *all* her children and grandchildren wouldn't arrive this year, some of them might.

And there were always the parcels to look forward to — large boxes containing all the delicacies she'd never have bought herself, but which her daughters seemed to imagine she might need. There were warm scarves and gloves, and pretty brooches to wear in the lapel of last year's coat. Even if Maureen and Ellen and Christine couldn't come this year, they didn't ever forget their mother.

Besides, there wouldn't have been room for them all in the cottage. It had been different when she and Jim lived in the roomy, family house.

Nearer Christmas there were some cards, and often a letter or two. The letter from her only daughter-in-law explained why they couldn't come to visit.

Robert hates driving in fog, she'd written. *We'll be up in the spring.*

And they always were.

Maureen sent a cheque, and more apologies, and photos of the latest grandchild.

"I don't blame them, Jim," she told her husband's picture. "We always wanted our children's family about us. It stands to reason

86

they're the same over their own grandchildren. Our great-grandchildren, I suppose."

She didn't think too much about Christine. Coming last, and a while after the others, maybe she'd been a wee bit spoiled. There'd been a large expensive-looking card from her this year, but no news. Christine had her career to consider, and even Gemma, her daughter, had always seemed too much for her to cope with.

There was an extra large cheque from Ellen, all the way from Canada. Maggie put it in the bank. There'd be lots of things it would pay for — new shoes or repairs.

As Christmas day drew nearer, and although it was clear she couldn't expect anyone to visit, Maggie added chicken joints to her list, just in case.

She only felt a little bit sad. Despite her preparations it was what she had expected. But she always kept on hoping.

Anyway, she thought, there are all those special programmes on television, and when did I ever get a chance to listen to the Queen's speech with all the family here, rushing about with never a moment's peace?

Maggie sipped her bedtime drink, her eyelids drooping. Maybe she was getting too old for visitors these days.

She was almost asleep when the knock came at the door. It sounded again, more urgently this time, before she'd hurried down the tiny hall to answer it.

WHEN a girl's voice answered her anxious query, Maggie couldn't believe her ears.

"Who did you say it was?"

"It's Gemma, Gran. You know, Tina's . . . I mean Christine's daughter. I know it's late . . ." The young voice began, but Maggie was already pulling back the bolts and opening the door.

"Gemma! What are you doing here?"

The child seemed to have difficulty standing upright and Maggie put an arm round her. "Come along in, lass. You look half starved."

Half starved was right, Maggie thought later, as she watched her granddaughter wolf down a plate of sandwiches. She had meant that Gemma looked cold, but now, seeing her small, thin face and the lack-lustre eyes, she wasn't sure just how close to the truth she had come.

At last Gemma sat back with a sigh.

"Ooh, Gran! That was good. I needed that."

She stretched her feet towards the warmth and Maggie noted the bare toes poking out from the shabby sandals. Sandals in this weather? The child didn't appear to have any proper clothes.

Under cover of clearing away the supper, Maggie studied Gemma. The long chestnut hair which Christine had been so proud of when her daughter was tiny, lay in tangled ropes down her back.

Gemma's hands and face were grey, but, Maggie reckoned, that could have been grime. She hadn't liked to insist the weary girl washed before eating. But the long, sack-like garment gave no clue as to whether Gemma underneath, was as ill nourished as the rest of her implied.

WHEN Maggie came back into the room Gemma's eyes were closed, but she roused herself on hearing her grandmother.

"I suppose I'd better explain, Gran. Mum will have told you I left home."

Maggie shook her head.

"Oh, I thought she'd have noised it abroad, but on the other hand . . . No, I suppose she wouldn't want to own to anything like that."

The girl leaned back in her chair.

"Dooley and I wanted to get married," she went on. "Mum didn't approve of Dooley, so . . ." Gemma spread her hands and Maggie wondered what was to come. She kept any expression from her face.

"We got wed, just the same, and Mum hasn't spoken to me since." She yawned hugely. "Well, it's a long story. Maybe I'll tell you sometime when I'm . . . not so . . . tired."

She started to slide from the chair and before Maggie could catch her, she was curled up on the rug in front of the fire.

Maggie leaned down beside her.

"Gemma! You can't sleep there. At least let me help you on to the sofa." She tugged uselessly at the girl's clothes. Gemma might be thin but she was too heavy for Maggie to lift.

"It's OK." Gemma flapped a hand at her grandmother. "Just leave me be. This is fine. If you saw where Dooley and I have been sleeping these last few months . . ." She gave a little giggle which ended in something like a snore as Maggie stared down at her helplessly.

There wasn't anything more she could do. Clearly the child was fast asleep — and if she was satisfied . . .! Maggie shrugged and went to fetch a blanket.

She worried about Gemma for all of 10 minutes when she got into her own bed. But she was tired, and life had taught her to be philosophical. What can't be cured must be endured, she told herself. Tomorrow I'll learn the whole story.

MAGGIE heard sounds in the bathroom before she was properly awake the next morning and lay there, gathering her strength for what the day might bring. She was still lying there when Gemma tapped at the door and came in, a tray in her hands and a smile on her face.

One couldn't say the girl looked well, but at least the weariness had receeded a little, leaving her face looking rather ethereal, Maggie decided. She accepted the dark coffee and thickly-cut toast with courtesy.

"I'm not used to breakfast in bed." She smiled, taking a sip of the hot, sweet coffee.

Gemma settled into the basket chair next to the bed.

"Well, you deserve pampering after last night. I wasn't sure how you would react when I arrived. I thought you might be really angry at first, but then I thought, not Gran, she's always coped."

Maggie smiled.

"You were a bit of a shock, you know."

Gemma looked down at her clothes.

"You mean this? Kaftans are easy to wear, and they don't take much sewing either. I made this one myself."

"Yes, I can see you did."

Gemma gurgled with laughter.

"I knew you were OK, Gran."

"It wasn't your clothes," Maggie explained. "I just wasn't expecting you. Your mother hadn't even said you were married."

"Mm! I thought she might have told you, but I guess she's disowned me." Gemma laughed lightly. "Well, I suppose I expected it. Tina's like that."

Maggie recalled Christine's last visit when she had tried to insist that her mother call her by this shortened version of her name.

"After forty years of calling you Christine, I'm too old to change now," she'd said, and that had been the end of it.

"What happened to Dooley?" she asked, pushing the toast nearer to Gemma.

"It's a nick-name," Gemma explained and Maggie waited. "He's . . . I've . . . We decided it wasn't working. You know how it is."

"No, I don't," Maggie told her, but there was no censure in her voice. "Have you come to stay for Christmas? I was hoping someone would come."

Gemma reached over and hugged her grandmother.

"Well, I guess I'm all the family you're going to get." She smiled.

"Well, I guess . . ." Maggie grinned, " . . . that that's one more than last year."

AS the child's face lit up, Maggie experienced a twinge of recognition and something close to panic. There had been so many signs, things she would have noticed if only she hadn't been so tired and worried last night.

"Where were you living? I mean, what part of the country?" Maggie wasn't certain she wanted to know any other details.

"Outside London," Gemma said finally, as if coming to a decision. "There were a lot of us in this great old house. It hadn't any what you'd call mod. cons." She laughed. "They made us leave." Again there was that intent stare.

"How did you get here, and . . . Well, you don't look, I mean, have you any money?"

It wasn't quite what Maggie had meant to ask.

"It's all right, I've got plenty of food," she went on quickly, "and you can stay as long as you like."

Gemma nodded.

"I hitched, and walked, and . . . Well, I'm here. I had to come, Gran. You were the only one I could go to. I knew you'd understand. Those tales you used to tell of when you were a girl, about the suffragettes and things you used to do, I thought . . . Gran will understand."

"I didn't . . ." she began, and then remembered the embroidered escapades she'd recounted to Gemma when she was small. Things got mixed up in a child's mind. She shrugged and said nothing. Serves you right, Maggie Webster, she thought, and smiled.

"And Dooley?" she asked at last. "Doesn't he know where you are? Why didn't he come with you?"

Gemma shook her head.

"He didn't want to, leastways, I never asked him."

Maggie leaned forward and put a hand on Gemma's arm.

"And the baby?" she asked gently.

It had been a guess, an educated guess, as they say, but still a guess, until Gemma's mounting colour told her she was right.

"It's due quite soon," she said quietly. "And I really want it, Gran. I really do. I love Dooley and want his child."

Maggie watched the escaping tear run down Gemma's cheek. The girl didn't even acknowledge its presence, not a muscle on her face twitched, nor did she lift a finger to wipe it away.

"Hasn't this fellow got a name, a proper name?" Maggie said at last.

Gemma chuckled.

"Edgar," she said, her eyes dancing, and Maggie laughed with her.

"I think I'd better be getting up," she said, lifting the tray to one side. "I've got some shopping to do."

M AGGIE wouldn't allow Gemma to come to the shops with her. "I can manage. Besides, you look to me as if you could do with a rest. When's baby due exactly?" she added casually.

"Oh, not for weeks! I'm not very big, am I?" Gemma pulled the kaftan tightly across her figure, but the result didn't ease Maggie's mind.

There was no doubt about it, the child was skin and bone.

"How many weeks?"

Gemma looked thoughtful.

"Well . . . I'm not sure."

"Haven't you seen a doctor?"

Gemma shook her head. "Having a baby's natural. Look at the women in . . ."

"I know all about that," Maggie interrupted, "but I think we'll make an appointment for you, all the same."

Maggie was very glad she'd had that cheque from Ellen, though large as it was it hadn't gone very far. Babies had clearly gone up in value, and clothes were dear.

Her granddaughter was lying on the bed in the spare room when Maggie got back.

"I've got this funny feeling," she told Maggie. "I started to make us some lunch, but . . ."

"Don't worry. You just rest. I'll bring mine up here, then we can talk a bit." She patted the girl's hand. "It's time we got better acquainted."

WHILE the soup was warming, Maggie phoned the doctor and put the tiny garments to air. She'd been a little mystified by the look of the all-in-one suits the young lady had recommended. What about nightgowns, and matinee jackets? But it seemed babies didn't wear such things these days. Maggie bought some extra, warm soft blankets, just to be on the safe side.

As she went back upstairs she remembered the date.

"It's Christmas Eve tomorrow," she told Gemma, watching her tuck into the food. "And I haven't got the decorations up, or the tree."

"A tree!" Gemma's eyes sparkled. "A real Christmas tree? With glass balls, and little presents?"

"I'm afraid it's not real, but there are glass balls, and presents," she added quickly, thinking of the tiny mittens she'd bought.

"I haven't decorated a tree for ages." Gemma pushed away the dishes, and twisted her feet to the floor. "I'm all right now. Can't we do it right away?"

They went out to the hall cupboard and took the tree from its box.

"It's only little." Gemma eyed the bright green fir tree critically. "Do you remember the great big ones you used to have? And there were always loads and loads of balls, and miles of tinsel! And we'd all put our presents underneath, the ones we bought each other."

Maggie saw the memories easing the strain from Gemma's face and forebore to correct her. The tree hadn't been very large and the tinsel often tarnished.

"We used to open them after Christmas dinner, remember?" Gemma smiled. "How you all must have loathed those pin-cushions and book-marks we made.

"And we kids got diaries and notepaper," she went on. "We only ever used the paper for thank-you letters." She giggled, draping coloured tinsel over the branches. "Have you got a fairy?"

Gemma seemed to hold her breath, as if she couldn't quite believe that her grandmother might have provided this memory as well as all the others. But then her face changed.

"Gran! Gran! It's . . . I think the baby's coming."

Maggie put her arms round the slight body.

"There's nothing to be scared of," she said firmly, though her own heart was thudding. "Come on, I think we'll get you into bed."

LATER, after phoning Dr Walker, Maggie went back to sit beside Gemma's bed. She had some knitting needles and a ball of blue wool.

"You can put a girl into blue, so it doesn't matter what you have, does it?"

"No, I don't mind," Gemma said. "Dooley wanted . . . I like blue, anyway. What are you knitting? I thought you bought clothes today.''

"Bonnets. I forgot to buy any and we might as well wait and see before we decide what else you'll need.''

"Gran?'' Gemma said later. ''I'm glad I'm the youngest of the grandchildren. When the others were all small, before I was born, there must have been such a crowd. But there was only me, wasn't there? We used to have some lovely talks, didn't we? When Mum had to go somewhere, to a conference, or something.''

Maggie needles clicked. There had been quite a few conferences.

"Don't talk so, child! Rest! You always did have too much to say for yourself.''

"Did I? Yes, I suppose I did.''

WHEN Dr Walker came he shooed Maggie out of the room.
"Go and boil water.'' He grinned. ''Isn't that what they always do in films at a time like this? You could brew a cup of tea while you're on the job,'' he added.

It was several cups of tea later that Maggie heard a baby's cry. All the strength seemed to drain from her.

Sinking down on to the edge of a chair she let the fears and hopes she had kept buried come to the surface. Let Gemma be all right, she prayed. And Dooley . . .

She didn't know whether she ought to want his return. What sort of a man was he to let Gemma come all this way alone? What sort of a father would he make?

She waited, summoning all the patience she had learned through the years, until Dr Walker called her name.

They met on the tiny square of landing, the doctor pulling the door shut behind him.

"She's all right. Your granddaughter's tough. She'll need rest and feeding up. But you know all about that sort of thing.''

He patted her shoulder. He and Maggie Webster had come through a few crises together.

"Gemma's asking for you,'' he said.

MAGGIE was bleary-eyed when she answered the door next morning to the young man's furious knocking.

"I know she's here!'' he cried as she opened the door.

"You must be Dooley. You'd better come in,'' she said quietly, leading the way into the sitting-room. ''You took your time getting here.''

Momentarily Maggie regretted the words as the man towered over her, his face suffused with anger.

"How was I supposed to know where she'd gone? She disappeared and didn't leave a word, not a note — nothing! How was I to find her? And that mother of hers!'' He gave a short, explosive snort. ''Gemma was better off without me, *she* said. I knew she'd head for you. You were the only one she ever talked of.''

He looked around the living-room.

The People's Friend Annual

"Where is she? She must be here or you wouldn't have known about me. She hasn't gone? I'm not too late, am I?" he asked earnestly.

Maggie smiled.

"No, I should say you're just about in time. You've got a daughter, Edgar Dooley."

She held her breath, not sure what reaction to expect but when, after his first startled gasp, Edgar began to grin, she knew her prayer had been answered. Everything was, as far as possible, going to be all right.

W HEN Maggie knocked at Gemma's door sometime later it was Dooley who opened it.

"Come in, Great-Grandma," he invited, catching her hands and drawing her forward. "I guess I've a lot to thank you for."

He helped her into the chair and perched on the edge of the bed, near to Gemma.

"Is it really Christmas Eve, Gran?" she asked. "I've lost count of the days."

Maggie nodded and Gemma smiled.

"I'm glad. When we all used to come to you for Christmas I always envied the little ones. My nephews and nieces, they were," she told Dooley. "They all got sacks from Father Christmas. And I could remember what fun it had been when I got one. Somehow the magic went when you were older, and you knew."

The other two kept silent, but probably the same thoughts went through all their minds as Gemma's face sobered. But then she smiled radiantly at them, pulling back the blanket from round the baby's face.

"Now I don't need to envy them. Margaret Christine Dooley is going to have the biggest sack Father Christmas has ever filled, next Christmas . . . Or maybe the one after." She giggled.

"There should be a baby in the house at Christmas, don't you think so, Gran?"

Maggie nodded, her eyes going to the cards on the dressing-table with their pictures of the manger.

"Of course. But what did you call the baby, Gemma?"

"Margaret, of course! Maggie for short." □

In 1675, nine years after the mediaeval St Paul's Cathedral was destroyed in the Great Fire of London, the building of the present cathedral was begun. The famous Whispering Gallery picks up a whisper from the other side of the dome, and the Stone Gallery gives a view out over the city. Higher still is the Golden Gallery at the top of the dome, and highest of all is the Golden Ball. The crypt of St Paul's contains the tombs of Nelson and Wellington, and Wellington's 18-ton funeral carriage.

ST. PAUL'S CATHEDRAL

R HONA FENTON put down her palette and brushes and wiped her paint-stained fingers on a piece of rag. A sound had interrupted her concentration, making her realise it was time for a break.

Flexing her aching shoulder muscles, she frowned critically at the landscape painting she had been working on. Then, as the door opened, Rhona realised that she'd been disturbed by sounds from the outer room of her studios.

She wasn't quick enough to rearrange her features into a conventionally polite expression, and her voice sounded hoarse from lack of use.

"Yes? Can I help you?" she asked brusquely.

The man who stood in the doorway looked indignant.

"I'm sorry," he said, so sharply that the words were an accusation rather than an apology. "The notice on your door says 'please enter,' so I did. But there's nobody in the office."

Rhona tossed the multi-coloured rag on to a table.

"I expect Ruby has gone out for her lunch," she said amiably. But she was conscious of the fact that he was looking at her stained hands,

Together From Now On

by
GRACE
MACAULAY

noticing with distate that wiping them had not improved the state of them.

"Lunch?" he said. "It's after six o'clock!"

"No doubt she's gone home, then." She resisted a ridiculous impulse to frown back at him. "Was it Ruby you wanted to see?"

"I came to see Miss Fenton," he replied awkwardly.

Rhona inclined her head. "I'm Rhona Fenton."

His stance altered and the impatience returned to his voice.

"I take it you have received my letter?" he said. "My name is John Livingstone."

The name meant nothing to Rhona, but she didn't let him guess that. Ruby was forever scolding her for being unbusinesslike. She would have been proud of the efficient manner in which she brushed past Mr Livingstone, led the way to the office and found his letter almost at once. It was clipped to several others which were awaiting her attention.

While her eyes scanned the page, she was acutely aware of the man's critical glance.

"I want you to paint my mother's portrait," he said sharply. "Why didn't you answer my letter?"

"Your letter would have been answered in due course," she told him primly. "But I may as well tell you now that if I do accept your commission . . ."

"But you must!" John Livingstone's eyes were fixed on her face incredulously.

Smoothly, she continued, totally ignoring his interruption.

"It would be at least a year before I could begin work."

"I see." He spoke the two words without any particular emphasis. "In that case I won't detain you any longer."

He moved towards the door, then swung round to look at her. He was about to say something more, then as his eyes encountered her serene gaze, he changed his mind.

RHONA waited until the clatter of his feet on the stairs had completely died away before she moved to close the door which he had left ajar.

Her actions were slow and stiff, almost as if she were afraid she might start to tremble.

She wasn't a mystic, nor did she possess a sixth sense, but in that instant when her eyes had met John Livingstone's a warning flash of intuition had told her that this man had the power to disrupt her entire life.

As she walked back to her studio, Rhona felt bewildered and a little frightened. She shivered as she recalled the aggression which had vibrated around them during the short duel of words.

You'll never see him again, her sensible inner voice told her. And the same voice jeered at her as she picked up a piece of charcoal and began to sketch his face on a large white pad.

Rhona was neither pleased nor displeased with the drawing. It was a likeness, that was all. She had simply transferred his image from her

G

mind on to the paper. But she'd done it with a kind of determination which was strengthened when she ripped the page from the pad and shut the drawing away in the store cupboard.

She didn't usually make tea before she went home, but tonight she did, adding extra sugar as if treating herself for shock. And as she drank it, she studied the painting she'd been working on earlier, realising quickly that the sky in the background was just too pale. No wonder she hadn't been pleased with it. Tomorrow, she would change it without any difficulty.

The thought lifted her spirits and she went to rinse her cup, thinking that an occasional shock was good for one's system. Not that she would like to repeat her encounter with that abrasive man.

R HONA didn't consciously think about John Livingstone after that, and yet his influence stayed with her. The next morning when she returned to her studios, she was immediately conscious of the disorder and neglect. But she realised that this was a recent state of affairs which ought to have been dealt with before now.

Going straight across to the long work bench where Ruby, her elderly assistant, was working, Rhona's eyes searched the lined face thoughtfully. It was difficult to ask a direct question; impossible to suggest that this dear little bundle of energy and vitality might not be up to fulfilling all the duties she had been in the habit of taking upon herself.

Before Rhona could frame a question, Ruby began to scold her, and Rhona listened sadly to the familiar voice which had been part of her life for so long. The words and phrases and the characteristic rhythms of Ruby's tones were unchanged, but they were slower, as if wound down by time and age.

"You should have left these cards, Ruby," Rhona broke in. "I would have trimmed them."

With an exclamation of anger, the old woman turned to glare at her.

"Rhona Fenton, you don't listen to a word that's said to you! I'm standing here telling you that the charity people want these cards today! It's all very well doing good works, painting pretty cards for a good cause, but as I said to you last year and the year before that . . ."

Rhona had propped herself against the edge of the bench, but now she straightened abruptly.

"I'll help you with these, Ruby," she said. "We can talk as we go."

If Ruby was surprised she gave no sign of it. She merely continued with her tirade of complaints and criticisms. Rhona listened, but part of her mind was going back to the day when she had first met Ruby.

Rhona had just left art college and had decided to invest her savings in this studio flat. She hadn't expected to find anyone on the premises when she arrived. But Ruby, having worked for the previous occupant, had been here, giving the place a final clean up.

Rhona hadn't reckoned on employing anyone. In fact, she'd had no real plans for the future, apart from a desperate need to immerse herself in work, to forget the heartbreak and disillusionment of her broken engagement.

Ruby hadn't known her background and Rhona herself hadn't given any information. But somehow it had seemed that Ruby understood. Like kindred spirits, the elderly woman and the young girl had taken a liking to each other.

When Rhona took over the studios and began work, Ruby had come to visit her every day. But after a couple of weeks, Rhona had decided that all the odd jobs Ruby said were a pleasure, must be paid for.

The deciding factor was the sale of a water painting. Rhona recalled how she had hugged her friend gleefully.

"I'm going to be a success, Ruby!" she'd told her.

"I knew it the minute I saw you." Ruby had smiled at her fondly. "We must keep a note of that buyer's name and address. You may want to borrow the painting for one of your exhibitions."

Rhona had laughed incredulously. "When do you think I'll have an exhibition?" she'd said.

"Three years," Ruby had answered solemnly. "Maybe a bit less if you continue to put your heart into your work."

Rhona sighed now as she reached for another card to trim. Ruby's faith and encouragement had never faltered. Over the years Rhona Fenton paintings had acquired a fine reputation and Rhona had the satisfaction of knowing that her work was greatly respected.

Ruby stayed always in the background, smoothing all the details, taking the real load so that nothing would intrude on Rhona's artistic vision. She was immensely proud of Rhona and fiercely protective and Rhona loved her for it. But now, with a pang of shame, she realised that she had been taking too much for granted. Ruby was looking pale and exhausted.

Gently, almost nervously, she glanced at the old woman.

"I'll finish this, Ruby," she said. "Why don't you go and have a seat and a cup of tea?"

Ruby didn't look up.

"I'll put the kettle on in a minute."

But before she'd finished speaking, the door flew open and they both turned to look at the newcomer.

"She smells the tea before it's made, that one," Ruby said tartly.

MELANIE MAIN came dashing in like a laughing whirlwind, bestowing lavish embraces on the two women.

"I knew you'd have the kettle on! I knew it!"

Grumbling under her breath Ruby stalked away while Melanie deposited an assortment of bags and folders on the work-bench.

"It's not often we see you these days, Melanie," Rhona said.

"I know. I'm sorry. I've been so busy." She lifted her hand to display an engagement ring. "You know how it is when I'm in the throes of a big romance!"

Rhona pretended to be dazzled by the flashing diamonds and emeralds.

"Congratulations, Melanie." She laughed. "I had no idea! When did this happen?"

"Last Saturday," Melanie trilled. "The most gloriously wonderful day of my life." Seeing her friend's smile, she went on. "I know you've heard that before, Rhona, but this time it's true. I didn't know what love really meant until now. He's the most fabulous man. He really is."

"So when is the wedding? Are you here to deliver an invitation?" Melanie giggled.

"We haven't planned that far yet. One ring is enough excitement for now. I'm so delirious, I feel almost giddy!"

Ruby's voice brought her down to earth. "You'll be needing this tea then."

Melanie linked her arm through Rhona's and she gave her a conspiratorial look.

"Ruby only tolerates me when I'm putting work in the way of her favourite artist."

A CHEERY VOICE

FIERY front and jaunty air, our
*   winter robin comes on site. His*
private territory, our garden.

Brave little chap, he asks so little.
Share of the crumbs the sparrows get –
an extra meal when one digs the bed.

But on winter nights! I think of him
out there. Where is his cheerless bed?
What shield for his tiny body when rain
is lashing; the snow driving? Bitter keen
the frost of the long, long night – only a
blanket of feathers to keep him warm.

Yet ere the winter dawn has broken,
I hear his cheery voice. Out there!

Life at times we say is hard to thole.
Think of the robin. Jaunty and braving
all the winter brings.

Rev. T.R.S. Campbell.

They sat down in the smaller studio.

"So that's what brought you here this morning," Ruby said.

"Some people don't believe that a person can make a purely social call on old and valued friends," Melanie retorted, in answer to Ruby's sharp words.

"And some people believe the world is flat," Ruby grunted.

Melanie decided to ignore that.

"Anyhow," she said, "I'm here on a mission of mercy."

Rhona's lips twitched into another smile. Melanie continued. "It's about Mrs Livingstone's portrait."

Rhona's smile froze and her heart gave a thud. Melanie went on quickly to explain that she had recommended Rhona to the Livingstones.

"Sorry, Melanie." Rhona shook her head. "I just can't fit anything else in. Not this side of the year."

Melanie gave a deep sigh.

"John made a bad impression on you last night," she said sadly. "I can't understand why, because he is a very charming man. Unless he disturbed you while you were working, was that it?"

Rhona felt colour coming into her cheeks, as she recalled that it wasn't her work that he had disturbed — it was her whole being. Instead of answering her friend, she looked at Ruby.

"It was after you'd gone home last night," she explained. "This man came in and demanded to know when I would paint his mother."

Melanie put a hand on Rhona's arm and smiled her most persuasive, friendly smile.

"He didn't mean it to sound like a demand," she said. "He was upset. We all are. You see, his mother is a sick woman. She isn't expected to live. The doctor's can't say exactly how long, but it may be only a month or two."

Melanie went on to describe the dying woman whose patient smile was an inspiration to everyone who knew her. She had been widowed young and had brought up a family of three sons and a daughter who adored her. They longed to have her portrait painted as a lasting memory in the years to come.

While she was speaking, Melanie was constantly twirling her engagement ring round and round and Rhona found herself wondering if John Livingstone was Melanie's fiance.

"Nobody but you could do justice to her," she said persuasively. "I told them that. And before John went back to London last night I promised him I'd get you to agree."

Rhona put down her cup. "OK, Melanie, I'll think about it."

In a delighted whirl of smiles of chattering thanks, Melanie collected all her belongings and hurried out.

R UBY looked at Rhona in a concerned way. "Will you manage to do it? She didn't give you much option, did she?"

Rhona pursed her lips thoughtfully.

"What makes it worse is the thought that the poor woman is dying. I don't know how I could keep that knowledge out of my mind. It would be bound to affect her portrait."

Silence settled on them until Ruby spoke in an unusually soft voice.

"We all of us have to go sometime. Even the longest life seems short compared to what someone like you can paint on a canvas. A gift like yours can make someone live for ever."

Suddenly, Rhona's eyes burned with tears.

"Ruby, you have many gifts," she told her friend. "I wish I could make you live for ever. And I intend to try." And as Ruby gazed at her in surprise, she went on firmly. "You've been working too hard, Ruby. I want you to get some rest. I know you can't stay away from here. So we shall get someone in to do the work. And you shall do nothing but supervise. What do you say to that?"

"I'm getting past it, Rhona. I'll be glad of a help."

Relief swept over Rhona.

"I was worried about you, Ruby," she confessed. "Will you promise me you'll take things easy?"

Ruby nodded.

"You may as well go away and see that woman. She'll be on your mind until you've made the first sketch."

"You know me too well." Rhona smiled.

A few minutes later, as she drove across the city towards the Livingstone's address, Rhona made a deliberate effort to recall the details of the sketch she'd made the previous evening. But John Livingstone's features were blurred and ill-defined. She was no longer angry and she was glad of it.

From some of Melanie's goodbye chatter she had gained the knowledge that he lived and worked permanently in London. So, thankfully, there would be no risk of meeting him. She could relax.

Mrs Livingstone looked much younger than Rhona had expected, and her outward appearance and manner gave no hint of the serious nature of her illness. Rhona wondered if Melanie had perhaps exaggerated. Later, she realised she had not.

But from the moment she began her preliminary sketch, Rhona believed that the portrait could turn out to be one of her best. Mrs Livingstone was an ideal subject. Her face was filled with character. She evidently had a strong personality which had been tempered by all the joys and pains which had been part of her life. When she smiled there was a glow which spoke of the inner tranquility with which she accepted her suffering.

Busy as she was with other work, Rhona always found herself looking forward to the sessions at Mrs Livingstone's house. Rhona always encouraged her sitters to talk while she painted and often a lasting friendship developed between herself and the person she was painting. And although this happened with Mrs Livingstone, there was more to it than that.

Rhona couldn't analyse the rapport which established itself between herself and Mrs Livingstone but somehow, she sensed that John was a central point in their conversation.

Mrs Livingstone had an extra special love for John, her youngest son. When she spoke of him, her expression was transfigured by a kind of proud adoration. She told Rhona that he held a responsible position in the Civil Service, that he was a modest, unassuming man whose promotion had been gained by his calm, reliable attitude to his work.

Rhona couldn't say so; but these tame words didn't in any way agree with the vitality of the sketch she had made of him. Sometime she would look at the sketch in a vaguely perplexed way and then return it to the secret darkness of the cupboard.

Very soon she discovered that Melanie Main was in fact engaged to Mrs Livingstone's oldest son, James. As a future daughter-in-law, Melanie seemed to be all that Mrs Livingstone could have wished for her son, and Rhona was surprised. She had always considered Melanie to be rather an extravagant slightly irresponsible person.

"Melanie has such a warm outgoing nature," Mrs Livingstone said. "It's easy to see why James loves her. Indeed, we all love her."

Rhona agreed with that and to her surprise she found herself revising her opinion of her friend.

WITH every sitting, Mrs Livingstone's influence seemed to enlarge and expand Rhona's thoughts and ideas. She knew that it affected the portrait and occasionally she wondered if it would spoil it or improve it.

But the finished work exceeded all her hopes. Mrs Livingstone and her family were delighted with it. But to Rhona that was of secondary importance compared to her own elation. When she looked at the framed portrait, she felt not only a better painter but a better person.

Before she left the family party which had been given in celebration of the portrait, Mrs Livingstone took her aside for a moment and apologised quietly for John's absence.

"John will love my portrait, I know he will," she murmured softly.

Overwhelmed by emotions which she could not voice, Rhona put her arms around John's mother.

"Thank you for everything," she said simply.

In the weeks that followed, Rhona often longed to see Mrs Livingstone again. But now that the contact was broken, she was wary of renewing it. There was no real reason to, and there were vague, uneasy reasons against it. Although, when she allowed herself to think of him, she knew that inevitably she would meet John Livingstone again.

She worked hard and lived in the way that she had always done, but at the back of her mind there was a new tense feeling of waiting, as if a small inner voice was telling her — sometime, somewhere.

S HE was working late in her studio on a summer evening when she became aware that there was someone in the outer room. Then she heard his voice and, like someone in a dream, she put aside her brushes, knowing that this was a dream which had been repeated times without number.

He opened the door, and their eyes met. Again she experienced an instinctive recognition of the power which could disrupt her life, but this time there was no fear, no threat.

He took a step towards, holding out his hands and she moved to meet him. At the same time she saw clearly the darkness of grief in his eyes and she knew without being told that his beloved mother had gone.

"I'm so sorry," Rhona murmured the words tenderly.

John seemed to take comfort from her voice and the warm pressure of her hands.

"She told me to come and thank you again for the portrait," John said unsteadily. "I think she knew that I wanted to see you again."

Their hands were still joined as they exchanged a long look of deep compassion and understanding. Tonight was a time for the sharing of sorrow. A sharing that would bind them together, forging strong links.

"The portrait is beautiful," John said.

"Your mother was a beautiful woman."

Then they were silent, as if together they were paying a tribute to the woman who had brought them together. In her letters to John, she had given him a deep insight into Rhona's character. In her talks with Rhona, she had created a feeling of enlightenment, a preparation for this second meeting.

It was as if she had known, Rhona thought, that this was a love that was meant to be. And now, their second meeting was a precious legacy which they would cherish for ever. □

If You
Were Mine...

by PHYLLIS HEATH

If You Were Mine . . .

J ANE cuddled Colin close to her and hummed a lullaby softly, her ears alert for the sound of her husband coming back inside the house. When Bob's tall figure filled the doorway, blocking the light from the landing, she raised a finger to her lips, and nodded an answer to his unspoken question.

Bob moved quietly away and Jane bent over the small bed as she settled the child under the blankets. She looked down at him a moment longer before following Bob.

"He seems to have settled down now," she told her husband as she walked into the sitting-room. Her voice was a little strained when next she spoke.

"I'll sleep here, of course. But you get back home, Bob."

Bob Southern glanced at his wife. She looked so young and vulnerable standing there, her face devoid of make-up, her hair tousled. He knew this was going to be hard on her.

"I could stay, love," he said.

Jane gave him a swift, unsteady smile.

"No, I'll be OK, and anyway, Colin's more used to me."

"Sure?" Bob hesitated. "You won't . . . you won't let it upset you?"

He watched as she shook her head, but when she turned to avoid his eyes he pulled her close.

"I'm sorry, darling," he whispered.

There was no point in saying anything more. They had gone over it all time and time again, and now wasn't the time to raise the idea of adoption once more. With another smile he walked out of the house, waiting until he heard the click of the lock behind him before crossing the lawn to their own home.

Bob made himself a hot drink when he got inside, and stood in the kitchen picturing Jane doing the same thing in the MacDonalds' house. He hoped she'd sleep, but he didn't think she would.

Ever since Rachel and Mike MacDonald had come to live in the adjoining semi, Jane hadn't been sleeping well. At first she had been thrilled to think that a young couple were buying the house, for most of their neighbours were much older. But when she saw all the paraphernalia which meant there'd be a child in the house she had lost interest.

Turning listlessly away from the window, she'd only said in a flat voice, that she hoped it was well behaved.

Bob had said nothing. He knew Jane didn't mean what she implied. Jane loved children. She wouldn't have minded how much noise one made, how much trouble it was . . . if only it had been hers.

They had married with such hopes.

"We'll have lots of children." Jane had laughed, walking round the rooms of the old-fashioned house. "Well, two," she qualified, catching Bob's horrified look. "This place is made for children. Large rooms, thick walls — and the garden . . ."

They had gone out to gaze at the wilderness she called a garden, and laughed giddily.

"Of course, we'll have to tidy it a bit," Jane said. "Or we might lose a child or two. But they'll love it all wild like this. You can do what you want with the front one." She dismissed it airly.

But now both front and back gardens were models of order. When the final tests had confirmed that they would never have any children to run riot there, she had attacked the jungle ferociously. Tired and weary after several weeks of hard work she had lain one night sobbing in Bob's arms. It was then he had first mentioned the idea of adoption.

"Maybe they could find us a baby. I know they try to match parents and children," he told her, ignoring the way her body stiffened in his arms. "Even if we took a toddler we'd grow to love it. I know we would."

"No!" Her answer came through tight lips and she sat up, pushing him away. "I don't want any other woman's child. I want mine. Mine! Do you hear?"

They hadn't spoken of babies again. Whenever the subject arose Jane would either walk out of the room or laugh shrilly.

"Children? Bob and I don't need anyone else."

WHEN Rachel MacDonald knocked on their door the day after moving in, Jane was ready for her. She walked with purposeful steps to answer the knock, her expression one of cool politeness. But then she opened it, and there on the step, red hair aflame in the early-morning sunshine, was Rachel Brown, the girl who had sat beside Jane at school.

"Rachel!" Her voice was a squeak of surprise. "Is it you?"

The other young woman's voice was equally amazed.

"Jane Makin! Little Jane Makin! Where did you spring from?"

"I happen to live here." Jane laughed. "But come on in." She held the door wide, forgetting her determination not to befriend this woman; this woman who had a child.

Rachel stepped inside, but not without a quick glance back to her own house.

"Just for a minute. Mike's minding Colin, and I can't leave those two together for long. Mike seems to think he's a teenager not a toddler." She laughed. "But I expect you're used to that."

Jane's smile froze.

"We haven't any children. Bob and I aren't the family kind." She realised how the words sounded and corrected them. "I mean . . . well, not yet. We wanted to get the house nice, and everything," she ended lamely.

"Gosh! I wish we'd thought of that." Rachel laughed. "But at least we've got a house now. When we were up in Scotland we only had a flat. Was I glad when Mike's firm transferred him down here — especially with the other baby on the way."

For the first time Jane noticed the loose dress and averted her eyes quickly, a stab of pain running through her. But her voice was bright and welcoming as she drew Jane into the dining-room and introduced her to Bob.

"You always were the prettiest girl in school." Rachel laughed as she was saying goodbye. "No wonder you got yourself such a good-looking husband. And nice, too!"

"Mmm! I kind of like him," Jane said.

They giggled as if they were still in their teens, and hearing the sound Bob's heart lightened. Having her old friend so close, surely Jane would relax. Perhaps Rachel would help him persuade her to consider adopting.

But as if she had guessed the way his thoughts would turn, Jane tackled him the moment she came back into the room.

"Don't say anything, Bob. Promise me! I don't want anyone's pity. Especially not Rachel's."

"But, Jane, she'd be sorry for you, and that's not the same thing at all. You do mean to be friends, don't you?"

"Of course! I always did like Rachel, she's fun, and so good hearted. But I'd sooner she didn't know that I . . . we . . . Promise, Bob. Please!"

So Bob had promised. Though when he saw the anguish in his wife's eyes when she played with Colin, or when the talk turned to the coming baby, he wanted to enlist Rachel's help.

It didn't take them long to discover what good friends and neighbours the other couple were, and if it hadn't been for Jane's secret unhappiness everything would have been fine. As it was, they spent lots of time with the other couple, and often baby-sat for them, so they could get out together. Bob had almost come to believe that Jane's hurt was easing, that she might even be persuaded to think of a solution.

Then there had been that furious knocking on the door one night, followed by the frantic pealing of the bell. Bob had tumbled out of bed to find a distraught Mike standing on the doorstep.

"It's Rachel," he'd said. "It's not time yet but she's started. I've rung for the ambulance, but Colin's crying and I'd like to go with her."

"Of course!" Bob was already fastening his dressing-gown and Jane was right behind him.

"Don't worry about a thing. I'll look after Colin. You know he's all right with me." Jane touched Rachel's forehead as the men carried her to the ambulance. "You always did like to be the centre of attention," she teased. "Never could do anything the quiet way like anyone else. Get along! And take this husband of yours with you."

Rachel tried to smile and gave Jane's hand a tight squeeze.

"Thanks, love. I'll do the same for you someday."

"I'll hold you to that." Jane summoned a smile. "Though I'm generally in command of the situation, not like you, you idiot!"

They watched the ambulance move away and turned back into the house where Colin was making his disapproval evident.

N EXT morning Mike came home, bleary eyed.

"A little girl . . . a very little girl," he told Jane, with an attempt at humour. "It was bad."

The bald statement brought Jane's heart into her mouth. "How's Rachel?"

"They've given her something to make her sleep, but she's fine, considering. She'll have to stay there a few extra days, and the baby. We didn't plan on this happening."

"Don't worry, Mike. I'll take Colin," Jane offered. "He'll be all right with me, you just take care of Rachel."

For a week and two days Colin lived with Jane and Bob. It made Bob's heart ache to hear her laughing with the child, and singing him to sleep. His heart went out to her when she held Colin, or kissed his tears away.

But when Mike brought Rachel home Jane handed the boy back as if he were a basket of groceries. Within minutes every vestige of his stay had been swept from the house, the toys from the living-room, the plastic boats from the bathroom. Life returned to normal — tidy, neat, ordered and empty!

Three days later Bob took matters into his own hands and contacted the adoption societies. It was only when the resultant letters began to descend that Jane discovered what he had done. She faced him one evening, the evidence clutched in her hands.

"How dare you?" she cried. "I've told you and told you. Don't you think it was bad enough having Colin here without you expecting me to take some other child into our home?"

"But you love Colin. You know you do."

"Of course I love him. But not the way I could love my own child, your child. Not the way Rachel loves her babies. They are a part of her. Won't you ever understand?"

B OB watched as she tossed the sheaf of papers into the waste-paper basket. He took a step towards her, murmering his apologies, but she backed away from him.

"Don't touch me. You of all people should understand. You're supposed to love me, yet you can do this. I didn't think you could ever be so . . . so insensitive." Her voice broke as she began to sob, but she turned away and ran from the room.

Bob watched her go. Was she right? Had he been unfeeling? But he wanted children, too. Having Colin had been hard on him, and now he missed the child's laughter and his welcoming scream of delight when he tossed him in the air.

For a long time he sat, his head in his hands, trying to decide what to do. Then, at last, he climbed the stairs to their room.

Jane was lying on the bed, her shoulders still trembling from the force of her sobs.

"I'm sorry, my dear. I'm everything you said. I won't ever say anything again."

He touched her shoulder tentatively and she lifted her face.

"Oh, Bob. I'm sorry. I was horrible. But I do love you."

He held her close. They had only each other. Nothing must spoil that, he vowed silently. Similar thoughts were passing through Jane's mind and she clung to her husband, vowing she would make him happy, that somehow she would make up for their lack of children.

If You Were Mine . . .

A S time passed, the pain receeded a little but there was a shadow behind Jane's eyes which her old friend noticed. She also noticed that Jane, though clearly fond of Colin, seemed scarcely aware of the new baby.

Seeing the way she avoided having any contact with the child, Rachel began to suspect that when Jane vowed she didn't want any children of her own, she wasn't telling the truth.

Rachel tried hard to get her to talk about it, but somehow the old companionship between them had slipped away. No longer did they confide everything to each other, as they had when they were younger.

If it hadn't been for the very obvious affection between Bob and Jane, Rachel might have thought that that was where the real trouble lay. But Bob and Jane appeared to be growing closer every day, ever more devoted.

But Rachel soon forgot about her worries over her friend as she looked after the new baby.

Y OU will be godparents, won't you?" Rachel was making plans for her daughter's christening. "You and Bob are our closest friends. It'll be a small party as there's only Mikes parents. They'll come down for the weekend. I want them to see Carrie before she gets much bigger. Later we'll have a holiday up there."

"They must miss Colin," Jane said idly. "It's a pity they live so far away."

"Yes," Rachel said, her voice rather strange, and Jane wondered if there'd been some quarrel. Perhaps the older MacDonalds had resented their son and grandson going so far away.

It took a lot of willpower for Jane to go through with the christening, keeping a smile on her face, saying all the right things, but somehow she managed.

However, when she got back to Rachel's house and had helped supply Mike's parents with food and drink, she sought a quiet corner.

She was sitting on the window-sill of the spare room, which would one day be Carrie's, when she heard a step on the landing. Feeling guilty at having slipped away, and conscious of her red-rimmed eyes, she held her breath, hoping the other person would pass by.

When the steps receeded and all was quiet, Jane crept out and headed for the bathroom to bathe her face. But as she turned towards the stairs again, a sound alerted her. She turned swiftly, giving a little gasp of surprise, before noticing the elder Mrs MacDonald almost running towards her. The two women halted, eyeing each other.

"I'm sorry," Jane began, and the other woman lifted her head. Recognising the signs of grief, so similar to those she had just washed away, Jane took a step towards her. "What is it? Can I help?"

"No, no it's nothing!" Mrs MacDonald's tone was angry, but her face crumpled and, impulsively, Jane put her arm round the shaking shoulders and drew her back into Carrie's bedroom.

"Rachel is well again," she said. "And she says they'll be coming up to see you quite soon. I do know how you must miss them, and baby Carrie. They grow so quickly, don't they?''

She was talking to give the older woman time to recover, not expecting any reply. She was startled when Mrs MacDonald spoke sharply.

"I've been such a fool! Proud and ignorant and . . . and stupid. Yes, stupid," she repeated, as if Jane had contradicted her.

"I'm sure," Jane began, a little embarrassed, "I'm sure Rachel doesn't . . . I mean, she often speaks of you."

Mrs MacDonald turned. "That's a lie! Oh, I know you meant it well, and Rachel's a good girl, truly good! Just look what she did, taking our Michael and the baby. I should have been thankful, but I wasn't. I was horrid and resentful."

"I'm sorry." Jane was puzzled, but she thought this was something she shouldn't be listening to. "I don't understand, but I'm sure if you talk to Rachel . . ."

"You don't know? I thought when Rachel said what friends you were, she'd have told you. But there, I should have known. She loves that boy as if he was her own. I think she believes he really is her child."

"Colin, you mean?" Jane said. "Please, I do have a reason for asking. Did they adopt Colin?"

Mrs MacDonald shook her head.

"Not really. You see, he's Michael's son. His first wife died when Colin was born, and he and Rachel had always been friends. Well, I think she always loved him.

"Michael came to us, his father and me, and I looked after Colin. Then, when Rachel and he got married . . . I'd begun to think Colin was mine, you see."

"You get attached to children so easily, you know. Little Colin brought such a lot of joy and laughter into our home and I just couldn't bear to part with him.

"I'm afraid I rather resented Rachel coming in and breaking up what I thought of as my family. Then when they moved away I didn't know how I would cope without them."

Mrs MacDonald looked down at her tightly clasped hands.

"I blamed Rachel for my life being so empty, all of a sudden," she admitted with disarming honesty.

"They moved down here," Jane said slowly, beginning to understand. This was why her friend had had that odd note in her voice. "I didn't know Colin wasn't Rachel's own child," she said slowly. "She never said . . ."

"No, you wouldn't. She's never made a scrap of difference. Even now! You can see she doesn't think of him as being any different from Carrie. Of course, she's not like me, bitter and jealous."

JANE'S own suffering helped her to understand the older woman's feelings. It wasn't that Mrs MacDonald had meant to be so heartless, it was just that emotions were so hard to control sometimes, as Jane well knew from her own experience.

"I'm sure you're not like that. Of course you miss Colin, he's such a lovely child. I love him, too."

"Yes, Rachel told me how good you'd been, and you with none of your own."

FOR once the words didn't hurt. Jane simply smiled, patting the other woman's hand. Mrs MacDonald looked at her.

"You know, you should have children. You've got a lot to give a child, a lot of love, I mean."

"Yes," Jane said. "You're right. Bob and I have so much. But you see, we can't have children." She managed the words with scarcely a quiver. "But we're going to adopt," she added firmly, all her doubts flying away. "I know I could love a baby, any baby."

Mrs MacDonald got to her feet and looked down at Jane.

"I hope you won't say anything," she began, then went on. "But of course you won't. Anyway, I just want to say thank you for listening. Sometimes it does us good to hear our own thoughts, don't you think?"

"You could be right." Jane smiled. "I know I've learned something today about myself." She turned to Mike's mother. "Come along. It sounds as if the party's really getting under way, and I for one don't want to miss it. Who knows, I might never have a christening to arrange, but at least I'll have a welcome home party, one day. One day when they find the baby that's waiting somewhere, just for Bob and me."

She linked her arm through Mrs MacDonald's.

"Come along, Grandma. You're an important person at this gathering. And . . ." She laughed happily. "I rate pretty high, too. Did you know, Colin calls me Manty? It's his way of saying auntie, and I love it."

But one day, she added silently. One day, some little girl, or boy, is going to call me Mummy, and I'll love that even more. □

One In A Million

by BARBARA COWAN

IT was my own fault. I shouldn't have left Aunt Letitia to make all the holiday arrangements. Yet, I always did and now, here I was, awkwardly standing at the door of the guest-house lounge, being stared at by row on row of seated on-shore oil workers; a diversion for them instead of the television which winked and blared cheerful sounds in the corner. And there was Aunt Letitia, ensconced in the middle row, chomping on the sweets the doctor said she shouldn't have.

The roar of welcoming approval settled my actions, I turned tail and ran back upstairs to the tiny bedroom Aunt Letitia and I were to share for the next week or so. Commonsense told me that any other reasonably young and

H

attractive female would have received the same treatment in this male-dominated establishment; but I knew coming here was just part of Aunt Letitia's plan to get me a husband.

For all she was an unclaimed treasure herself, as she put it, she was determined to see that I wasn't. And what better way than pitching me into male company? And where in all Britain would that be found more than in oil-rich Aberdeenshire?

I was sure that this was the real reason for choosing the area for our sight-seeing holiday, and not because she wanted to see the land of her Gordon forebears.

I sat dismally on the bed. Nothing and no-one would persuade me to go down to that room. By now every man there would know what a good marriage prospect I was. Aunt Letitia didn't hide my light under a bushel. She was an ardent crusader on my behalf. Although we'd only just arrived, I knew she would have been at it. And it was humiliating and embarrassing.

J UST then a cheerful rap at the bedroom door made me jump. I opened it cautiously and a cup of tea was thrust at me.

"Couldn't see you missing your last cup of the day." The blond giant I last glimpsed sitting in the middle of the front row grinned. "Sleep well!" He nodded, turned on his heel, and walked quickly along the corridor.

Cup in hand, I watched him go, feeling vaguely disappointed. Usually I was coolly distant when young men approached me after Aunt Letitia had been working on them, but this one didn't give me the time. It was a bit unsatisfactory, really, for on reflection he was about the only eligible-looking male in the whole bunch. The rest looked like kindly, family men, enjoying an evening's viewing. Perhaps tomorrow I could show him I was no man-hunting female.

As I expected, Aunt Letitia didn't appear until the television programmes finished for the night. Bleary eyed, I got up to open the bedroom door, and thank the two kindly men who had helped her stout, little, pear-shaped form upstairs.

"Lovely viewing this evening, Lucy, my dear," she greeted me. "Pity you're so shy in company," she said over her shoulder for the benefit of her assistants.

I closed the door at once. She was the limit. I turned on her.

"Where are they?" I put my hand out. Sighing, she pressed a crumpled bag into my hand. As I expected, the packet was completely empty.

"Now, my dear, we are on holiday," she said. "A few little sweeties don't go amiss at such a time. I'm sure the doctor would agree. They're very relaxing — something you should do more of."

"I was asleep!" I growled, helping her off with her layers of clothes and into her bell-like nightie. But I didn't pursue it. I was tired after driving all day to get here. So I climbed back into bed and left her happily shuffling round the room, hither and thither like a Russian doll, bobbing backwards and forwards.

One In a Million

I N the morning, between six and seven o'clock, the guest-house rever- berated to the sound of male voices and heavy footsteps as the oil-men left for work. They wakened me but sleep soon took possession once more.

Abruptly, I was awake again when the door was rapped loudly. I struggled up into a sitting position just as a fully-dressed Aunt Letitia opened wide the door. There, grinning broadly, was the blond giant of the previous evening. I gave a little squeal and slipped back down under the covers.

"Last call for breakfast, ladies!" he announced in a transatlantic drawl. "It's almost nine-thirty."

"Thank you, young man!" Aunt Letitia purred. "I let my niece sleep on this morning. She desperately needs the rest on holiday, has such an exacting job." She was cosily confidential with him. "We'll be down in a moment. She's really very efficient once she's awake."

When the door closed, I was out of bed, showered, dressed and ready in under 10 minutes. I would dearly have loved to dawdle to show my independence but I was starving, and breakfast at these establishments wasn't a meal to miss — especially as our combined finances didn't run to lunch.

The big square dining-room was full of tables with cheerful, seer- sucker cloths. We were the only two guests present, and had hardly sat down before the blond giant appeared with two steaming plates of por- ridge. It surprised me, for with his transatlantic accent I automatically associated him with oil, certainly not with the domestic arrangements of this establishment.

"Dugald Jablonski at your service, ladies!" he said, laying a plate in front of each of us. I accepted with a cool little nod in his general direction, but didn't look at him. Fruit juice would have been my preference, but when I was being "coolly distant" with young men, I never started conversations with them. But Aunt Letitia — she would talk to anything that moved.

Now she was into a discussion as to whether medium or fine oatmeal made the best porridge. By the time Dugald went to fetch our bacon and eggs, she had discovered he was the grandson of the guest-house owner, over from Canada to do a post-graduate sociological thesis. His mother, once the daughter of the house, had married a Polish soldier during the war and afterwards emigrated with him to Canada. Dugald, their youngest, unmarried child was born in Canada. This was his first visit to his mother's country.

Then by the time he brought our tea, toast, bacon and eggs, he knew what I did for a living, and that Aunt Letitia looked after me and our three-roomed flat in London. To help save for the holidays she baby-sat during the day, and he was told in detail how much planning it took on her part to make our available money stretch to a touring holiday. Today we hoped to go to Culloden and perhaps Cawdor Castle, too.

While all this was going on, I ate my way steadily through my break- fast, offering nothing to the conversation. It was always safer that way. It let men know that although Aunt Letitia was measuring them up as husband material for me, that I was in no way co-operating. Perhaps it was a bit rude, but it worked.

So I was somewhat startled when Dugald Jablonski confronted me on my way into the hall.

"Have I said something to offend you?" he asked politely.

"Why of course not!" I spluttered, feeling the colour rise in my face.

"Good, because I have a proposition to make," he said, and went on to ask if he could accompany us in the car over the next few days. He too had to watch his money, and yet he had to study people in their leisure hours, and where better than as tourists? He would happily pay one third of the petrol and expenses.

I was embarrassed. He was so polite, and I had been rude. But a stranger as a third? Would it work? I looked helplessly at Aunt Letitia, but she was in one of her infuriating docile moods this morning. She smiled sweetly, her head coyly on one side.

"It's your car, dear, so the decision is yours. But it would mean we could afford lunch with the extra one sharing."

She was no help, so I shrugged.

"Well, if you don't really mind being in the company of two strange females, you can come," I said, very ungraciously.

"Thank you. I will get my note-book."

"Oh, good!" Aunt Letitia breathed, as she watched him hurry off. "I do like a man about the place." And she waddled out of the front door, a strange little figure dressed as always in a navy blue dress with a white lace collar and starched white apron and little white cap. It was a smart and practical outfit, she always said.

WHERE to first?" I asked when the three of us were in the car.

"Cawdor Castle!" Aunt Letitia said thickly.

"You're eating sweets again. You know what you've been told. You must lose weight."

"Oh dear! I'm on holiday. It's my only pleasure." Aunt Letitia was at her most pathetic.

But I steeled myself. I knew they weren't budgeted for.

"Where did you get them?"

"They were a gift from me!" Dugald Jablonski's voice came from behind me.

"You're very kind, Mr Jablonski, but my aunt knows she shouldn't have taken them." I sounded thin, prim and shrewish, so to signal the end of conversation I revved the engine. I couldn't very well demand them from her with the donor sitting in the back of the car — and didn't she know it!

The sun was shining and we were soon bowling along country roads, rich farm lands on either side. We always, Aunt Letitia and I, sing folk songs when we're out in the car, but I felt shy of joining in when Aunt Letitia started "Hey Johnnie Cope." To my surprise Dugald Jablonski sang along with her, and before I knew it I was singing, too. By the time half a dozen songs had been sung, I could tell our extra passenger had fitted in surprisingly well.

IN Cawdor Castle, Aunt Letitia gave up by the second room. Pathetically she informed us that she knew there would soon be narrow, winding stone staircases to be climbed, but we must go on ahead and she would wait for us.

I couldn't persuade her to come further. Normally she loved being punted upstairs by other tourists. Allowing people to help her, she maintained, put everyone in a good mood. But now, there was an opportunity to get me alone in a single male's company. These days she would forgo anything for that.

But it was difficult to stay annoyed as we went from room to room and read the descriptions from the official little notices. They were very witty and dryly humorous, and I found myself giggling. By the time we finished our sight-seeing in the castle we were laughing together. It was difficult then to try to regain my original, stony, un-interested look. Somehow to my surprise, I didn't want to now.

Of course, it shouldn't have surprised me that Aunt Letitia was not where she promised to be when we came out. She seldom was. But after five minutes searching I began to panic that she might be ill again.

"I hope she's all right. She hasn't been well." I tried to keep the hysteria out of my voice.

Music

GOD gave me ears that I might hear,
   so I must use them well,
To mark each crash of timpani, each
   tiny tinkling bell.
The hammers of a xylophone like
   little, scampering feet,
The brush of hand on bongo drum,
   in rhythmic, haunting beat,
The woodwind, with its clear-cut
   song,
The trumpet's clarion call,
The brass, with noises fat and round,
   I'll memorise them all.
I'll float upon light breezes conjured by
   the gentle strings,
And call to mind a summer's day
   spent where the skylark sings.
I'll listen with my very soul when I
   hear music play.
Commit it well, in case the Lord
   should take his gift away.
               Sylvia Hart.

"Let's try the tearoom. Seems a likely place," Dugald offered, steering me over the courtyard to a low-slung building.

"Oh no, our finances don't run to tearooms mid-morning!" I gasped, trying to keep up with his long strides. "One thing Aunt Letitia will never do is over-spend on our budget." I tried to explain, but Dugald was hustling me in the door. And there was Aunt Letitia beaming a welcome to us from one of the tables.

"Just did a quick calculation and we can manage morning coffee."

There was nothing for it but to sit down. I couldn't argue. Budgeting was Aunt Letitia's department. There was none better, despite her air of woolly vagueness. Of course, the vagueness was just a front. There was no-one with sharper reactions.

Outside, the sun was shining, and it was pleasantly warm. I suggested we find a quiet place to sit, and allow Dugald to make notes. We found a pleasant spot under an old tree and settled Aunt Letitia comfortably on a folding chair from the car. I stretched out on a tartan rug, while Dugald sat on a cushion, his pad leaning on his knee.

Some Highland cattle in the next field came over and stood at the fence, their eyes barely visible through their red straggling hair. It was restful just lying staring back at the oddly dignified, behorned cattle, the sun dappling through the branches of the trees. A lovely drowsiness stole over me, and I laid my head on my arms.

The next thing I knew was Dugald Jablonski shaking my shoulder. "It's starting to rain," he said. "Best go for lunch now."

It took me a moment or two to surface and I shivered. It was much cooler now. Then I realised to my horror that I had been sleeping in my usual position — crouching with my knees almost touching my forehead and my thumb in my mouth. I felt positively humiliated. How long had I been like that? How could I be on my dignity now?

I was grateful when Dugald didn't remark on it, but then, perversely, it began to irk me. Slowly it dawned on me he was different. Was he, perhaps, doing a little distancing act of his own? He was very pleasant and most courteous, but our earlier companionship had gone.

Strangely, I felt let down. I had never come across this response before and wasn't very sure how to handle it. I was so used to being stiffly on guard I didn't know how to be just myself with young men. But I would try with Dugald.

"There's a good film on television tonight," he remarked as we drove up the drive of the guest house. "I'll keep you both a seat if you like."

"Yes, please." Aunt Letitia answered for us both. "Make it the front row because I couldn't see over some of the heads last night."

Aunt Letitia had obviously made a big hit with the oil workers. To a man they stopped at our little table to enquire if we had a good day. They were so open and friendly, I felt a little ashamed of my disappearing act last night.

I knew it would be unneccessarily churlish not to go into the residents' lounge after our evening meal, especially when Dugald had gone to the trouble of booking us the best seats.

A few minutes after the film started, Dugald came and sat beside me. His presence was strangely comforting. He laid a box of chocolates on my lap, and I was glad everyone was engrossed in the film as I stammered my thanks. He raised his hand in slight acknowledgment, never taking his eyes from the screen. And I sat then in a daze of silly happiness, so aware of his arm lolling round the back of my chair.

OVER the next days we toured all the places of interest, Aunt Letitia became quite emotional on our visit to Huntly Castle, the ruined seat of the Gordons. We stood silent and awed listening to the white-robed monks in the restored ruin of their monastery at Pluscarden.

But at least once a day Aunt Letitia disappeared and I found myself panicking. That last attack of Aunt Letitia's had frightened me. It made me suddenly realise I might have to face life on my own without her, the pivot of my life since I was 10 years old. Life for me without Aunt Letitia was unthinkable.

Saturday was a perfect day when I wakened, feeling vaguely excited. The guest-house was almost empty as most of the men went home for the weekend. Today was the town's annual Highland games. This was the event Dugald was really anxious to attend. His mother had told him all about it.

It seemed the whole town turned out for the games. Bunting danced and shook in the breeze around the fence which circled the grounds. The spectators stood, sat on rugs or just lay on the grass.

It looked like cheerful chaos as a knot of brawny, kilted men took turns at throwing the hammer. And nearby on a raised dais, children in Highland dress danced to the music of a couple of pipers.

T HE three of us explored the edges of the scene and Aunt Letitia and I plied Dugald with questions.

Then once again, despite my vigilance, it happened. Aunt Letitia was no longer with us. As usual I immediately started to look round for her, trying to quell the feelings of fear and dread which always engulfed me. Was it an attack this time, I wondered. At once Dugald was aware of my worry.

"Don't panic!" He sighed. "I'll show you where she is." He took my hand and led me up through the watching people to the top of the bank. The touch of his hand almost put Aunt Letitia out of my mind.

"There she is sitting at the end of the front row."

I followed the line of his pointing finger and there was Aunt Letitia in the middle of the arena with the judges.

"Oh, help! How did she get there?"

"Relax. I arranged it," Dugald said, lowering himself on to the grass. "Now sit down and be at peace, and stop putting me on edge, worrying over your little relative. I'm sure it's totally unnecessary — she's a tough old bird." He tugged at me and I sat down beside him.

"Actually, she isn't a relative," I murmured, pleased yet bright pink. Had he done this to be alone with me? I hoped he had.

"She's not a relative?" he exclaimed. "Then why all this possessive concern?"

It was difficult under his unwavering gaze, but I tried to explain what Aunt Letitia meant to me, how she came into my life at a night-mare time when my parents' marriage was breaking up. They were rowing over me constantly, seeming to even resent my existence. Neither wanted to look after me, especially if it meant forgoing some of their own interests.

"So, you see, I was a moody, miserable ten-year-old, convinced I was totally unlovable, when Aunt Letitia came on the scene. She was just another in the long line of domestic helps, I thought then. But she stayed and immediately filled my empty life." I paused, then went on a little stronger for he was listening so intently.

"That first week was the school holidays and she decided we would make believe we were tourists just visiting London to see the sights. We pretended the flat was on loan from friends, and out of politeness we had to keep it clean. So each morning we rose early and hurried through the housework. Then went off for the day.

"That week, I remember, we watched the Changing of the Guard at Buckingham Palace, tip-toed through St Paul's and the abbey and visited the Victoria and Albert Museum. Aunt Letitia loves sight-seeing." I laughed to keep emotion at bay, remembering how my life then was suddenly full of colour. How for the first time in my childish life I was securely loved. I had never spoken so much about myself to anyone before.

"Where are your parents now?" Dugald asked quietly.

"My mother is on her third husband, and my father is between div-orces. They're not too keen on being seen with me. I betray their age." I tried to be flippant. "How about your parents? Do they come back here?"

"No, never!" Dugald said, his eyes roving now over the arena. "My father's health couldn't take the journey, and my mother won't leave him."

THE simple statement of devotion silenced me. How fortunate he was.

"But they've got a camping van and at weekends and holidays they go to the Great Lakes. Dad says it's like being back in Poland and Mum says it's like Scotland. So they're both happy. We've had a cabin up there since I was a kid. It's special."

"You're lucky having a family like that. All I've got is Aunt Letitia, and she's one in a million.

"You see," I tried to explain my anxieties and panics, "recently, since her heart attack, I've realised my life would be so empty without her. I suppose it's because she's the only person in the world that cares about me." I tried to laugh lightly.

Dugald turned and looked at me. "No, Lucy, she isn't!"

I stared at him for a moment, then my eyes dropped under his intent gaze. I felt the blush rise from the base of my neck and flood up over my face. I was tongue-tied, yet I longed to hear more of the same.

"After all." He grinned and covered my hand with his. "I'd sure need an ulterior motive to travel folded up in the back seat of a Mini for days — all to be with a tense, shy girl who drives at a mad thirty-five miles an hour singing off-key, who worries herself sick over a wilful old woman and sucks her thumb when she's asleep."

I gulped, but couldn't take the happy smile off my face.

"Come on, they're starting to toss the caber." He yanked me to my feet and towed me along behind him to a better viewpoint.

I looked over towards Aunt Letitia and she raised her hand in acknow-ledgment. But strangely it looked like a gesture of benediction on us both. And although, at that distance, I couldn't be sure, I'd almost swear there was a smile of triumph on her face. □

LET THERE BE LOVE

by
ALICE MACKIE

PLEASE change your mind, Mummy!'' Julie Morton's clear young voice was shaky as she gazed at her mother.

Carolyn Morton's eyes were equally distressed. Julie was far too young to get married, in her opinion.

"You're only seventeen, darling,'' she protested.

"Eighteen in another month. You know that means I can marry if I like, Mummy, but Craig and I don't want to go against your wishes. Anyway, it isn't age that counts, it's how much you've packed into your life, and you know I've seen more and done more than most girls of my age.''

Carolyn nodded and sighed. It was probably true that Julie was older than most girls her age. Her father, Graham, had been an officer in the Army and they'd never had a settled home. They'd lived abroad for most of their married life and Julie had mixed in with children of all creeds and colours.

She'd packed a great deal of experience into her 17 years, but Carolyn felt her maturity in emotional matters was still not as developed as she would have liked.

A year ago Graham had been killed in an accident involving explosives, and Carolyn had decided to return to her old home in Scotland, and try to settle down with Julie. Her parents had died and the last tenant had now vacated their house, but it was hard to make a new life alone after 20 years of marriage.

Was she trying to hold on to Julie because she didn't want to be left on her own, Carolyn wondered uneasily. Yet even as she looked at her daughter's sophisticated figure and saw how beautiful she was, she couldn't help seeing through to the child underneath. There was a look on Julie's face she'd seen before when she'd wanted a special doll's pram, too expensive at the time. Then there'd been a row over riding lessons and a desire for her own horse.

Underneath, Julie was still just a child, Carolyn thought. She'd soon tired of her wants after they'd been gratified, but if she tired of Craig Robson, then that would be a great deal more serious.

I STILL think you should wait for at least a year, Julie," she said evenly. "I'm asking that of you. After all, you've only known Craig a short time and although I know you love him, there's more than one kind of love, and in marriage you are going to encounter them all."

"Perhaps there is more than one kind of love . . . but a whole year!" Julie cried. "Oh, Mummy, Craig and I just couldn't wait for a whole year!" She stood up and began to stroll about the room.

"You know, Mummy," she said carefully. "Craig and I *want* marriage. We don't want to have to live together."

"That's enough!" Carolyn said sharply. "There's no need to say any more. What you're saying is that it will be my fault if you and Craig decide to forego a wedding ceremony and I'll only get what I deserve. Well, if that's how you want to behave, Julie, I will not accept the blame."

"But, Mummy . . ." Julie was near to tears.

"I give in," Carolyn said, all at once exhausted by the argument. "I'll arrange a wedding for you, even if it is very short notice. You can let me know which date you choose."

"Oh, Mummy!" Julie threw her arms round her neck. "I'll tell Craig straightaway. And if you're worried about being on your own, you can come and see us as often as you like. We'll be living above his father's shop in Eglinton Street. Mr Robson doesn't mind Craig getting married soon either, and Eglinton Street isn't far away."

Carolyn nodded again, her heart heavy. Shouldn't she be protesting a little more? But she knew that Julie meant every word she said.

"I only ask one thing, darling," she said. "I'm going up to Edinburgh this weekend, as I think I mentioned to you, and I want you to come with me."

"I thought you said you were going to stay with friends."

"I'm going to a silver wedding anniversary. I was bridesmaid to my friend Heather. She and Daniel are celebrating their twenty-fifth anniversary this weekend. I'd like you to come along, too."

"You don't have to keep an eye on me, Mummy."

Again Carolyn flushed. Was that what she had in mind when she wanted Julie with her? Perhaps it was, a little. She didn't want Julie to be left on her own in the empty house, but in a vague sort of way, she also wanted Julie to see what 25 years of marriage had meant to her friends.

"I hope I can trust you, dear," she said evenly, "but Heather and Daniel have extended their invitation to you. If you're going to be married soon, we won't have any more opportunities of going out together."

"No," Julie said, "I can see what you mean."

"The celebration will be a quiet affair," Carolyn went on. "Dinner at their house on Saturday evening."

"It sounds exciting," Julie said rather dolefully, then she brightened. "Have they any children? I don't remember you talking about them very much."

"I was bridesmaid to four of my friends before marrying your father. Heather was first. She never had any children."

"How old was she when she married?" Julie asked.

"Nineteen."

"Not much older than me."

"Not much. By the way, I'd better tell you that she's in a wheelchair now. She's got polio."

"Oh, Mummy, that's tough." Julie's face was full of sympathy. "Of course I'll come with you."

"Here's her wedding photograph!" Carolyn had been turning over the pages of an album.

Julie stared at it. The bride was beautiful with clouds of dark hair and delicate sensitive features. Her young husband was tall and equally handsome. Julie's eyes went to the bridesmaid. How young her mother looked . . . and the bride. It was the fashion of the times which made them both look like little girls dressed up.

"She's very beautiful," Julie said, handing it back. "You look lovely, too, Mummy."

Carolyn smiled as she put away the album.

"Yes, it's a pity we have to grow old."

D ANIEL and Heather Campbell lived in a one-storey house next to a corner shop which had windows facing on to two streets. Both windows were filled with finest-quality antique furniture, and Julie learned that Daniel was an expert on the subject.

Carolyn and Julie called in at the shop after they arrived in Edinburgh, and Daniel Campbell greeted them with delight.

He's aged a little, Carolyn thought, but he's still very handsome . . . perhaps more so now than before.

"I didn't know whether to go straight round to the house," she said, awkwardly. "I mean, I know Heather is in a wheelchair now . . ."

"She's waiting for you in the lounge," Daniel said pleasantly, then turned to Julie. "I can hardly believe you've got a grown-up daughter, Carolyn, but you've brought the evidence with you. You're most welcome, my dear."

"Thank you," Julie said politely. "As a matter of fact, I'm getting married in a little over a month."

"Then I must offer my congratulations. Heather will be delighted, too. Just come through here; this door connects us with the house. It means I can be easily available for both the house and the shop."

The house was bright and full of sunshine. Julie noticed that the doors were especially wide and that there were ramps for a wheelchair instead of steps. No doubt Heather Campbell was able to do everything she could do normally with the aid of a light wheelchair. It was rather wonderful how people could live normal lives under such a handicap.

But when Julie followed Carolyn into the sitting-room, her heart jerked when she looked at the woman who lay on a specially-made bed-cum-wheelchair. She would never have recognised the beautiful young girl from the wedding photograph.

THE CLEANSING SEA

WALK upon a lonely beach. Around the golden halo of the bay, where sea meets land. Lovely to stroll where, gentle as the hands of healing, each tiny wavelet caresses the sand as the cleansing sea bathes the margin of the land.

Stroll there and muse. Is not life a walking on a beach?

To port is the land of the life we live. How stained by our imperfect natures. But to starboard – what? The great attendant sea of God's pure spirit. Whose waters clear and crystalline, tireless as ocean, wash away the stain of our shortcomings.

So the gentle hands of God, gentle as the breathings of the merest wave, make us clean again.

Clean as the sands upon the shore.

Rev. T.R.S. Campbell.

Heather Campbell's hair was now in snow-white curls and there was a tracery of lines on her white face, yet her dark eyes were still bright and full of interest.

Her slender hand was held out and as Julie took it in her own strong young fingers, she knew a pang of compassion for her mother's friend. Heather was severely paralysed. It was obvious that she wouldn't be able to do anything for herself.

It was Daniel Campbell who settled them in comfortably, and Heather and Carolyn began to talk eagerly about the old days.

"Will I help Mr Campbell?" Julie asked, standing up when Daniel went through to the kitchen to make a cup of tea.

"If you like, darling." Her mother looked enquiringly at Heather.

"Daniel won't mind," Heather said, laughing, "though he's probably quite well organised."

Julie walked through to the kitchen and found it spotless. There wasn't a thing out of place.

"This looks better than the one we have at home," she said ruefully. "I'm hoping Craig and I can have a nice modern house one day."

"It does make life pleasant." Daniel grinned. "Since you've come to help, you'd better find me a couple of sandwich plates in that cupboard."

"Do you have help?" Julie asked. "I mean . . ."

"I know what you mean. I have a cleaning woman twice a week.

Apart from that, Heather and I rub along together really very well.''

"But . . . but isn't she completely disabled?''

"Completely,'' Daniel assured her. "I thank God every day that she's here at all. I think this bowl needs a little more sugar, my dear. It's in a plastic container up in that cupboard.''

Julie did as he asked, then looked again at Daniel Campbell. He was humming cheerfully as he measured tea into a beautiful old silver teapot. He looked years younger than his wife.

"Then . . . then she won't get any better? I mean . . . how long is it since she took polio?''

"We had only been married six months,'' Daniel said simply. "We were both building up the business then.''

Julie's eyes were wide with shock and disbelief. "And you've looked after her ever since?'' she whispered.

"We made our vows to love, honour and cherish, in sickness and in health. It was very sad that it should be sickness, but Heather would have done the same for me if it had been the other way round. Now, my dear, I'll carry the tray if you go ahead.''

Julie went into the living-room, speechless from all she had learned. To think that Mr Campbell had looked after his wife for almost all their married life!

As she sat drinking a delicious cup of tea, she could see the love between them as Daniel helped Heather to drink her tea from a special cup, all the time keeping up a cheerful conversation with her mother and herself.

Julie knew that she was seeing a very special kind of love. It was something completely beyond anything she had ever experienced.

C AROLYN MORTON noticed her daughter's preoccupation during the weekend and wondered if she'd done the right thing by insisting that Julie should come with her. Was the child depressed by what she had found in the Campbell home?

Surely she must see that it was a happy house, full of sunshine and light. Heather's body had been spoiled by her illness, but her good spirits and keen sense of humour had not been lost, and even amusing tales of incidents which had happened to her and Daniel as a result of her disability had them laughing helplessly at times.

Daniel had booked outside caterers and a few more friends had been invited to the wedding anniversary dinner. Carolyn and Julie had bought them a modern silver marmalade dish and Carolyn presented it with a rueful laugh.

"It's almost like coals to Newcastle,'' she said, "except that it could never compete with your lovely antique silver.''

"That's to sell to other people,'' Daniel said. "This will be in constant use. Heather and I like to have nice things, and to use them.''

Julie listened, and her eyes went to Heather Campbell. She wore a garment made of pale pink silk, trimmed with finest creamy lace at the neck and wrists. It enhanced her ethereal look, yet it brought colour to the delicate face. There was a small pink bow in her hair.

The People's Friend Annual

"You look very nice," she said wonderingly, and Heather smiled and thanked her for the compliment.

"Daniel chose this for me," she said. "He also put the bow in my hair."

"She's always been beautiful," Daniel said with pride, and Julie looked at him again. She suspected that he only saw his bride in Heather. She still looked just the same to him!

Julie was still quiet for a day or two after they returned home, but it was now Carolyn's turn to be busy. She'd been brushing up on her typing and shorthand now she was applying for jobs.

"I think I'll have to accept a part-time job at first," she said to Julie.

"Yes, perhaps you might," Julie answered absently.

Craig had been busy, too, but they were planning a visit to Glasgow to look at soft furnishings. Julie hadn't seen much of him since her weekend in Edinburgh, and each day found her longing more and more for a serious discussion with him.

ON Saturday Craig picked her up in the car and hugged her as though he hadn't seen her for weeks.

"I missed you last weekend, darling," he assured her. "I had to go to Stephen Cairns' twenty-first birthday party on my own. We had a great time. You'd have loved it."

"Perhaps I would," Julie said rather slowly.

"What's the matter? You don't sound too sure."

"Oh, I guess I'm sure. It would have been fun, only . . . I just wanted to ask you something, Craig. Just suppose . . . suppose, mind you . . . that I got ill or something a little while after we got married, would you . . . do you think you'd be able to look after me?"

"What are you talking about?" Craig was astonished.

"No, I mean it, Craig." She was silent for a moment. "Last weekend I met a couple who had to cope with that." She told him about Heather and Daniel, and Craig was appalled.

"Six months after they were married!" he echoed. "That's appalling. You mean they haven't had a . . . well a proper married life together all this time?"

"Oh yes, they've had a proper married life together, but not the way you mean," Julie said. "Heather only had Daniel, and he's looked after her so well for twenty-five years."

"Doing the cooking and everything for her? Poor chap."

"And poor Heather!" Julie put in quickly. "It's fallen on both of them."

"Yes, well . . . anyway, what are we worried about? It won't happen to us and you'd always have your mum to help. Of course I'd stick by you, Julie. I'm mad about you," Craig said confidently. "We'll have a great time together."

But will we also have a dull time together, Julie wondered. She listened to Craig's reassurance that he would look after her in sickness as well as in health, then she seemed to hear an echo of Daniel Campbell's voice.

126

If it had been the other way round, I know she would have done the same for me.

Would she be able to look after Craig if he became helpless so soon after their marriage? Julie bit her lip. She didn't know. Suddenly she was afraid, but she pushed her fears behind her and tried to enjoy her day.

They called in at several stores, and Julie looked at pretty wallpaper with matching curtains and bedspreads.

"Which do you like, Craig?" she asked.

"Oh, any really," he said, off-handedly. "I'll leave that to you, darling. Whatever you decide."

"But we'll both have to live with it."

"I know. But that sort of thing doesn't interest me much. I tell you what, I'll be down at the record department. You choose patterns and I'll see you downstairs."

"OK," Julie said. "I'll see you there."

She leafed over a few more designs, then left it all. She wasn't in the mood to choose designs today.

I T was a week before Carolyn had a chance to talk to Julie again. She'd found a part-time office job which suited her and she was beginning to enjoy life again. It was nice to feel that she had something useful to do.

Julie had finished her school examinations and was now at home most of the time.

"Can you write out a list of the other people you want to invite to the wedding, darling?" Carolyn asked her. "There isn't much time, but I'm sure I can do something about a celebration. The dining-room is quite big and we could have it here and copy Daniel's idea . . . have outside caterers."

"I've put it off." Julie turned away from her.

Carolyn thought she would have been happy to hear such words, but she wasn't. She'd been worried ever since the weekend in Edinburgh that she might have given Julie some rather strong medicine to have to swallow.

"Oh, Julie," she said. "I'm sorry. Have I spoiled things for you? I've frightened you by showing another side to marriage. But you know, Heather and Daniel are unique. That sort of thing is very rare. Most people just have an ordinary marriage and if you and Craig really love one another . . ."

"We do," Julie said. "We've talked about it a lot, Mummy, and we do. But as you said, there are many loves in marriage. This is only our first one when we want to enjoy ourselves and each other. I think we ought to wait for the second one, when we want to settle down before we arrange our wedding. And Craig agrees with me."

Carolyn was unable to hide her relief.

"So I don't have to rush things so much after all?"

"No," Julie said earnestly. "We're going to wait till we're really sure . . . at least three months!" □

SUNSHINE and SHADOWS

by GILLIAN FRASER

I TURNED to face the woman behind the reception desk.

"My name's Blake," I said. "I have a reservation."

Her smile was welcoming.

"I hope you enjoy your stay with us, Miss Blake. Your room's number eleven on the second floor."

I registered then followed her upstairs into a warm sunlit room, pungent with the smell of flowers."

"Will this be suitable?"

"Delightful, thanks, and the flowers are lovely."

"I like to welcome my guests with a homely touch. I'm Mrs Ritchie, the manageress. Is this your first visit to Scotland?"

"Yes, I've always meant to come, but never found the time."

"You must make the most of your stay then. If there's anything you want, don't hesitate to ask," she said kindly.

Left alone, I stood wrapped in the silence of my room. I couldn't bring myself to believe that I was hiding myself away in a remote Highland village. Four days ago when I'd driven out of London, my plans had been made in my usual organised way. I would spend a few days in Scotland away

from the pressure, make the decision about my future, then return to London. It was all going to be so easy, I thought.

How wrong I was! I arrived in Scotland during the best summer weather for years, each day hotter than the next. My usual driving speed had been reduced to a meander from place to place. The hypnotic effect of the scents and sounds of summer were dulling the edge of my reason, making finding a solution to my problem no easier. My desire to return quickly to London had vanished as everything seemed to be telling me to stay a while.

But maybe I was using that as an excuse for not going back at once. The speed with which events had overtaken me in the last few months had left me scared and uncertain. That was why I'd registered into the hotel as Miss Blake rather than Dr Blake. I longed to be myself for a change, not someone who was always on call in a busy London hospital.

I stood before the long mirror, a shaft of evening sunlight slatning across my forehead. I noticed a few grey hairs hidden discreetly among the abundance of brown, and tiny worry lines about the eyes, but no more than that. I'd never had time to give my attractiveness much thought, far less now I was 35 years old. For 12 of these years I'd been a doctor, during which time I'd to think more of others than myself.

Only recently, when things began to pile up on me, did I pause to take stock of my life. Had all the studying and effort been worth it? Had I been right not to pursue my musical career, my first love? I might have shrugged off my uncertainty as just a phase if Malcolm Harris hadn't come into my life on a day when I really began to question my ability as a doctor.

Lynn Williams had been brought into hospital seriously injured from a car crash. Yet despite her injuries, she'd shown a tremendous will to live and was one of the cheeriest patients in the ward. Lynn was so young and vibrant. I hated the thought of losing her. It seemed she might just pull through, but she slipped away from us when complications set in.

I hid myself away, crying hot bitter tears; the culmination of the pressure which had been building up inside me for a long time. My boss, Gordon Willoughby, found me. He placed an affectionate arm round my shoulder, pushed a cup of sweet tea in my hand and invited me to talk about it. He listened patiently while I poured my heart out.

"She was only fifteen, Gordon. I should have been able to do more for her."

"Don't blame yourself, Roslyn, we can only do so much."

"I know, Gordon, but —"

He was suddenly my senior again. "Forget it, Roslyn. Your responsibility is to the living who're relying on you."

I would have forgotten the tragedy if it hadn't been for the incident on the way home. The lift in the block of flats where I lived had always been temperamental, and this time it ground to a halt between the second and third floors. I turned to smile ruefully at the lift's other occupant and he smiled back. He was a man of about my own age who lived on the top floor. I'd seen him often, but we were only on nodding acquaintance.

"What happens now?" he asked.

"I'm not sure. Aren't we supposed to tell each other jokes or sing songs until help arrives?"

"The jokes I know are terrible," he confessed.

"And I can't sing," I told him.

We looked at each other for a moment then burst out laughing. He pressed the emergency button and we waited.

"Strange," he said. "We've been neighbours for a long time and never really become acquainted, I'm Malcolm Harris."

"Dr Roslyn Blake."

"What shall we talk about?" he asked.

I found myself pouring out the story about Lynn.

"What rotten luck," he sympathised. "I'm really sorry. You must be feeling awful."

Suddenly the lift started to move.

"This is my floor," I told him. "Goodbye, Malcolm. Thanks for your company."

"But you can't go yet," he protested. "You must be feeling terrible. You shouldn't be on your own. Come up to my flat for a while, I make the best cup of tea in the block."

He looked so sincere that I just had to accept, and he was right, I couldn't face my own company.

MALCOLM'S flat was on the top floor with a fine view over the London roof-tops. It turned out to be a home-cum-studio for his work as a free-lance artist. It was comfortable in a free and easy way, typical of Malcolm, as I would find out when I came to know him better.

"Whatever you do, don't bump into the baby grand," he warned. "It belongs to a friend of mine who's overseas and he didn't want to put it into store. I said I'd look after it. D'you play the piano?"

"I had grand ideas about a musical career once, but medicine took over," I said.

"Try the piano if you like while I make the tea."

I played my way through a couple of Beatles' ballads, rustily. Malcolm grinned round the kitchen door. "I haven't heard 'Yesterday' for years — shades of my mis-spent youth."

We had tea in the sunshine by the window. Malcolm pointed some of London's landmarks out to me and I felt quite ashamed. Though I lived within easy distance of some of them my life had been restricted to the flat and the hospital. Malcolm was the first person to raise my eyes above mundane everyday routine, and I was enjoying the experience. Our conversation was relaxed and easy, but I still hadn't forgotten what had happened at work that day.

Malcolm dismissed it. "Crisis of confidence, that's all. We've all wanted to go down different paths at some time, but never really regretted the one we've chosen. I had ambitions to be a musician once, too, but I went to art school instead. Mind you, I look at that piano now and again and feel terribly frustrated. You wouldn't like to give me a lesson or two, would you?"

"Only if you teach me how to paint."

He laughed. "Agreed."

SOMEHOW this set the seal on our meeting. I found myself taking to Malcolm Harris. He had a lovely dry sense of humour and didn't take himself too seriously, which was good for me in my present lack of confidence. But I didn't realise just how vulnerable my present dissatisfaction with my work had made me.

As the weeks passed, my deepening feelings for Malcolm only added to that vulnerability. As a doctor I was able to make instant decisions, but a love affair, the first serious one of my life, was something I had no training for. When Malcolm asked me to marry him, I was completely unsure, but he was patience itself.

"I know we haven't known each other too long, Roslyn, so I don't want you to give your answer till you're absolutely sure."

"I wouldn't want to be half a wife to you, Malcolm," I said thoughtfully. "If I marry you, I'll give up medicine."

"No, Roslyn, that's too big a sacrifice to make. I'd rather you didn't marry me than give up your career."

I snuggled deeper into his arms.

"Dear Malcolm, just at this moment there's nothing I'd like better than to walk straight out of the hospital."

"That feeling will pass. What you need is a holiday. Can you get away from the hospital for a few days? It'll give you time to think things over."

Which is why I found myself standing before a full-length mirror in a hotel bedroom wondering what on earth Malcolm Harris could see in a very care-worn Roslyn Blake.

Endlessly my mind returned to its questioning. Did I really love

Malcolm enough to marry him or was I just looking upon marriage as an escape from the pressures of my career? I felt isolated and lonely. An absurd prickle of tears filled my eyes. For the first time I wondered if leaving London had been a ghastly mistake.

M RS RITCHIE was waiting to greet me in the dining-room. "Sorry I haven't an individual table for you. You'll be sharing with Miss Hammond, one of our regular midsummer guests. Come and I'll introduce you."

I felt slightly disappointed. In my present depressed mood I'd have preferred my own company. Yet despite this, I found myself liking Miss Hammond at once. She was an older woman, slim, white haired, but her eyes were compelling, full of light and love of life.

"Have you had a chance to look round the village yet, Miss Blake?" she asked, and I explained I hadn't. "You must take time to soak up the atmosphere," she enthused. "Blackwell's very small, but it's very special to me."

I thought she was going to tell me why, but she changed the subject.

"Will you be putting your name down for the walk?"

"What walk?" I was mystified.

"Tomorrow is Midsummer's Day. No-one seems to know how or why the custom started, but every midsummer there's a walk to the summit of Ben Vereen to watch the sunrise — the earliest one of the year before the days start drawing in again." She smiled. "Are you up to an early start at three a.m. for the sunrise at four-thirty?"

I shook my head and smiled ruefully.

"I'm afraid mountain climbing's not my forte, certainly not so early in the morning."

"Oh well, never mind, but if you change your mind, give your name to Mrs Ritchie." Miss Hammond sighed contentedly. "I'm looking forward to climbing the Ben again." She chuckled. "He looks black and fierce from down here but he's a canny old fellow really, with a good path to the summit." She rose to go. "Maybe I'll see you in the lounge, Miss Blake, and we can talk some more."

I found myself grateful to her. She'd deliberately kept our conversation to generalities, no probing to find out anything about me. Miss Hammond, despite our brief acquaintance, had made a deep impression on me.

After dinner, I met Mrs Ritchie, and complimented her on the quality of the meal.

"How did you and Miss Hammond get along?" she asked.

"What a charming woman," I replied.

"Yes, she's a much-travelled lady but always comes back to Blackwell to climb the Ben on Midsummer's Morning. No-one knows how many years she's been doing it, but I've heard it's a kind of pilgrimage for her. She's never divulged her reasons and I've never asked." Mrs Ritchie smiled. "How many of us will want to climb mountains when we're Miss Hammond's age, seventy-five?"

I gasped, remembering how sprightly she looked.

"When I reach that age I think I'll just sit in a rocking chair and watch the world go by!"

"Me, too." Mrs Ritchie laughed. "Are you sure you don't want to go on the walk? The forecast's good for the morning."

"Thanks, but no. I've been working very hard lately. I'm trying to catch up on my sleep."

"Very well then, if you want coffee, it's being served in the residents' lounge."

I wasn't too keen on inflicting my doubtful company on anyone, but I felt the need of a few friendly faces. Miss Hammond insisted on taking charge of me, giving me coffee, introducing me to the other guests. I was drawn immediately into the cheerful conversation of the other guests. I was just ordinary Miss Blake again, another faceless person on holiday. My problems in London were beginning to seem a long way off when Mrs Ritchie came in to clear away the coffee cups. She didn't look her usual composed self.

"Are you all right, Mrs Ritchie?" I enquired.

"Archie the barman's had an accident, I'm afraid. He's fallen over and hurt his ankle. It's badly swollen. I've phoned Dr Honeyman but he's attending a patient down the glen and his wife doesn't know when he'll be back."

"I'll come." My response was automatic. "I'm a doctor." I was conscious of a sudden stillness in the room, but I didn't feel sorry that my identity was out, just an urgency to deal with what I was trained for.

I examined Archie's ankle carefully.

"What's the verdict, Doctor?"

"Favourable," I told him. "Your ankle's only sprained. I'll put a cold compress on it, that should reduce the swelling."

"I'm grateful, Doctor. Sorry you've had your holiday broken into like this."

My Choice

SOME people, when the snow is on the ground
And winds blow cold, seek warm and sunny lands,
Where skies are cloudless blue, and all around
They see but shimmering sea and golden sands.

I do not envy them, nor, sighing, say,
"I wish that I could fly to lands afar!"
I'd miss the snow, the rosy children's play,
The redbreast's song, the shining evening star.

The cosy blaze of hearth-fires, when day ends.
The lamplight shining down each frosty street,
The warm goodwill of neighbours and of friends.
Old-fashioned winter? Maybe, but so sweet!

Claire Ritchie

I DIDN'T return to the lounge but went straight to my room. I left the room in darkness and opened the window wide. The night was heavenly, the air heavy with the scent of flowers. The only darkness was in the deep hollows of Ben Vereen. Above, the all-night twilight, midsummer's coat of many colours, such a peaceful scene compared with the turmoil in my heart.

I'd felt so wretched today without Malcolm that I'd almost decided to marry him. Yet the satisfaction from practising my medical skills again, if only on a small scale was something I didn't think I could live without. The answer to my dilemma seemed further away than ever. Which way was I going to turn?

I was about to prepare for bed when there was a knock on my door. Mrs Ritchie stood there.

"May I speak to you for a moment, Doctor Blake?"

"Come in, please," I called.

"Your coming to Archie's help was a generous gesture which cost you your privacy. But we're very grateful."

"It came as rather a relief," I admitted. "I've been Dr Blake for so long I'd quite forgotten what Miss Blake was like."

Mrs Ritchie came straight to the point. "I'm asking a favour of you, Doctor. I've had a phone call from Ken Honeyman our local G.P. He's to be with that patient down the glen all night and will be unable to come on the walk. He usually comes in case of accidents. I know it's an imposition, but . . ."

"Don't worry, I'll be pleased to come."

Mrs Ritchie sighed with relief. "I'm very grateful."

Alone again, I didn't have to ask myself why I'd agreed. I just accepted that my services were needed. Before turning in, I glanced at the Ben with a certain sense of anticipation. Perhaps I was looking forward to challenging something bigger than my own problems.

Being a doctor I was a light sleeper, so I was out of bed the instant Mrs Ritchie called me. I dressed quickly and joined the others.

Miss Hammond looked pleased. "So you've decided to come, Dr Blake, I'm so glad."

"I'd rather you called me Roslyn. Doctor sounds so formal."

"I agree." She laughed. "I'm Eleanor."

She was by far the oldest member of the party so I decided to keep an eye on her. I needn't have worried. Despite the semi-darkness, Eleanor Hammond was the life and soul of the party. Her hand was on my elbow several times as she chided me.

"Come along, Roslyn, you're lagging behind."

I was at first, my legs rebelling against every step. Once I'd found my second wind and my stubbornness, my stride opened out and the walking was quite easy.

UP there on the summit, the world was suspended between day and night, yet even as we watched, the fragile summer night was receding, silhouetting the eastern peaks against the ever brightening sky.

The talking amongst us had stopped. We felt a breathless hush of expectancy, of something wonderful to be witnessed. Red sky to orange, then the sun climbing over the rim of the world filling the corries with liquid gold. Words were inadequate to describe this miracle. I felt very small and humble.

Then as the sun's disc cleared the mountain tops, the party began drifting away down the Ben. I thought I was last until I saw Eleanor sitting some distance away.

She looked up and smiled. "Still here, Roslyn?"

"I'm loth to leave."

"Me, too."

We sat together. It seemed as though time itself was standing still, and a strange sensation I'd never known before enfolded me. It was a kind of awareness that there was a presence in this place, and with it came a sense of blissful peace I'd never experienced before.

"What's worrying you, Roslyn?" Eleanor's question didn't take me at all by surprise. She'd sensed my mood. "I'd like to help," she added. "You looked so sad at dinner last evening, I knew something was wrong."

I FELT no sense of intrusion into my private affairs, just relief that someone was sympathetic to listen to my problems.

"My emotions are in rather a tangle and I don't know how to unravel the threads. I thought if I separated the 'miss' from the 'doctor,' I might find my own identity again. I was wrong. I've been Dr Blake for so long I've lost Miss Blake beneath that white coat I wear." My story tumbled out about Malcolm and the dissatisfaction with my work.

Eleanor listened patiently.

"Mother and Father always came to Blackwell for their summer holidays," she told me. "At first I was too young to make the midsummer climb of the Ben, then came that wonderful moment when I was allowed to accompany my father." She chuckled. "He used to carry me on his shoulders but I always felt secure. Oh, the excitement of looking forward to that first attempt. Then came disaster — rain and gales made the ascent impossible. I was heartbroken.

"That was when my father offered some valuable advice. We stood by the window looking up at the mist-shrouded mountain. 'Look how the Ben's covered in clouds, Eleanor,' he said. 'They look as if they'll never clear away, but they do, sometimes quickly, often a little longer, and you see the sunshine again. Life will surround you with clouds of disappointment, just like this morning, but you've to learn patience and accept the things you can't change. But everything will come right for you eventually.' "

All the time Eleanor had been speaking, she never looked at me. Her eyes seemed to be gazing abstractedly at some distant point on the horizon. Yet although she'd been speaking of her own experience, I knew her words were meant for me.

"The Ben's been a good friend to me, giving me the chance to see

The People's Friend Annual

what the world's like high above my problems. Somehow they all seem smaller when I go down again."

Soothed by Eleanor's guidance and the tranquillity of my surroundings I felt my life slipping into perspective. I could see things much more clearly now.

"Malcolm once told me that we all wish we'd gone down different paths from time to time yet never really regret the one we've chosen. Despite recent events, I love my calling and so many people depend on my skills. I could never give it up."

"And where does Malcolm fit into your scheme of things?" Eleanor asked.

"I told him I couldn't be half a wife. If I married him I would give up my doctoring. I was wrong, Eleanor. I love him deeply and realise I can't do my job now without his support. Maybe I'll become a better doctor for it. I'm going to marry him."

"Then you must let him know right away." Her eyes twinkled. I could see she was enjoying the moment of decision as much as I was. I couldn't wait to tell Malcolm.

"I'll phone the minute we return to the hotel."

We lingered on the summit looking down to Blackwell far below. In the ensuing silence, a curlew with its urgent call winged down the mountainside.

Eleanor sighed.

"This is my last climb. I'm seventy-five now and I think my old bones deserve a rest. Time for me to leave the Ben to younger people like you, and Malcolm of course."

Malcolm. The very mention of his name was enough to fill me with tremors of anticipation and I felt ridiculously young and in love. "He would love this place," I told her.

Eleanor laughed.

"Could you think of a more beautiful place for a honeymoon, Roslyn?"

Her words seemed to be telling me that the best part of my life was about to begin, that it still lay, dark and mysterious and inviting before me.

"No, I can't," I replied, "and you'll receive the first invitation to our wedding." □

Originally a burgh of barony, under the Argyll family, Inveraray became a royal burgh early in the 17th century. When the 14th-century castle was rebuilt in 1745, the then Duke of Argyll also rebuilt the town. North of Inveraray, which is the county town of Argyll, lies the hill of Duniquaich, a favourite viewpoint. Inveraray Castle itself stands on the west bank of the Aray River. A pleasant walk through the castle grounds leads north to the 17th-century dovecot at Carlunan and, three miles farther on, to the pretty Falls of Aray.

INVERARAY CASTLE, ARGYLL

The Start Of Something Special

By
HELEN
REID

MY name's Gillian Ashcroft. I'm thirty years old, have a business school diploma and own a florist's shop called "Bouquets."

I thought of myself as a good example of the modern independent woman who'd worked hard for success and enjoyed the battle.

Now as I drove home on Christmas Eve, I wasn't so sure any more. Was the contentment I enjoyed merely some illusion? I tried to convince myself that I was just exhausted after the Christmas rush, that my mood would wear off as the holiday progressed.

But in my heart I knew there was a deeper reason. For the first time in my life I was facing a real crisis of confidence in myself, an emotional one. This was something I wasn't used to or quite sure how to handle.

It all began when Hugh and Mary Bell, life-long neighbours and close friends, broke their news to me that they were leaving Walker Terrace.

I was deeply upset, for I'd always jokingly referred to Hugh and Mary as my second parents. When my own mother and father died within two years of each other, Hugh and Mary more or less adopted me, despite my being in my twenties and embarked on a business career. Because of their love for me, I lost none of my security, and life in Walker Terrace continued much as before.

Their news was even more of a shock coming so close to Christmas. It was always our happiest time of the year, when we looked forward to our never varying routine. Christmas Day began for us always with a visit to the peaceful Watch Night Service in our local church. Those carols so joyfully sung became a reminder of the real meaning of Christmas.

We visited each other's houses on alternate years for Christmas dinner. Afterwards we would gather round the tree, where our presents were placed, enjoying the pleasure of giving and receiving. There was satisfaction in another year turning full circle. It was a time to pause, take stock of our lives and count our blessings.

N OW it seemed, I'd nothing left to look forward to. Hugh and Mary had decided to live with their married daughter in Australia.
"We'll miss you, Gillian," Mary said sadly. "You've been like a daughter to us, keeping Hugh and me young in mind, if not in body."

"Our old bones aren't taking so kindly to these colder winters," Hugh said with a smile. "Our decision hasn't been an easy one. However, we've made up our minds, though we'll have nightmares about tearing up our roots at our time of life."

I felt the bottom dropping out of my secure little world.

"What am I going to do without you?" I managed to stammer in a little-girl-lost kind of voice.

"You've done very well up till now," Hugh assured. "A business of your own, that's quite an achievement."

"There are more things in life than being successful in business, Hugh Bell," Mary scolded him, and sighing, added, "Your mum and dad hoped you'd settle down one day and marry. I've looked forward to that too, dear."

"I'm grateful for your love and concern," I told them. "But I value my independence. I'm very happy as I am, my life is as I want it." The strength of my statement took me by surprise. I was sure I was trying to convince myself of this as well as Hugh and Mary.

As the weeks passed, I steeled myself listening to the plans they'd made concerning their new life. I watched with dread each step in the leaving process — the big furniture van, the emptying of the house, the front door being locked for the last time.

I tried to keep calm at their departure, but afterwards I ran frantically into the house and wept uncontrollably. Forever it seemed, the house stood silent and empty. I felt my independence to be somewhat shaky, I needed company more than I realised and longed for a sight of my new neighbours.

T HEY moved in just before Christmas, though I saw little of them at first. I was out early in the mornings and came home late in the evenings. I arrived home on Christmas Eve to find the girl standing at the gate looking anxiously up and down.

"I've lost my husband," she told me, laughing. "He went to buy a Christmas tree. Maybe he's caught up in the traffic."

"I expect so."

"You're Miss Ashcroft, aren't you?" she asked me.

"Yes."

"Well, I'm your new neighbour, Louise Clark. The missing husband is Brian. I meant to speak to you before, but somehow with the upheaval of moving in I haven't had the chance."

My heart sank. Though I'd been desperate for new neighbours, I'd somehow pictured them as being of my own age group or older. This girl looked too young with her untidy, shoulder-length hair, faded jeans and shapeless jumper. I made some flimsy excuse and fled into the house, deeply disappointed. Could I ever find anything in common with her?

MY only gesture to Christmas this year was a token one, just a small tree with the minimum of decoration. I realised how much I'd lost with Hugh and Mary going. This year I would have been the hostess to our Christmas dinner. The house would have been filled with love and laughter.

Suddenly I felt desperately lonely and wanted to rush out and apologise to the girl. When I did look out, she'd gone. Dejectedly I toyed with my tea. Nothing on television suited my mood. I wondered at the emptiness within me, my emotions seemed to have reached a low point and stopped there.

Then the carol singing began. Like most of Walker Terrace's residents I was slightly reserved once behind my own front door. I didn't take kindly to strangers on my doorstep, even at Christmas. Yet there was something compulsive about the plaintive singing. Something about it spelled out the whole meaning of Christmas which I'd forgotten in the depth of my self-pity.

Wisdom

I'M growing older, this I know,
　　The busy days slip by.
Perhaps a lot of younger folk,
　　Could learn from such as I.

I've gleaned a lot of wisdom
　　And I've stored it through the years.
But youngsters never listen,
　　So my words fall on "deaf" ears.

It's then that I remember
　　When I wasn't very old,
You couldn't tell me anything,
　　I just would not be told.

So I shall try to keep my place,
　　As humbly as I ought,
And may I never give advice,
　　At least, until it's sought!
　　　　　　　　Irene Bernaerts.

When the bell rang, I almost ran to the door. There, I received quite a surprise. The carollers were my new neighbours, Brian and Louise Clark. I could see they were frozen and invited them in.

"That was lovely," I told them. "Now take off your coats and warm yourselves by the fire. I'll make some coffee."

"Please don't go to any trouble," Lousie pleaded. "We don't want to interrupt what you're doing."

I looked at the girl, pretty and animated now, regretting my earlier hasty judgment. Brian, too, was quite a handsome young man.

"No trouble," I told them. "After all, if I'm to know my neighbours, I must start off in the best possible way and repay your kindness in singing to me."

"The carol singing was Brian's idea," Louise said, as we sat chatting by the fire. "He thought it would be a novel idea of getting to know our neighbours."

"I'm grateful," I told them. "You've cheered up a decidedly dull Christmas Eve."

"Mr Stone told us that as well," Brian added with a laugh.

"Mr Stone," I echoed unthinkingly.

"He lives a few doors down on the other side. Like you, he welcomed us into his home. D'you know him?"

I WAS ashamed to admit I didn't know him all that well, but the people in Walker Terrace had an unwritten rule about other people intruding into their privacy. All Mr Stone and I ever had was a nodding acquaintance when we passed each other in the mornings, on the way to work. Any information regarding him had come through Hugh and Mary Bell.

"I believe he works in some branch of telecommunications, and isn't married," I told Brian and Louise. "But I really don't know anything else about him, I'm afraid."

"When we told him we were coming here, he volunteered as much information about you, Miss Ashcroft," Louise informed me. "You own a flower shop and you're unmarried."

I found myself surprised at this because I'd never thought anyone interested enough in me to know that. For some reason I felt pleased, and this made me open up my heart to the young couple.

I told them about Hugh and Mary leaving to go to Australia and how I dreaded being without them.

"I don't find it easy to make new friends," I admitted.

I gave a little laugh and shrugged my shoulders.

"I'll get used to it, I expect," I said, beginning to feel hopeful about the situation for the first time. "After all, there's really nothing much I can do about it, is there?"

"You must miss the Bells very much," Brian sympathised. "It sounds as if you were very close to them."

"Yes, we know what it's like," Louise went on. "We're finding it rather difficult to adjust, too. Our families are quite a distance away now and this neighbourhood is so different from our old one. We're having to start all over again and learn where everything is — shops, doctor and dentist. You know the kind of thing."

I looked at them in surprise. In my self-pity, it had slipped my mind that they might be experiencing difficulties, too. I'd become so terribly wrapped up in my own problems that I hadn't even thought that others might need help. I felt ashamed of myself.

"If there's anything you want any time, please ask me," I told them. "I really mean it. I'd be more than happy to show you round the place."

"Thanks, Miss Ashcroft," Louise said sincerely. "It's very kind of you."

"And I'd appreciate being called Gillian." I smiled, thinking that it would be fun getting to know this young couple. I was so grateful my

The Start Of Something Special

new neighbours were such an out-going pair. They really were nice.

C ALLING me by my first name broke the final barrier of reserve between us and they talked freely about themselves. They'd been married for one year and had lived in a cramped flat; now they were excited about their first house. Both were commercial artists working for the same firm and they'd plans to convert their attic into a studio.

I was won over by their bubbling enthusiasm, which reminded me of myself at their age. I felt rather ashamed, too, that some of my interest in life had slipped away since the Bells went.

Louise's eyes shone.

"I'm glad we've moved in now because we can have a double celebration, Christmas and house warming."

Brian laughed.

"Louise is a 'Christmas Freak'," he said. "She goes absolutely mad over everything. No matter that our house is only half furnished as long as we have a Christmas tree with presents underneath."

I felt a lump in my throat remembering other Christmases past; the brightly-lit tree, the masses of paper decorations, holly with bright red berries.

"That's how I like to think of Christmas," I told them. "And it always started with the Watch Night Service in our local church."

"Louise and I are going. You could come with us, Gillian. What a lovely start that would make to Christmas Day." He looked fondly at his wife. "You see, Louise and I have a lot to be thankful for, a new house and a new friend next door."

I blushed at this reference to me. I wanted to go to the service — I always had done so with my parents and then with the Bells. Should I go now? I decided against it, for the service had always been very personal to me, something I knew I couldn't share with anyone else yet.

"Well if you change your mind, Gillian, we're leaving at eleven-fifteen."

M Y excuse about being tired however seemed a very shallow one. I watched them go hand in hand down the path and found myself wondering if independence was worth the loneliness I suffered sometimes. I closed the door and found myself wandering round, restlessly touching this and that, letting the aching misery flow from my fingers.

I glanced from the bay window over to the Clark's house. The curtains were pulled back, their Christmas tree a reminder of those times when I'd enjoyed those supreme moments of giving and sharing. Now here I was, giving nothing, sharing only unhappiness with myself.

I made up my mind. Tidying myself up, I put on my hat and coat and went next door.

"You're coming after all," Louise exclaimed delightedly. "Brian and I'll be ready in a jiffy, you can wait in the sitting-room."

There, I came face to face with someone whose name had cropped up earlier. I walked over to him and smiled shyly, not sure what to say.

"Oh, Mr Stone, good evening," I said.

"Good evening, Miss Ashcroft. Pleasant young couple, aren't they?"

"Yes."

"I enjoyed their singing."

"Me, too."

"Quite an ingenious way of getting to know their new neighbours," he said with a grin.

"I thought so."

We stood there flat footed and unsure of what to say next. Mr Stone broke the silence.

"I always was partial to Christmas carols. We had super Christmases when I was young."

I laughed excitedly at finding this in common with him.

"But I did, too. I miss them now." I explained about my former neighbours.

"I was looking forward to going to my mother's for Christmas again, but she died three months ago," he explained.

"I'm sorry."

"That's why I'm at rather a loose end this Christmas," he told me.

"Just like me, Mr Stone."

"Please call me Philip."

"All right, then I'm Gillian."

He laughed and reached out to shake my hand.

"Pleased to meet you, Gillian. Isn't it ridiculous you can live so near to a person and never get to know them? Are you going to the service?"

"Yes, Philip."

"Me, too. I wasn't, but I feel I'm searching for something in life at the moment, maybe the service will provide it."

"I feel that way, too."

THE tiny picturesque church had always been a centrepiece in my life. It had a warmth and intimacy which could be almost overwhelming. The sound of the organ and the carol singing was quite enchanting, filling every corner of the building with glorious sound.

Music had always played an important part in my life. I could be moved to tears or have my spirits lifted quite easily. Carols especially filled my mind with pictures which would never fade of that time in Nazareth all those years ago when Jesus was born in the humblest of surroundings. They made me realise I'd so much to be thankful for.

One carol was my favourite — *In the bleak mid winter, frosty wind made moan.*

I loved its vivid description of the darkest time of year, yet with its message of hope for the future. I glanced at Philip. For a moment our eyes met before looking away and I was surprised to find my heart beating just that little bit faster.

The four of us emerged from the church into the early hours of Christmas Day. We walked home quietly as if unwilling to break the spell the service had woven round us. Brian looked lovingly at Louise, commenting on how much they were looking forward to spending their first Christmas in their new home. Philip and I watched them walking hand in hand to their front door, two young people deeply in love, standing strong against the world.

D ID you find what you were looking for in the service, Gillian?'' Philip asked.

"Yes," I replied. "Some restoring of faith, that's all I was needing. I'm glad Brian and Louise persuaded me to go. Somehow their love and good neighbourliness reminded me of what Christmas is all about." He nodded in understanding. "And what about you, Philip, did you find the service helpful?"

"Yes, it's given me the courage to ask if you'd care to share my Christmas dinner with me," he said with a smile. "I've a chicken far too large for one, a plum pudding and a bottle of wine."

My heart gave a little lift of joy.

"I'd love to, Philip."

Suddenly there seemed to be so much for me to look forward to. I'd have to find a little gift for Philip. Perhaps I could make an attractive arrangement from holly and berries — or maybe I could bake a cake.

I turned to Philip and all the previous awkwardness between us melted away.

As we spoke, snow began to fall, large creamy flakes which covered our heads and shoulders in no time at all. We shared the excitement of children instead of two mature people. Philip smiled.

"Merry Christmas, Gillian."

"Merry Christmas, Philip."

The magic of this moment seemed to be telling me that a new chapter in my life was just beginning and the future lay mysterious, yet exciting, before me. □

Because I Care

By LAURA CALDWELL

SHIVERING in the chill of the February morning, Janet Browning put on her nurse's uniform, wondering all the while if perhaps her daughter Marjorie was right.

Give up, Mum. You're due a rest at your time of life. Marjorie had written in her last letter.

Janet had smiled to herself. Goodness, you'd think she was 90! But of course, there must be no thought of retiral yet. Janet needed the money. Everything seemed to be getting more and more expensive, and besides, she was saving hard for the flight-fare to New Zealand to visit Marjorie and Tommy.

The young couple hadn't returned to Scotland since their marriage three years before. Marjorie had met the handsome young New Zealander when he was over for a year on an exchange visit from the school in Wellington where he taught.

Janet Browning missed her daughter. She wrote to her every week, and they exchanged the occasional phone-call around birthdays and Christmas. Sometimes, though, Janet had to fight a feeling of self-pity. It was unfortunate that her daughter, her only child, had settled so far away. But she knew this was a situation shared by many other loving parents. She wasn't the only lonely widow, by any means.

FRASER BROWNING had been tragically killed in a road accident years before when Marjorie was still a schoolgirl. Janet had taken a refresher course and gone back to nursing. Now she was a staff nurse at Russet House, a small hospital for the elderly.

But this particular type of nursing was heavy, involving a good deal of lifting and moving, and during the past winter Janet had come home some evenings feeling tired and washed out. Still, she thought now as she pulled on her winter boots, in a few weeks' time it'll be Easter, and Easter, somehow, brings its own new hope.

After a quick cup of coffee and a slice of toast, Janet opened her front door and plunged into the bitter, sleet-laden wind. The hospital was half-a-mile's walk from Juniper Grove. There was no bus which went up the long hill, but summer and winter Janet had become accustomed to the walk. It braced her for her day's work.

Juniper Grove was just a sprinkling of houses in a leafy cul-de-sac. In the dark of the morning, the milkman was on his rounds, his clattering float stopping and starting while a boy ran in and out of the gardens delivering bottles.

Janet drew level with the float as the lad dashed out of the garden of The Pines. In his hurry he left the gate swinging and creaking in the wind.

As she stopped to close the gate, Janet's eyes were drawn to a splash of white on the doorstep. Three full pints of milk stood there, yet she was certain the milkboy had been carrying just one bottle. She walked on a few paces. It looked as if old Mrs Frew hadn't taken in yesterday's milk, or the previous day's.

The elderly lady who lived alone in The Pines was a source of mild mystery to her neighbours. She never seemed to have a visitor, and went out only on a Saturday morning when she walked to the post office.

And always, a beautiful copper-coloured cat would be stepping daintily alongside her. The cat would settle on a low wall to wait and would then skip down to rejoin her mistress as she crossed from the shops. The lady and the cat would then make their way to the local park.

ONE Saturday morning Janet Browning had deliberately hurried to catch up on Mrs Frew. She'd stooped to stroke the beautiful cat.
"What's her name?"
"Miss Jenny."

Miss Jenny! It seemed an odd name for a cat, yet, somehow, it suited the old lady's pet. Its coat was like burnished copper and its eyes like amber beads.

"She is rather a special cat," Mrs Frew confided. "She and I are never apart. Miss Jenny is a true companion. She comes with me to the park every Saturday. In the summer we sit in the rose garden, in winter we find shelter in the gazebo."

Gazebo? Janet had to think hard to recall what a gazebo was. Some kind of Victorian summerhouse? Trust an old-fashioned little lady like Mrs Frew to use that out-of-date name.

Janet stood and chatted for a moment.

"I'm going to the shops. Is there anything I can get for you?" she'd asked.

"Thank you, no," Mrs Frew replied. "Good morning." And she and Miss Jenny had walked slowly on. Clearly she didn't want to become involved with neighbours.

BUT Janet stopped to speak to her another day.
Mrs Frew was carrying a letter. "I write to my son every Friday evening and post the letter on the Saturday," she explained.

Janet would have liked to hear more about this son who never appeared, but there was something about this elderly lady's manner which forbade questioning.

Nevertheless, faced with the evidence that all was not well in The Pines, with three days' milk left on the doorstep, Janet didn't hesitate for long. She hurried up the garden path, and at once noticed something else — a folded newspaper stuck in the letterbox bearing yesterday's date!

She pressed the bell. There was no response. She tried again, but only its harsh echo sounded through the house. Now she stooped to peer through the letterbox — and there was old Mrs Frew, huddled on the floor of the hall.

Janet turned and ran like the wind back to her own house and the telephone.

T HE doctor was with Mrs Frew, an ambulance on its way, and while she waited in the icy parlour of The Pines, Janet studied a photograph of a handsome man with expressive dark eyes.

He was lounging in a garden chair against a rich background of flowers. The words *With all my love, Mum, Scott. Perth, summer '81* were written across the top.

So, here was the son old Mrs Frew wrote to so faithfully. Janet was lost in puzzled thoughts about this son who lived no further away than Perth, and yet had never once been seen to visit his mother in the two years she had rented The Pines.

She was startled out of her reverie by the touch of something soft and warm brushing her ankles. It was Miss Jenny. Janet hurried to the kitchen to fill a bowl with milk, and watched the beautiful, small cat lap hungrily.

Presently the doctor joined her.

"Do you know if Mrs Frew has any family near?"

"There is a son," Janet said. "He seems to live in Perth. I'm afraid that's all I know. My neighbour kept very much to herself."

The doctor shook his head.

"Ah well, no doubt the social worker at the hospital will find out how she's placed."

The doorbell rang. The ambulance had arrived.

Mrs Frew was being taken to Janet's own hospital, so she went with her in the ambulance. During the short journey the old lady opened her eyes for the first time.

"It was my own fault," she whispered. "I was putting a new light bulb in the hall. I must have toppled off the chair. I don't remember . . ."

Gently Janet reassured her. The doctor had shocked Janet by telling her the old lady appeared to be neglected. This news made her blood boil. Here was a loving, caring mother living alone in that depressing house, while her son basked in his luxurious garden in Perth, less than 100 miles away!

"Mrs Browning?" The old lady stirred again. "What will happen to Miss Jenny?" Her voice shook.

"I've left plenty of bread and milk for her," Janet said kindly. "She'll be all right. You mustn't worry. I'll look in again on my way home. I'll take good care of Miss Jenny."

"My poor little pet. She will miss our weekly walk into the park . . ." Mrs Frew closed her eyes again.

L ATE that afternoon, on her way home from work, Janet opened the front door of The Pines with the key Mrs Frew had given her, and switched on the lights. But there was no response to her calls for Miss Jenny. No small copper cat hurried to rub itself against her ankle.

Janet searched the house. She went out into the darkening, overgrown garden and called again and again but there was no response.

Here was a real predicament. Old Mrs Frew would be asking every day about her pet. What was she to tell her? Janet searched further. She walked slowly along one side of Juniper Grove and back on the other. She kept up the call, but only the scruffy one-eyed tom cat from number seven came lolloping up to her. There was no sign at all of the dainty Miss Jenny.

Three days slipped by. Janet asked at the post office and shops, but drew a blank. It was becoming increasingly difficult to keep up a pretence with her patient. Janet knew that the old lady, in the weak state she was in, might pine away if she knew the truth.

"Mrs Frew is a difficult case," the doctor confided. "She's under-nourished. It's plain she hasn't been preparing proper food."

Janet told him about the missing cat.

"Don't tell her yet," he warned. "She mustn't be worried just now, Nurse."

"How is Miss Jenny?" Mrs Frew asked regularly. "Are you taking good care of her, Mrs Browning? I ought to have told you her favourite supper is a little smoked haddock steamed in the top of the milk. She's also fond of a saucer-full of custard now and then. I do worry in case she isn't getting enough to eat."

The truth was Mrs Frew wasn't proving an easy patient. The office staff at Russet House reported that she'd been totally unco-operative about her son. They had to prod and coax from her the tiny bits of information she was willing to give about Scott.

"My son has his own life to lead," she'd said. "He is an extremely busy and important man and must not be disturbed at present. I will write to him myself when I am well enough."

When Janet heard about this she felt enraged, and not for the first time. If black thoughts could harm Scott Frew, then he was in for a very bad time!

Janet wrote to Marjorie about it.

There's no sign yet of Mrs Frew's cat. I don't know how long I can keep up the pretence that everything's all right. Also – and this is far more serious – there's been not a single visit from that despicable son of hers . . .!

It was a relief to unburden herself.

A T dusk one evening after a week had gone by, Janet came off duty and made her way again to The Pines. The house looked depressing, the windows closely curtained, the uncared-for garden wet and wild.

Janet called the little cat, but there was no response. She shivered. The house had begun to smell musty.

Back in the kitchen she decided to open the window wide to let some air circulate. She parted the curtains, stretched a hand to unfasten the snib, then froze with shock. A man's face was framed in the darkening window.

Janet only just managed to stifle the impulse to scream. She dropped the curtain, her heart thumping. Here she was alone in this deserted house and there was a prowler right there in the back garden!

S HE stumbled her way to the front door. She must get out before the man had time to make his way round. But her hands shook so badly she found the key difficult to manipulate. It turned at last, and stealthily she opened the door. And there, blocking her way out, stood the prowler.

The colour drained from Janet's face. For a long minute they stared at each other.

"Isn't Mrs Frew at home?" the man said at last.

Janet managed to shake her head.

"I'm sorry," he went on. "I see I've scared you. I didn't mean to. I rang and rang at the bell; then I decided to go round the back and investigate. It was then I saw the lights go on. I'm Scott Frew. I'm Mrs Frew's son." And the handsome grey-haired man held out a hand.

With an overwhelming sense of relief, Janet realised that this was, indeed, Scott Frew.

He came in and closed the door.

"You must be my mother's companion?"

Janet was puzzled.

"Oh no, I'm just a neighbour. Mrs Browning. Your mother asked me to collect any mail." She led the way to the kitchen. "Also I happen to be a nurse at Russet House." Her voice had gone cold. "Surely you know your mother is in hospital?"

"No, I didn't know," he exclaimed, shocked. "No-one told me anything about it. What happened? Was it serious? Is she all right?"

"She had rather a bad fall," Janet explained, "but we think she'll be all right. She just needs good care and lots of rest."

Scott's gaze went slowly round the shabby kitchen.

"This doesn't look like the house my mother described in her letters. I'm beginning to wonder if I've come to the wrong address."

"You haven't visited her here before then, Mr Frew?" Janet's voice was icy.

"Not here. Never. Otherwise, do you think I'd have allowed her to rent a run-down place like this?" He sounded angry.

This man has a nerve, Janet thought. He comes to visit his elderly mother, and admits quite calmly he's never visited her once during the two years she's lived alone at The Pines. She hoped he would notice her contempt. But he still looked very puzzled.

"Then where's Miss Jenny?" he asked. "Why isn't she here?"

"I'm afraid Miss Jenny is lost," Janet confessed.

S COTT FREW looked as if this was the last straw.

"*Lost*! Miss Jenny lost?"

"I'm sorry . . . I promised I would care for her," Janet

explained, "but she disappeared the day after your mother went into hospital. I — I feel so terrible about it."

"Mrs Browning, I guess we're not on the same wave-length," Scott Frew said evenly. "How can Miss Jenny be lost? She's been here since my mother moved in, hasn't she? She's been a wonderful help, a wonderful house-keeper. I don't understand."

The truth broke over Janet.

"Did you not know Miss Jenny is just a cat?" she exclaimed.

It was clear Mrs Frew's son had not known. As far as he was concerned, Miss Jenny was the little lady who was friend and help to his elderly mother while he, Dr Frew, carried out the secret scientific experiments he had been appointed to do two years ago.

There had been a bad misunderstanding, Janet could see that, but she wasn't prepared yet to forgive him.

"I can't imagine how you come to be so much in the dark, Mr Frew. Surely if you live in Perth you could have kept in much closer touch?"

Scott thought this one over.

"Perth? Yes, that's where I've been for the past twenty-four months, but Perth, Western Australia! At least, the station is hundreds of miles into the outback, but we call it Perth. And I did keep in touch, I can assure you. And so did Mother. I had a letter every week from her."

Scott Frew pretended not to see Janet's blush of confusion. She should have guessed from the photograph that this particular Perth wasn't in the middle of Scotland — the background of exotic flowering trees should have told her!

"I'm not the ogre you obviously thought I was." Scott smiled at her kindly. "The truth is my mother was determined I took up the Australian appointment though she knew I'd be away for two years at least. I insisted she found a live-in companion-help, and that's how all this nonsense about Miss Jenny arose."

He took out some letters from his pocket.

TRUE TREASURE

*P*LENISHING *of the Lord's Table. Silver bowls from which generations have partaken of the Communion wine.*

The sacred supper ended, the cups return to the bank's dark vault. Because, long now in the Lord's service, their silver has become antique and precious. Earthly treasure to be laid up "where thieves shall not break through and steal."

But what of Christ's heavenly treasure? Laid up in the safe deposit of the heart whose doors are open wide — a cup for others to partake. Wine from the grapes of love and compassion.

To charm away another's gloom. To dispel fear and turn darkness into light.

How precious beyond price is this heavenly treasure. Immune to the rust of time. No thief can steal it from us.

Rev. T.R.S. Campbell.

"Look, you must see these. I want you to read them — please."
He handed a letter to Janet.

It has been very cold here today, she read. *But now Miss Jenny and I are seated cosily by the fire having just had our supper. We had fish pie made with smoked haddock. This is Miss Jenny's favourite supper, and mine, too.*

We went to the park for our usual walk. It is quite deserted in winter. We sat in the gazebo for shelter and the little sparrows and robins gathered for their treat. Miss Jenny and I keep a supply of biscuit crumbs.and bread hidden under the seat for them. It is our little secret.

But I think there is snow coming. It has been dark today. How strange to think of you basking in that amazing Australian sun. I am so glad you are happy and having such an exciting life.

J ANET raised her eyes to look at Scott Frew. How wrong she had been about this kindly man.

"It's funny," he was saying, "but I've been up to the very same caper. I deliberately described my life in Perth as splendidly exciting, when the reality was simply a vast, red-dust landscape and a merciless sun in a brassy sky.

"And it was a case of work, work, work, because there was nothing else to do so far out in the outback. But I made sure Mother never guessed the truth."

For a moment he was silent, then he went on.

"Don't you agree most of us tell some little white lies at sometime or other to shelter those we love from the not-so-pleasant side of our lives?"

Janet thought about this. How right he was! She herself, in her letters to Marjorie, tended to make out all was well, that she had few problems, no money-worries, no nights of sad loneliness.

It was so true. Loving mothers, fathers, sons, daughters, all play the sheltering game.

"I must go and see Mother at once," Scott Frew was saying. "I've a car out there. I hired one meantime to get me around quickly. Will you guide me to the hospital, Mrs Browning? Please say you'll come with me."

His smile was warm, his firm grasp of her arm totally reassuring. This clever scientist, Janet decided, had rather a generous measure of charm!

M RS FREW'S recovery speeded up amazingly after the surprise of her son's visit.

"Yes, Mother," he told her, not once, but many times, "I knew my stint in Australia was coming to an end, but I deliberately didn't tell you. I just wanted to appear one day on your doorstep, rather like the good genie in the pantomime."

Scott had, Janet noticed, a way of gently teasing her, a way which filled the old lady with a kind of happy exasperation.

But if Mrs Frew recovered in spirits, the damage done by her fall remained. She had to face the fact she would never again be able to get around in the way she had been used to.

The doctor broke the news to Scott.

"Your mother will need skilled nursing from now on. I suggest we move her to Russet House Annex. It's pleasant and she'll be able to have as many visitors as she wants, and at the same time be well cared for."

To her son's relief he didn't need to coax her. Mrs Frew was tired. She had reached a time of life when it is pleasant to dispense with the small worries of shopping, cooking and housekeeping.

Russet Annex, Janet was able to tell her, had large sunny rooms, comfortable chairs, good food and books. Secretly, the old lady welcomed all these things.

But one thing still tormented her.

"Janet," she confided in a whisper, "you know how precious Miss Jenny is to me. It would make me so happy if she could come to live in the annex, too.

"I'm afraid to discuss it with Scott. He was quite angry with me, you know, for deceiving him over me having a companion! But if you would speak to someone about my pet, I'd be so very, very grateful. Will you, Janet?"

"Oh, what are we to do?" Janet moaned to Scott Frew. "It's all my fault. I feel just terrible about Miss Jenny. How are we ever to tell her?"

"Well, first you must get rid of this ridiculous guilt-complex you've developed." Scott was having supper with her, not for the first time, by any means, since he returned to Scotland.

IT was strange, Janet Browning thought, how completely at ease they were with each other — as if they'd been old friends. She found herself telling him of when Fraser was alive and Marjorie a bonnie bairn.

And, in his turn, Scott Frew confided he'd once been engaged to a girl who, on the eve of their marriage, ran off with someone else.

"It took time to get over that," he confessed. "But I did, of course. In fact, she did me a good turn really. I reacted by putting my head down and working till the cows came home! I've had a highly-interesting career. I've travelled all over the world — worked in America, Australia, New Zealand —"

Janet felt a surge of excitement.

"Did you go to Wellington, Scott? What's it like?"

"Ah, that's where you daughter is, isn't it? Sorry, I only passed through it on my way to more remote spots. But it's a fine city. Why don't you go out to see it for yourself, Janet?"

"I will, one day, I hope . . . It's just a question of . . . " Janet didn't want to discuss her financial problems with anyone, not even Scott Frew. Quickly she changed the subject.

"It's all very well to say it isn't my fault Miss Jenny has vanished, but I'm afraid your mother might have a relapse when she learns the truth. You just don't know how attached she was to that cat."

"I can assure you I do know!" Scott insisted. "You saw, Janet, that her letters were full of the amazing Miss Jenny. Mother certainly pulled the wool over my eyes! She even described in detail the walks they took . . ." Mrs Frew's son was silent for quite a long time.

"I wonder . . ." he murmured. "It's an idea . . . I think it might be worth following up."

To Janet's exasperation he stopped there and would say no more even when she pleaded with him.

"Wait," he said. "We'll see. Wait."

The next morning, while Staff Nurse Browning was busy at Russet House, Scott Frew walked smartly in the direction of Victoria Park. It had snowed in the night and the little park had taken on a fairy-tale look. It was deserted. He passed the duck pond his mother had so often described, the empty rose-garden, and the arbour of trees where the log summer-house stood — the shelter his mother called the gazebo.

The door of the little round house was closed, the windows thick with frost-flowers. But would the door be locked? Scott put out a hand to try.

IN the afternoon of that same day, old Mrs Frew was moved into Russet House annex. Scott helped, bringing for her room a car-load of favourite bits and pieces. Janet Browning saw to her clothes.

"Did you ask Matron?" Mrs Frew asked hopefully. "Did you ask if Miss Jenny could come here to stay? Oh, how she would love that beautiful garden to sun herself in — and so many other folk around to spoil her."

She talked so much about her pet poor Janet's heart sank very low indeed. For her the situation had become a small nightmare.

But Scott appeared to have no such qualms.

"Now, Mother," he told her briskly, "first things first. We want to see you settled happily before we think of cats."

"Cats!" Mrs Frew exclaimed. "How can you be so cruel, Scott? Miss Jenny is not just any cat!"

"I only want you to pay attention, Mum." He brushed her remarks aside. "Look, where do you want this picture hung?"

Janet was dismayed at Scott Frew's attitude. It was if he didn't care tuppence for Miss Jenny. She brooded, then decided once and for all that if he wouldn't take the plunge and tell the truth then she would, for the time had surely come.

"Mrs Frew . . ." Her voice was shaky. "About Miss Jenny — I really think you ought to . . ."

She got no further. Scott stretched an arm and pulled her quite roughly towards him.

"Help me here, Janet. Hold this steady for me, will you?"

He was frowning, shaking his head, too. Janet felt her temper rise, and then to her complete astonishment he gave a big comical wink.

"Wait," he whispered.

"Do you think you could bring Miss Jenny tomorrow, Scott?" his mother asked later. "I want Matron to see what a very special little cat she is."

"Not tomorrow, Mother." His voice was firm. "Let me see now, this is Tuesday . . . What do you say we bring her along on Saturday?"

The old lady happily agreed.

B UT as soon as they were seated in Scott's car Janet turned on him. "Really, I think it's quite wrong of you . . ."

"Don't talk to me just now," he cut in. "I find it rather tricky getting out of this drive-way."

"Yes, I'll talk," Janet barged on, "and not before time. Surely it would have been much kinder if . . ."

"Quiet!" He had edged his car on to the road. "Is anything coming?"

Oh, he was totally maddening, this man, Janet decided. She sat beside him speechless. It was *his* mother he was hurting. If he wanted to go on making a charade out of Miss Jenny's disappearance, then let him!

It didn't take Janet Browning long to realise Scott wasn't heading for Juniper Grove.

"Please, may I know exactly where we're going?" Her voice was cold.

"Certainly. To Silverbanks. It isn't far. Don't fidget."

Silverbanks? Janet wouldn't demean herself by enquiring where that might be.

Presently Scott drew up at the gates of a big old farmhouse.

"We're here." He opened her door for her.

There was a large plate on the gate. *J. K. Massie. Veterinary Surgeon. Kennels. Cat-Hostel.*

"Don't get too much of a shock, love," Scott whispered. "We're calling to see how Miss Jenny is!"

In a moment they were looking down at a pathetic little scrap of copper-coloured fur lying in a basket in the vet's surgery.

"She's doing very well. She's going to be fine," the vet told them. "I suggest you leave her for two or three more days. I guarantee she'll be back to her former glory then." The vet stroked the cat's thin little neck. "She's rather an appealing little scrap, I think."

Janet could scarcely hold back the tears.

L ATER, at home, she made supper, while Scott filled his pipe and talked.

"Yes?" she was saying. "You went to the park? And what did you find?"

"Well, the door of the summer-house — Mother's famous gazebo — wasn't locked, although it was shut tight. Almost at once I heard this weak little squeaking noise."

Scott smiled at her surprise.

"My hunch was right, Janet. There was this wee object lying under a bench, hardly alive! And do you know what had kept her ticking over? Remember Mother said how she and Miss Jenny hid a bag of crumbs and things there for the birds in winter? Well, that, and the trickles of water from the roof was our amazing puss's survival kit!''

Smiling happily Scott put strong arms round Janet and drew her close to him.

''Life can sometimes come up with some wonderful moments, my love.''

''It can, it can. It does,'' she said. ''I suppose Miss Jenny must have gone to their gazebo looking for her mistress?''

''That would be it.'' Scott nodded. ''But she was trapped when the door slammed shut in the wind. And one more day would have been too late.''

Janet looked up at Scott with a smile of relief.

''Thank goodness you thought of going there,'' she said. ''It would have been terrible if you hadn't found her.

''Your mother will be so pleased to see Miss Jenny again. It'll do her the world of good. We'd better not tell her what happened, though. It would upset her to think that her little friend had such a terrible experience.''

Scott nodded.

''Yes, I think you're right about that, Janet.''

S COTT leaned over and picked up a card he had placed on the coffee table. He handed it to her.

''Here's mail for you, Janet. It was lying in the hall. I don't think you noticed it.''

Janet studied the vividly-coloured photograph of Wellington Airport.

''It's from Marjorie!''

Dearest Mum, she read, *we fly out from here on April the 1st on a wonderful Easter trip home! I didn't tell you before in case our plans went wrong and you would be so disappointed. All's well. We have our tickets and can hardly wait. See you soon. Love, Marjorie and Tommy.*

Janet couldn't speak. She handed the postcard to Scott. He read it over then took her hands in his, enjoying the look of pleasure which had lit up her whole face. Tears of happiness were glinting in her eyes.

''Oh, my love, this is fantastic news for you.'' His kind eyes shone. ''Janet, it's just what we were talking about the other day — the little white lies of love. The way we protect those close to us, keeping hurts and disappointments at bay.'' He kissed her wet eyes, and gently stroked her hair. ''Janet, let me protect you from now on, my dearest, please.''

Janet nodded, but said nothing. She felt too happy for words. Suddenly she knew exactly what Scott meant about ''little white lies.'' And she would be perfectly happy to let him shelter her for the rest of their lives.

Like the Easter promise, a bright new hope flooded Janet Browning's heart. □

Hats Off To Alex!

"MUM! I've got news for you!"

Jess Marshall, busy at the cooker, looked round to see her son at the kitchen door, his brown eyes twinkling.

"Are you listening?" he demanded.

"Yes. I'm listening, Roy."

"Well, here goes! Ailsa and I are getting married."

Jess turned back to the potato pot, mashing furiously.

"Oh, you are, are you? When was this decided?"

"Last night," he told her. "You seemed so tired when I came home

by Margaret Nicol

that I thought you might bite my nose off, so I waited until today."
Jess hid a smile.

"Your nose is quite safe," she said. "Away ben to the room and I'll bring your meal."

"Anything I can do?" Roy lingered by the doorway.

"Yes, go and wash your hands. Shoo!" Jess ordered.

H E was still a boy to her and yet, here he was, going to be married . . . leaving her alone in the flat they'd lived in since his father died twelve years ago.

They had been a one-parent family, he and she. That phase was about to end now, as she had known it would one day. She had made up her mind she would accept it cheerfully when it came, and yet —

From now on, she realised, they would be living different lives. Ailsa Garrick's people were wealthy and would expect Roy to fall in with their ways. She had never mixed with people like that. She'd had to work hard and count every penny, especially when Roy was younger.

Now that he had a good position in electronics, it wasn't so necessary, but habits were hard to break: so she had kept on her afternoon job at a local tearoom.

It was here she had first cast eyes on the girl Roy was to marry. Serving at her table, she had been struck by the poise and beauty of the popular young girl. Not for Ailsa the scruffy jeans of the town's teenagers. She knew how to dress, did Ailsa. Everything she wore was just right.

Jess sighed a little as she dished up the potatoes. Oh, that she had that gift of elegance that came to some women naturally!

Perhaps if she had been given a different name at birth? But plain Jess she was and plain Jess she would remain. She thought she had come to terms with that fact long ago, but now the truth loomed up again to make her feel uneasy and inadequate.

T HE wedding was fixed for a day in June. It was to be in Ailsa's home town, some distance away, so few of their friends would be able to attend.

"What is so rare as a day in June?" Roy kept quoting. "Then if ever come perfect days."

Jess wished that all Roy's days could be perfect but of course nobody, not even her son, could expect such dispensation.

But, Jess determined, she at least wouldn't spoil his wedding day. For once she would live up to the image she had conjured up for herself. Smartness and sophistication would be her aim.

One afternoon she picked up a glossy magazine that one of the customers had left behind in the tearoom. Opening it at an article entitled *Weddings: What The Bride's Mother Should Wear,* she read on with interest.

The one essential in her outfit should be a really smart hat, a hat to catch the eye.

What applied to the bride's mother, Jess thought, probably applied to the bridegroom's mother, too. And on the spot, she decided to get a really super, eye-catching hat.

A small pang of guilt accompanied the thought. A few months ago she had attended a cousin's wedding in a completely new outfit, not worn since. The blue two-piece with a frilly blouse had been quite expensive and was very suitable for the coming occasion. Yes, she would wear it; but the hat!

The sober, blue beret-type hat that went with the suit simply wouldn't do. It was as plain as putty, as her mother used to say.

Before, Jess had hardly cast a glance at the Linbrook hat shops, but now all that was changed. She began to linger at the windows in an agony of indecision, till at last she plucked up courage to enter a new establishment that seemed to offer an up-to-date selection.

THE owner was a tall, stately lady and Jess found her confidence ebbing. But she managed to state her business.

"A wedding hat? Certainly. We have an excellent choice."

A choice indeed, Jess thought. There were hats in all colours and shapes. It was quite bewildering.

"I'll be wearing it with this blue two-piece." Taking off her light coat, she displayed the wedding outfit.

The lady surveyed it.

"Well, almost any colour will go with that blue. Oyster or shrimp are very fashionable just now. I think I know the very hat!"

From a deep drawer she took out the hat in question. A bright, almost violent pink, it was topped by a group of fluffy feathers. Eye-catching was the word for it.

Jess tried it on before the mirror. The hat sat high up on her head, making her inches taller. It wasn't very comfortable, but what did comfort matter? Elegance was the thing.

"That type of hat is worn at all the fashionable weddings," she was told.

That clinched it. The price was staggering and she would never wear the hat again, she was sure; but she mustn't let Roy down, price or no price.

That evening, Jess could hardly wait to her her son's verdict. Vanishing from the room, she appeared again, all dressed up.

"How do you like me?" she demanded.

He looked up from his book and gasped.

"Mother, that can't be you!"

"It's me in my wedding hat. What do you think?"

Roy got to his feet, smiling.

"You're tremendous," he said, giving her a hug.

"Watch my hat! So you think it will do?"

"It'll knock them flat."

Jess laughed tremulously.

"I've got to keep up with the Joneses, you know."

He pulled her down beside him on the sofa.

"If you mean Ailsa's relations, you needn't worry. Please don't stand in awe of them, Mum! Granted her parents are well off, but they are genuine folk, and so are the other relatives. Have you met her Uncle Alex? You'll be paired off with him, I expect.''

Jess shook her head.

"Not yet. What's he like?"

"Breezy bachelor type. Heart of gold," Roy said. "You'll like him."

"Really." She didn't care much for breezy types. They made her feel withdrawn and inarticulate. She would certainly need that hat to give her confidence!

THE big day dawned at last. It wasn't as perfect a day, weatherwise, as they had hoped for. There was a blustery north-west wind with some heavy showers, but in between them, the sun shone brightly. But, for the bridal pair there had never been a day like this, and Jess was happy in the knowledge that these two were deeply in love.

Roy was taking his mother to the wedding in his own car, picking up the best man on the way. The car stood at the gate now, spick and span, as Jess waited in the hall for her son to come downstairs.

Never had she taken so long to get dressed. She was glad that the years had left her looking young for her age. If not beautiful, she was at least presentable. She would put it no higher than that!

But the hat! A small niggle of doubt had crept in. Did the colour really blend with the blue of her suit? Would the tightish rim give her a headache? She could almost feel it coming on now . . .

"Hurry, Roy!" she called. "Time we were away!"

He appeared on the stair.

"Just coming!"

"I'll go out to the car, before the rain comes on again," she told him.

From the door, she made a dive for the car. At the same moment a gust of wind came swirling round the house. Jess clutched at her hat, but it was too late. Torn from her head, the gorgeous confection went flying in the breeze, with her panting after it.

After some suspenseful moments, the hat came down to earth, landing in the middle of the road. She stood frozen as a big lorry came hurtling along. When it passed, what remained of the hat was just not worth picking up.

"My hat," she sobbed, as Roy made his appearance. "Oh, my hat!"

He took her arm comfortingly.

"Leave it, Mum. We'll be late for the wedding."

"But I can't go without a hat!"

"Wear the other one, then. I'll fetch it for you."

ROY ran upstairs, then brought down the original blue hat she had so despised.

"It's so plain!" she moaned.

"Never mind. Nobody will notice," Roy assured her.

That was what he thought, but she knew better. In the car she fell silent. Men simply didn't understand what being properly dressed meant to a woman at an important function like this. Instead of being

upsides with Ailsa's people, she would probably be a laughing stock.
"Cheer up," Roy rallied her. "Don't let it spoil your day!"
But that was just what it was going to do.

ENTERING the church was an ordeal. Jess was so conscious of her plain little hat that all the others seemed to shine out with extra lustre; large hats, small hats, straw hats and silk hats, hats feathered and hats be-ribboned, all worn with poise and confidence by Ailsa's female relations.

Only during the solemn marriage ceremony did the recent calamity fade into insignificance. Once the knot was tied, however, and the congregation rustled into action, hats came into prominence again.

As Jess stood hesitant, she heard a voice at her elbow.

"Are you Jess Marshall, the bridegroom's mother?"

"Yes," she admitted. "And you must be Uncle Alex."

"That's right." He held her by the elbow. "I'm told we've been paired off for the reception. I'll take you to the hotel with one or two others. Will you come?"

"Yes, of course."

Uncle Alex had the sort of face to give one confidence. Square chin, shrewd grey eyes, a hint of laughter in his voice. He seemed to have the gift of rallying people and soon had his car filled with his quota of guests.

Red Rose Of Love

GLANCING through an ancient book
I found a flower there
Faded, fragile, lovely still
    And pressed with loving care.

Did you adorn a buttonhole
    Or grace a lady's gown
When going to an old-time ball
    In carriage, through the town?

Were you alone, the precious one
    Plucked from a bride's bouquet
To keep as a memento of
    A lovely wedding day?

Or gesture of repentance, when
    True love was torn apart?
Peace offering, the tears to stem
    And heal a wounded heart?

Red rose of love, you speak to me
    Of love, and joy and tears.
Whispering of memories
    Across the bygone years.

Dorothy M. Loughran

They were a merry group, all radiant in their finery. One of the cousins, Clare, wore a hat not unlike Jess's late lamented. She wore it with an air which Jess could never achieve, no matter how long or how hard she tried.

"Lovely to see so many smashing hats," Clare chortled. "I do think that for a wedding one should go the whole hog and hang the expense!"

Her glance rested for a moment on Jess's modest headgear. It was a pitying sort of glance, or so she imagined. Jess sank into herself, wishing she could disappear.

Among the guests at the reception, she still felt self-conscious, especially when they put her at the top table beside Uncle Alex. Everybody seemed to be looking at her hat.

"Are you always so silent?" Alex asked, his eyes twinkling. "You've hardly said a word all day."

"I'm just a bit overwhelmed," she replied.

"You're not the only one!"

But he was just saying that to comfort her, she thought.

Alex was that kind of person. Mixing in with this crowd of people and joining in the fun was obviously no bother to him at all. She was sure he'd be relaxed and happy in anyone's company.

AFTER the speeches were made and the toasts drunk, Roy sought Jess out in the corner where she had taken refuge. In his dress kilt, bronzed and happy, she had never seen him so handsome, nor so remote from herself.

Don't go away from me, she thought wildly. You're all I've got!

But, smiling, she simply put her hand in his.

"It's been a lovely day," she said. "You've got a lovely wife. Be good to her!"

"I will." Roy bent to kiss her. "Thank you for all you've done. Need I say more?"

"No, you've said enough." Jess laughed. "Off you go!"

When the gaily-decorated taxi drew up to take the newlyweds away, she stood on the steps with the others. It was a colourful scene, full of laughter and high spirits.

Jess tried to share in the jubilation, but as the car moved off, her spirits sank lower and lower.

She went back up the hotel steps, intending to get her things and slip away. But a hand touched her arm and there was Uncle Alex smiling at her kindly.

"Let's get out of this crowd," he suggested. "I hear they're serving tea in the lounge."

"Well . . ." She hesitated.

But he was propelling her gently into the quiet corner.

The lounge was comfortably furnished and not too busy. It would be pleasant, Jess had to admit, to get away from the noise and bustle for a while. The celebrations would probably go on for hours yet.

"It will do you good. Going home to brood will just finish you."

She sat down with a breathless laugh.

"How did you know I was going home?"

"I've been watching you all afternoon," he said.

She flushed.

"Oh dear, I wonder why. Was it my awful hat?"

He gave the hat a quizzical look.

"I like your hat," he said honestly. "It's different from the others. I'll tell you something. I'm scared stiff of all these dames in their fancy hats, but yours is nice. It goes with your face. And I'll bet you feel very comfortable in it.''

"Now you mention it, I do," she confessed. "But it's not what I intended to wear."

O VER tea she related the sad story of the new hat. It seemed less of a tragedy now; in fact, she was able to laugh along with him and her spirits rose accordingly.

Though highly amused, Alex's laughter was kindly. Breezy he might be, but it was in a nice, humorous way that encouraged her to talk.

"I can imagine what you must have felt at the time," he told her. "I'm glad you've got over it so well. And," he added in a low voice, "you'll get over that empty feeling of Roy leaving you, too."

"So you guessed about that."

A remarkable man, Uncle Alex.

"I told you I'd been watching you," he said. "I have also heard the saying about 'a son's a son till he gets him a wife.' It's only natural you should feel left out."

"Perhaps." She lowered her eyes. "You're a very understanding person, Alex."

"I do try," he replied soberly, "especially when I meet someone I like. We've got to get to know each other, Jess. Tomorrow's Saturday. Will you lunch with me here?"

"I'd like to." Jess's eyes danced through the tears. "Just as I am, in this hat?"

"Especially in that hat," he confirmed.

Home again, Jess looked round the familiar surroundings without the pang of loneliness she had expected to feel.

"What is so rare as a day in June?" she quoted to herself.

Truly, it had been a wonderful day, a pointer to more wonderful days in the future.

It wasn't such a bad little hat after all, she decided, removing the blue beret and stroking it tenderly. She owed a lot to it. She would certainly wear it more often.

Probably she had only imagined the pitying glances at the wedding. Ailsa's relations were really quite nice folk — especially her Uncle Alex. □

The popular holiday resort of Helensburgh, which takes its name from the wife of Sir James Colquhoun of Luss, stands on the lower Clyde, near its junction with the Gare Loch. This loch, Loch Long, Loch Lomond and Glen Fruin may be visited by road in a round trip of 35 miles. Helensburgh was the birthplace of John Logie Baird (1888-1946), pioneer of television. An obelisk on the sea front commemorates Henry Bell, provost in 1807-9, who in 1812 launched the Comet on the Clyde — the first practical passenger steamer in Europe.

HELENSBURGH, DUNBARTONSHIRE

W AKING from a long, refreshing sleep, George Nicolson stretched
luxuriously and thought how wonderful it was to be back on land
again, and to be a welcome visitor at the home of his married
sister.

"Look upon this place as your home till you get married yourself,"
Sheena had said in her kindly way, and that was just what he had done.

So he was home for Christmas this year and it was marvellous. He
smiled drowsily at the thought of last year's Christmas when his ship
had been trapped in ice for a week in the Arctic. Br-r-r! How cold it
had been! How much more pleasant it was to lie here so comfortably,
with nothing to do but get up at his leisure and laze about all morning.

In the afternoon he did have something to do, he remembered. Sheena
had asked if he would mind looking after the children for an hour or
so while she was out.

"I've a lot of last-minute shopping to do," she'd explained. "It isn't
easy with two youngsters around, and it's boring for them, poor darlings.
You'll be good, won't you, you pair?"

The children who sat beside her, looking at their almost unknown
uncle with interest, nodded in agreement.

"Of course I'll see to them," George had promised. "We'll get to
know each other."

"Yes, it's strange to think that it's nearly two years since you were
last home." Sheena had sighed. "Jessica was just starting to walk then."

Thinking about his nephew and niece now, George felt rather pleased
with them. Four-year-old Gavin was as bright as a button, and Jessica
was a pretty little thing with a delightful smile. Both talked splendidly,

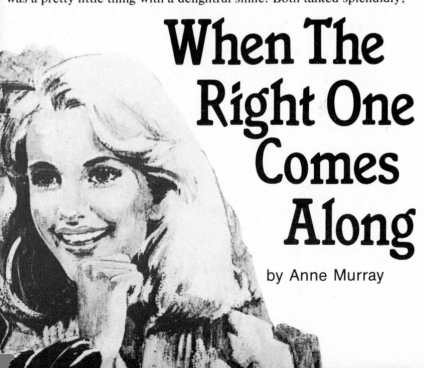

When The
Right One
Comes
Along

by Anne Murray

The People's Friend Annual

and Gavin had been absolutely thrilled with the present George had brought him.

"Ships!" he'd shouted as he opened the big box. "Oh, super!"

"Gavin's going into the Navy, too, when he grows up," Sheena explained. "You couldn't have brought him anything better."

Well, with a father and uncle both in the Navy it was no wonder Gavin's ambitions lay in that direction. Jessica had been pleased, too, with her gift — a toy lamb which she'd decided to call Benny. Funny little thing, George thought. She seemed to want the lamb to wear socks . . .

SUDDENLY, George became aware of sounds outside his bedroom door. He pulled himself up on the pillows and listened.

"Mummy said we weren't to wake him up," came the voice of his nephew.

"Let's look at him," Jessica responded in a loud whisper.

The door opened cautiously and two rosy little faces appeared.

"It's all right. I'm awake," George told them. "You can come in."

Hand in hand the two entered, looking at him shyly.

"Are you going to get up soon?" Gavin said at last.

"Oh, yes, in a while."

"You's lazy," Jessica stated. "Mummy says it's lazy to lie in bed."

Well, really! George was taken aback. Hadn't Sheena urged him to lie as long as he liked? Still, the child was only three . . .

"He was tired," Gavin informed his little sister. "Mummy says when you're old you get awful tired."

George sat bolt upright.

"Here, that's enough," he began indignantly.

"How old is he?" Jessica asked.

"I don't know," Gavin said. "About sixty, I suppose."

George nearly exploded. Fortunately Sheena appeared at that moment and chased the children out of the room.

"Go and play downstairs," she ordered firmly.

Gavin ran off, but Jessica lingered, asking if socks for Benny had been made.

"Jessica, I haven't time to sit knitting socks," Sheena said impatiently. "I phoned Auntie Linda and she's very kindly going to make them this morning. Now do run away."

"What's all this about socks?" George inquired.

Sheena laughed.

"At the Christmas service tomorrow the juniors are singing a carol," she said. "It mentions a lamb that wore little red socks, so Jessica is determined that her one will do the same. It's lucky our baby-sitter has time to do them, but then she understands how important this sort of thing can be to a three-year-old."

"Sheena," George said, slowly, "Gavin seems to think I'm sixty. Do I really look that old?"

"Of course not!" his sister exclaimed. "Small children don't understand about ages. Sixteen or sixty sounds much the same to

168

them. You shouldn't take what they say so seriously, you know."

George relaxed. "I didn't think I looked quite so ancient!"

"You look splendid!" Sheena assured him warmly. "And I've got some nice girls looked out for you this time."

It was an old joke between them that she was going to get her brother married, but so far her efforts had been unsuccessful. In the meantime, however, she realised that all George wanted to do was to laze about and do nothing. For a start, she would bring him breakfast in bed.

GEORGE had another nap after that. Then he got up for lunch and discovered that he still felt short of sleep. Of course, before reaching home he'd had three gruelling nights at sea, while his ship fought her way through a storm. But he must stay awake now.

He listened to Sheena giving instructions to the children.

"Just play quietly with your toys and don't bother Uncle George," she ordered. "If you're good there may be something nice for you when I come back."

"Chocolate?" Jessica asked hopefully.

"Ice-cream?" Gavin cried. "I like pink . . ."

"There'll be nothing at all if you aren't good," Sheena warned, then hurried away, while George stifled a few tremors at the thought that he was now in sole charge of these two youngsters.

It was just that he'd never had anything to do with children. They didn't fit in with a life at sea. Now here was his chance to get to know them better.

It was nice of Sheena to trust them to him. Some mothers wouldn't have dreamed of it, he felt sure, but then she was a sister in a thousand.

"I'll just play with my ships." Gavin sat on the floor beside the big box which held such an exciting collection of naval ships.

Jessica was in a corner of the room playing with some dolls and her lamb.

Nothing to it, George thought contentedly as he settled into a comfortable chair and picked up the newspaper.

The room was warm, the children's murmuring voices had a soothing effect, and after five minutes the paper slid to the floor and George fell fast asleep.

TWENTY minutes later he woke with a start. What a way to baby-sit! But all was well. Gavin was still in front of him, pushing the ships about. But Jessica —

Where was she? The dolls lay neglected in the corner and there was no sign of the little girl or her lamb. George sprang up.

"Gavin, where's Jessica?"

Gavin looked up vaguely.

"She's gone to get Benny's socks," he said.

"Gone where?" George demanded. "Not out, surely?"

"She had to go out," Gavin pointed out calmly. "She went to Auntie Linda's. Didn't you hear Mummy say Auntie Linda would make socks for Benny?"

Oh, no, George thought. Out in the gathering dusk! Into that street with cars going to and fro! He tried to fight down a rising sense of panic.

"Where does this aunt live? Is it far away?"

"She isn't a real aunt," Gavin explained brightly. "She's our baby-sitter. She comes to look after us when Mummy goes out."

"Do you know the way to her house?"

" 'Course I do. So does Jessica."

George waited no longer. Seizing Gavin by the hand, he pulled him out of the room, then outside through the front door which was standing open.

"Come on, then. Show me the way to this house."

It took five minutes to reach the entrance to a block of flats. They went up two flights of stairs, then Gavin jerked his hand free and ran ahead to peer through a letter flap.

"Jessica's here," he announced. "I can hear her talking."

Thank goodness for that, George thought in relief. He'd been badly scared at the thought of his little niece out on her own. He rang the bell, which was too high for Gavin to reach.

"Jessica can't reach the bell either," Gavin said. "She would just kick the door, I expect."

"Kick the door?" George gasped.

CHILDISH DREAMS

*A*S a little child on Christmas Eve,
   I lay a-bed and gazed upon the sky.
   The wind was driving clouds like sheep,
   The moon shone when she could.
   This the night that Santa rides!
   Would I hear the sleigh bells overhead?
   At our chimney would he halt –
   and then deliver,
   As the milkman brings the milk.
   Then a wondering child became a sleeping child.
   And in the morning? Santa had delivered.
   O mystery unfathomable!
   The years bring truth; childish dreams are shattered.
   No Santa rides the midnight skies.
   How sad!
   Until you think. Are we not Santas all?
   Thronging the Christmas sky.
   A sackful of gifts and greetings to deliver.
   Dropping happiness down the chimney
   Of others' lives.
                              Rev. T.R.S. Campbell.

He was beginning to think he knew less about children than ever. But the door opened and a new kind of shock hit him. The slim, fair-haired girl who stood there was the prettiest he had ever seen. She really was lovely. But her deep blue eyes glinted back at him coldly.

"Are you Sheena's brother?" she demanded. "I suppose you've come looking for Jessica. How could you let her come along here all by herself?"

"I didn't let her," George protested. "I didn't know a thing. I . . .

I fell asleep for a moment, that was all. I was really tired, you know."

"Fell asleep!" Linda Gray exclaimed. "Don't you realise you've got to be on the alert all the time when you're in charge of children? What made you fall asleep? I can hardly believe it."

"Well, if you'd had three nights in succession without any sleep you might do just the same," George retorted.

Jessica appeared, clasping her lamb. Four little red socks now adorned his stubby legs and she displayed them proudly.

"I'm going to take Benny to church tomorrow," she said. "I'll hold him up when we sing the bit about his socks."

"Well, come along home," George said shortly, wishing he'd never thought of buying a lamb for Jessica.

It was a few minutes before he could get the children away. Jessica had to kiss Auntie Linda goodbye, then Gavin wanted to do the same. George managed a stilted word of thanks to Linda for taking the child in, and in return received a puzzling remark.

"Goodbye. It was nice you had such a good time in London," she said disapprovingly as she shut the door.

WHAT on earth did she mean by that, George wondered, as he hurried the children along the street. He hadn't even spent five minutes in London on his way here. It was true that at one time he'd thought of having a night there, but when his ship docked so late he gave up the idea.

Did that girl imagine his lack of sleep was due to living it up in the city? Yes, that must be it. How could someone who looked so lovely, who by all accounts was such a help to his sister, jump to such a conclusion? He shook his head in perplexity.

They were nearing the house now and he gave Gavin permission to run on ahead. But only a moment later the boy came racing back, his eyes almost popping out of his head.

"Uncle George, there's a man in the house!" he cried. "I heard him walking about upstairs and then he coughed, so I knew it was a man. You didn't lock the door when we came out and it must be a burglar."

Gavin was right, George thought in dismay. They'd come out in such haste that he'd left the door standing wide open. This was the end! Sheena would never trust him again to see to things in her absence. But at least he'd deal with this intruder . . .

Ready to do battle, George burst in through the open front door, the children at his heels. All three stopped short as a man came down the stairs.

Jessica stared at him in delight.

"Daddy, Daddy!" she screamed, rushing forward to clasp her father round the knees. Gavin was only a second slower in giving his boisterous welcome.

"Hello, George. You here for Christmas? Fine!" Robin Sinclair said hospitably. "I didn't expect that I would make it, but plans changed and here I am. I suppose Sheena's out. But, George, old chap, if you take the kids for a walk you really mustn't leave the door wide open."

"It wasn't exactly a walk," George explained. "Sorry, Robin, it was desperately careless of me. It's plain that I'm no earthly use left in charge here."

Sheena came home at that moment, overjoyed to see her husband. Both seemed very amused when they heard all that had happened, and relieved that nothing had gone wrong.

"But don't worry." Sheena smiled at her brother. "I'll put things right between you and Linda. She's really the nicest girl I know, and very much on her own."

"She wasn't very nice to me," George broke in. "You should have heard the way she went on at me for falling asleep. No, Sheena, if you've looked her out for me, then just forget it."

For once he thought his sister a little unfeeling when her only reply was to laugh at him.

THE next morning the house was in an uproar. The children were excited over their presents and looking forward to going to the gift service in the church. It was there that they would join the others in the junior class to sing about the lamb who wore socks.

Sitting in a pew near the front of the church, George felt happy again. Yesterday had been a bit of a disaster, but it was in the past. He really felt full of Christmas goodwill this morning, and was even ready to say a polite word to Linda Gray if he met her.

From where he sat he could see her helping with the small children, as they took up their position in front, Jessica clasping her lamb proudly. A stillness fell on the church as they began to sing.

The best birthday party of all,
Had three strange guests, I recall.
A donkey and an ox, and a lamb who wore red socks,
Because it was very cold in the stall.

As the lamb was mentioned, Jessica held her lamb as high as her short arms allowed. A murmur of appreciation could be heard on all sides. Then they got on with the next verse.

Lord Jesus, He wanted them there,
Invited them in for a share.
A donkey and an ox, and a lamb who wore red socks,
As they stood together in prayer.

Once again Jessica held up the lamb. But George noticed something. Slowly, but steadily, one of the lamb's socks was coming off. He watched helplessly as it slid downwards, wondering if they'd get through the last verse before it fell to the floor.

The three wise men sat on a seat,
And warmed their hands and their feet.
And the donkey and the ox, and the lamb who wore red socks,
Added hee-haw, moo, and a bleat.

Down went the sock and as Jessica hoisted Benny up she saw what had happened. Her face puckered and it was obvious she was going to cry. It simply wouldn't do if Benny wore only three socks!

But help was at hand. Quickly Linda Gray went forward, so quickly

172

that not everyone saw her deft replacement of the sock. Jessica was all smiles again as the beginners were led away and older children came forward to sing.

George found himself approving of that quick action. It was a pity he'd got off on the wrong foot with that pretty girl. She really was lovely, he admitted to himself, with her shining fair hair and those deep blue eyes.

But how coldly these eyes had looked at him yesterday! He winced at the remembrance while he listened to the older children singing "Away In A Manger."

WHEN the service was over, people congregated to exchange good wishes outside the door. Sheena and Robin seemed to know everyone, and for a few minutes George stood by himself, feeling rather out of it. Even the children were chattering to other small friends about the presents they had received.

All at once George became aware of someone pausing in front of him. He felt his heart give a jump as he looked into the blue eyes of Linda Gray.

There was no coldness in these pretty eyes today, just a sort of appeal he didn't quite understand. It made him feel protective, so that he wanted to help her.

"Please forgive me for yesterday," Linda said awkwardly. "I shouldn't have spoken so crossly to you. It was just that I was so frightened."

"Frightened?" George repeated in astonishment. "What frightened you?"

"It was the thought of little Jessica being out by herself," Linda confessed. "She could have been lost, or run over. I thought you had fallen asleep because you'd been hitting the high spots in London. Sheena told me this morning it was because your ship had come through a dreadful storm. It was no wonder you fell asleep."

George discovered he had completely changed his opinion of this girl. He admired her for making that apology. It wasn't an easy thing to do.

"I was frightened, too," he told her gravely. "When I realised Jessica had gone out alone I felt in more of a panic than any time during the storm."

"It was Jessica who deserved the scolding, not you." Linda sighed. "She's a naughty little thing, yet such a darling."

An understanding smile was exchanged. And when George heard that Linda was coming along to share Christmas lunch with his family, he was delighted.

Yes, being home for Christmas was wonderful, George thought, as he walked along beside Linda, with the children running around them and Jessica's lamb proudly wearing his little red socks. □

Printed and published in Great Britain by D. C. Thomson & Co. Ltd., Dundee, Glasgow, London and Manchester.
© D. C. Thomson & Co. Ltd., 1983.
ISBN 0-85116-289-4

DURHAM CATHEDRAL